CW00920113

THE KILLING RITUAL

RANDOLPH CASEY HORROR THRILLERS
BOOK 5

ROCKWELL SCOTT

THE KILLING RITUAL

PROLOGUE

Our Lady of Redemption Cathedral stood large and imposing at the center of the small town. It had been there since the municipality had been established in 1902. The bell tower reached toward the cloudy sky.

That night, the aura of calm, holy silence was broken.

The front of the cathedral was rushed by a SWAT team wearing bulletproof vests, assault rifles ready. They moved in unison with fluid precision as they lined up near the entrance. After everyone was in place, the lead man slammed his heavy boot into the door and forced it open. The armed unit surged inside.

A lone woman was among the many empty pews, head bowed in prayer. She barely had time to recognize what was happening before one of the squad swept her up, a hand covering her mouth, and pulled her away from the unfolding scene to safety.

The team reassembled at the front of the sanctuary, their guns trained on a simple wooden table that held nothing more than a thick Bible and a crucifix. The cast-iron Jesus statue seemed unfazed at having so many weapons leveled in his direction.

Two men hefted the table by its ends and carried it away. A third pulled back the edge of the embroidered rug on the floor, exposing a hidden cellar door.

A symbol had been etched into the wood: a distorted pentagram, each point of the star a different length.

One man flung open the cellar, revealing a staircase that led down into a basement. The SWAT team descended into the darkness, guns ready.

The beams from the flashlights affixed to the ends of their rifles cut through the shadows, so it didn't take long for them to find the cages. Inside were dozens of children, faces dirty and hair disheveled. Many were quite thin from malnourishment.

Although no one on the SWAT team spoke, they all shared the same thought in that moment: they were in disbelief. The outlandish tip they'd received was *real*.

1

It was one of those days where Rand Casey was physically there, but mentally elsewhere.

The only sounds in the hushed classroom were pens scratching on paper and Professor Sharma's heels clacking on the tiled floor as she slowly paced back and forth, scanned the students, and ensured everyone kept their eyes on their own papers.

Clack... clack... clack...

The steady rhythm only heightened Rand's sleepiness as he struggled to stay awake.

It had only been three days since his return from the Herron House. What he'd thought was just another case had turned out to be a carefully laid trap. He'd only narrowly escaped with his life and was now burdened by new, disturbing revelations— the existence of a network of corrupt, influential people allied with powerful demons.

The stadium-style lecture hall was more full than Rand had ever seen it. A ceiling leak next door had forced

Professor Sharma and her students to share Rand's class-room for the afternoon. Fortunately, it was a test day for both classes, so combining everyone wasn't an issue.

Even as Rand sat behind the desk at the head of his classroom, he ached from the lumps he'd taken in the decrepit mansion. The large purple bruises underneath his clothes were nowhere near faded. Every few seconds, he had to consciously force his eyelids open. It frustrated him how badly his body wanted to sleep *now,* but when he laid down in bed at night, he was suddenly alert, constantly imagining figures shifting in the shadowy corners of the room.

Maybe I should get up and walk around with her, Rand thought. *That might keep me awake.*

Rand considered Professor Sharma's militant demeanor during test-taking a bit much. But then again, she taught World Religions—one of the core classes in the Religious Studies department. From what Rand had heard, her class was notoriously difficult, and many students had to repeat it. Rand eyed the current batch as they pored over their essay tests, scratching their heads, chewing on pen tops, and correcting their work with white-out.

Another wave of fatigue blurred his vision, so he clenched his eyes shut for a few moments before opening them. Doing that almost felt like a reset, and he hoped it would buy him about ten more seconds of forced attention before his brain dozed off again. Staying alert was vital because there were important things he needed to do after class.

And during. *Focus,* he told himself.

Rand turned his tired eyes back to his laptop on the

desk in front of him. A few hours prior, his friend Miller Landingham had emailed him a link.

'This is the website where I found Arthur Briggs,' Miller had written underneath the link. *'Take a look, but keep an open mind. I really think he knows what he's talking about.'*

Rand felt a familiar resistance well up within him. Despite Miller's good intentions, Rand was reluctant to admit there might be someone more knowledgeable about the supernatural world than him.

Not only that, but Arthur Briggs was arrogant and dismissive. He'd called Miller after they'd escaped the Herron House and had been unimpressed by Rand's new knowledge that demons could be killed.

"No shit," he'd said.

What had been one of the biggest breakthroughs of Rand's life might as well have been an overplayed pop song on the radio to Arthur Briggs.

And that's probably why Miller thinks he's reliable, Rand reminded himself.

Despite his misgivings... Rand knew Miller was right. Rand needed to keep an open mind about Arthur Briggs if he really wanted the best chance in his fights against the demonic. It was important to learn all he could from anyone who might be able to help, even though it sounded to Rand like Briggs wasn't at all interested.

"This is not my fight. You stirred up *this trouble. There's nothing I can do for you."*

As far as Rand was concerned, Arthur Briggs had made his position clear. Yet Miller wanted to disregard that and see if there was a way to get Briggs to assist them anyway.

Despite his hesitance, Rand needed help. The events

of the other night inside the Herron House had proven he was in over his head.

Rand's thoughts were interrupted when his student—Jimmy Newson—started walking down the stadium steps towards him, completed test in hand. Rand had been so distracted by his rambling mind that he'd lost track of time. Jimmy placed his test on the stack of other and left.

Was he the last one? Or the first? Rand cast a hopeful glance around the room, looking for any of his students among the dozens of Professor Sharma's that remained. If everyone had finished the test, then he could leave early—which would be a big help, because he'd planned to meet with Miller and Libby to discuss their next steps.

But then Rand spotted Kurt, seated at the edge of the room and still engrossed in his papers. His brow was furrowed as he pondered over the questions.

Come on, Kurt, it's not that difficult, Rand thought.

Kurt was always the last to finish his test, usually taking the entire hour. He second-guessed everything.

Normally, Rand appreciated his meticulousness. But on that day, with so many other things on his mind, Rand wished that just once, Kurt would trust his knowledge and turn the test in. Especially since the multiple-choice questions weren't difficult.

Professor Sharma approached the stack of turned-in tests. Rand could see the overwhelming curiosity on his colleague's face as she picked up Jimmy's test and scanned the first page. Her interest was quickly replaced by skeptical confusion.

Although Rand didn't socialize much with the other professors and instructors, he was aware of the rumors surrounding his class, as well as the ire from the ones who didn't consider his subject matter "real."

But Rand had nothing to hide. What he taught was just as real and important as the material in other classes. Professor Sharma could peek at his tests all she wanted. She—and everyone else in the world—could greatly benefit from knowing the safest way to banish a demon from your home, or the best strategy for leading a lost spirit to the afterlife. Those were questions two and seven, respectively.

The inclusion of Intro to Supernatural Studies on the Religious Studies roster three years ago had always been controversial. Rand was under no illusion that the other professors and instructors in the department *actually* considered him a serious teacher. Although he didn't know for sure, Rand suspected that Professor Sharma might have been his biggest detractor.

Rand refocused on his laptop screen. He clicked the link that Miller had sent him the day before, which took him to a website that looked like it was from the early 90s. The background was black, the text was white, and two cheesy skulls at the top of the homepage rotated round and round—probably the most complex feature in the site's code.

He understood the website's appearance didn't matter. Sites like this were what Miller perused quite often. Its users had been discussing the paranormal and supernatural online since the earliest days of the internet. Updating their websites to modern styles wasn't important—they were all about exchanging information and ideas.

The link led to the forum thread Miller wanted him

to read. Rand skimmed through to see how long the post was before he started. Posts from a user named "AB"—which Rand assumed to be Arthur Briggs—were the longest, and they seemed to be met with positive responses in the comments.

As he scrolled, one phrase jumped out.

The Lords of Hell.

Arthur had mentioned that when he'd called Miller; Rand had never heard of them before. This was another reason why Miller felt Briggs was credible—there were things the man spoke about that neither Miller nor Rand knew of.

Rand tried to not let his ego take a hit. He'd spent half his life immersing himself in the supernatural world, fighting extremely dangerous demonic entities and nearly dying on multiple occasions. He even taught a damn *class* on the subject. He was very hesitant to consider the idea that there was someone out there who knew more than him.

Before Rand could start reading through the forum posts, Kurt rose from his desk and started toward the front of the classroom.

Rand didn't hesitate. He snapped his laptop shut, shot up from his chair, and shoved the stack of test papers into his bag. He met Kurt halfway and took his test from him, earning an odd look from the boy.

Professor Sharma also eyed him strangely. After being sluggish and tired all hour, he'd suddenly come alive.

"You'll lock up and turn the lights off?" Rand asked her, keeping his voice low to not disturb her students who were still working.

She responded with a stiff nod.

So, Rand headed toward the exit. His arms were full and the things he carried were precariously loose even when clutched to his chest.

He felt something drop.

The black cube landed with a heavy *thud* that reverberated off the classroom walls and ceiling, breaking through the silence more than he would've thought possible for an object that was only the size of a Rubik's Cube. Professor Sharma's students all looked up from their exams, startled.

He'd taken it from the Herron House and no matter how many times he tried to get rid of it, it always reappeared either beside him or in one of his pockets. This time it had been inside his interior jacket pocket, even though he'd locked the cube in a drawer in his office before class.

It rested on the tiled floor between him and Professor Sharma. Rand knew what was coming—seeing that Rand's arms were full, she went to pick up the black cube to hand it to him.

"No," Rand said, a little too sharply. He quickly set everything down and rushed to snatch it up before Professor Sharma could touch it.

Rand knew hardly anything about the black cube— what it was, where it had come from, what it was made of, or what dark energy it held. But he knew that it brought some kind of curse on anyone who touched it. He'd learned that at the Herron House—James Herron had been its previous victim.

Professor Sharma gave him a peculiar look as he tucked the cube into his jacket pocket and ensured it was securely inside and would not drop again. He wasn't sure how it had fallen out in the first place. The thing seemed to have a mind of its own.

"Sorry," Rand added quickly, now aware that every eye in the room was on him. He scooped up his stack of tests and rushed out of the classroom.

Now, the unpleasant part of the day would begin— facing his friends and family, who were counting on him to protect them from the evil he'd stirred up three nights ago.

2

The sun was setting on the chilly day, painting the sky orange, purple, and yellow. Under different circumstances, Rand might've enjoyed the view. But that night, his attention was needed elsewhere.

Out of habit, he nearly took the turn heading to his own house, but caught himself. He snapped back into awareness and straightened his steering wheel, passing the street. His house was totally unlivable at the moment.

He and Miller had returned from the Herron House to find that Rand's home had been completely desecrated. Demonic symbols had been gouged into the walls. His furniture and belongings were destroyed. The intruders had even drawn a magic circle onto his living room ceiling. There was no doubt in Rand's mind that what had happened within his home had brought some very negative energy with it.

He'd emerged from the Herron House victorious...

but that victory seemed hollow. He'd angered many people that night—powerful, evil people.

' At first he'd planned to check in to a hotel, but the cost was a deterrent. Once Tessa, his ex, had found out what had happened, she'd invited him to stay at her fiancé Bill's house until Rand could figure out what to do about his own home.

Rand drove his Jeep through the gated entrance of the finest neighborhood in the city. Every home was nearly a mansion. Man-made lakes with fountains welcomed him as he traveled the spacious roads to Bill's house.

When he arrived, he saw familiar cars had filled the wide driveway: Miller's yellow truck and Libby's blue Mini Cooper. Bill and Tessa were also home. Presumably they were all inside, waiting for him.

And wondering what exactly I've gotten them all into now, Rand thought.

Rand went to the front door of Bill's massive house. Again, out of habit, he tried to press his own key into the lock. He sighed at his tired mind and found the newest key on his ring—the copy of Bill's house key Tessa had given him—and used it to let himself in.

I hope I don't end up staying here long enough to get accustomed to this, Rand thought as he entered.

Bill's massive living room was empty, and Rand couldn't hear anyone inside. But he'd seen all the cars parked out front, so he knew everyone was there. That was the thing about big houses—even when full of people, they could still seem so vacant sometimes.

Rand was about to drop his bag on the plush leather couch, but stopped himself. He didn't want to start feeling *too* at home in Bill's house. He was merely displaced, and his intention was to only stay there as long as he had to.

There was no telling how much time it would take to get his own house back to normal. It was more than just cleaning—he'd have to remove all the negative energy the blasphemies, desecrations, and curses had invited into the home.

There was also the possibility his house would never be habitable again. Expert though he was, even Rand did not fully understand the depths of the evil magic that had been used there. It was entirely possible it was so powerful the darkness would be there forever.

But Rand hadn't allowed himself to consider that outcome yet. He simply didn't have the energy; there were too many other things on his mind.

When he entered the kitchen and looked through the sliding glass door, he spotted everyone seated around Bill's outdoor entertainment area. Even Bill was there.

You left work early for this, Bill? Rand thought. Though he knew he shouldn't be surprised. The man would do anything to support Tessa.

Rand slid the door open and the sound brought everyone's attention to him. The back patio was nicer than most things in Rand's own home. There was a wrought-iron table with matching chairs underneath an awning. Nearby was a grill, a sink, and even a mini fridge filled with soft drinks and beer. Bill's pool and hot tub both had impeccably clear water.

Miller and Libby sat at the table while Bill stood near the head, arms folded. The sleeves of his white shirt were rolled halfway up his forearms. He'd also removed his tie and opened his collar. Tessa was beside him, her body rigid and tense.

With all eyes on him, Rand couldn't help but feel like this was some kind of intervention.

Maybe it is, he thought.

"How was work?" Libby asked. It was clearly a courtesy question, something simple so she could ease him into what she actually wanted to talk about.

"Test day," Rand replied. His voice croaked, which only happened when he was exceptionally exhausted.

"You okay, buddy?" Miller asked. "Have you been sleeping?"

"Honestly... not really." Despite how tired he was, Rand wasn't able to fall asleep at night. If he did, it was never for long, and shadows always filled his dreams.

"Maybe we should talk about this another time?" Miller's voice spiked mid-question, as if he'd realized it wasn't the best idea before he even said it.

"No," Tessa said. "Look, Rand, I'm sorry you're not feeling great, but there are some things we need to know."

She was right. They'd given him a few days to rest and gather his thoughts after what had happened in the Herron House, yet he felt like he hadn't recovered at all. He may have even gotten worse.

Plus, with the dire circumstances at hand, there simply wasn't time for them to wait around for him to "feel better."

"Let's start with this," Tessa went on. "Is our daughter safe?"

Libby swung her soft gaze from Tessa back to Rand.

Rand hated to see her like that. He'd tried to keep

Libby away from the Herron House, though she'd still ended up going there on her own.

But if she hadn't, then I wouldn't have survived, Rand thought. *Even though her getting involved has put in her a terrible situation.*

Libby had insisted time and time again that she wanted to help with his cases, and that at sixteen years old, she could make her own decisions about her level of involvement. She'd always been confident she could handle the demons Rand constantly fought.

Now, for the first time, she looked totally unsure.

SLAYER OF AKHUBEL.

Rand remembered the words that had been scrawled into the walls of Libby's bedroom at his house. These people—whoever they were—somehow knew Libby herself was the one who had slain their demon. And that message told him they were planning to hold her accountable.

Tessa had heard about it—even seen the pictures of the writing on the wall, which Libby had taken on her phone.

These people would not leave them alone. Would not let them get away with what they had done.

Rand wished he could go back in time so he could be the one who'd killed Akhubel. Not from a place of ego, but so that he would be the target instead of Libby.

Tessa had always told him it was only a matter of time before his work with the supernatural would put their daughter in danger. It actually had In his last few cases, but they'd still emerged victorious and relatively unharmed. He figured his good fortune would continue —that maybe God was protecting him all along.

But that had ended. Now, some of the world's most evil people wanted Libby to pay for killing their demonic servant. And they had the power to make it happen.

"I don't know," Rand said. "But probably not."

He hated to say it, but it was the truth. She *wasn't* safe. A heavy silence lingered around the table. Tessa's jaw clenched, and now it was she who seemed like she might start crying.

"What have you done, Rand?" she asked, her voice pinched. "What happened in that mansion?"

Miller's eyes fell.

Rand set his bag down and took a seat. The metal chair was rough against his back and thighs, but he just needed to be off his feet.

Bill cleared his throat. "Word has been circulating around my office and a few other businesses in town. They're all saying Jackson Herron committed suicide."

Rand had found out yesterday that Bill had actually known Jackson Herron. Rand had even suspected as much when he'd first met Jackson; wealthy business owners seemed to know each other and run in the same circles.

"He didn't," Rand said. "After all his plans failed, he... was punished."

The image of Shindael shoving Jackson Herron off the tower flashed in his mind.

Bill shifted where he stood, unable to meet Rand's gaze. This was the first time Rand had spoken openly about his supernatural experiences with the man. *I have no clue how much Tess has told him,* he thought. His guess was not a lot, since she likely wanted to keep her old life as separate from her new one as possible.

"Besides Jackson, I was the only person left up there on the tower," Rand went on, "and I was the only one who saw what happened to him. When you say that word is getting around your office, that means someone is *intentionally* spreading that story. They're covering up the truth."

Bill hung his head. Rand could tell he desperately wanted to resist the reality of the situation, to protect his comfortable bubble where all the businessmen he knew were honest, hardworking, and successful on their own merits. He didn't want to hear that one of them—and possibly many others—were dabbling in supernatural evil.

Rand would never forget Jackson Herron's words:

"These are the people who control everything and everyone on the entire planet. They decide who gets elected. They decide who wins wars. They decide which nations rise and which ones collapse. Yet no one has a clue they even exist."

Before, if someone had told Rand that world leaders, politicians, and prominent businessmen were summoning demons and using their power to influence the masses, he would've dismissed the notion. Now, he couldn't deny it, no matter how uncomfortable it made him.

To Rand, it seemed his fight was no longer simply with the demonic. He was up against some of the most influential people in the country, and perhaps even the world.

"What about Carmen?" Libby asked.

Rand's shoulders slumped. Carmen Herron was Jackson's nine-year-old daughter, and the man had attempted to sacrifice her to Akhubel in return for acceptance into the Bale family. Rand had foiled that ritual and Carmen had survived; however, her mother Miranda and grandfather Bernard Bale had the girl in their custody. That meant she was still very much in danger.

"I agree that she needs our help," Rand said, speaking slowly so he could choose his words carefully. He knew his daughter was very concerned about Carmen. "But I'm... not sure how to pull that off right now. But I promise I'll find a way."

Libby held Rand's gaze. She looked like she didn't believe him.

I don't believe myself, Rand thought. He wanted to do everything he could to save the girl from her twisted, evil family, but he simply didn't know how yet.

"This all sounds like something you shouldn't stick your nose into," Tessa said.

"It's complicated, Mom," Libby snapped. Tessa seemed taken aback by Libby's sudden reaction. "Trust me, this girl needs our help."

Rand frowned and met Tessa's gaze. He could hear how strongly his daughter felt about helping Carmen, but it was entirely possible that there wasn't anything they could reasonably do. It might be entirely out of their hands.

"You've already brought enough crazy supernatural stuff into our lives," Tessa said tersely. "The least you could do is not get us into any legal trouble as well."

"Noted," Rand said with a sigh.

"What if..." Bill began. All eyes went to him and he paused, as if nervous about suddenly having everyone's attention. He eyed Rand. "What if you just... stopped?"

"Stopped what?"

"All of these cases?"

Tessa scoffed. "I've been suggesting that for years. If *you* asking him is all it takes for him to stop, then great. But Jesus, I wish I'd known that a long time ago."

"Something clearly happened this time that's made you very uncomfortable," Bill went on. "And... has possibly put some of us in danger." He glanced at Libby. "What if we just say... enough is enough? And let it be."

"It's a nice idea, Bill, but I don't think it'll work that way," Rand said. "These people, they... they won't let it be."

"Do you know that for sure?"

"You've seen the pictures of my house, haven't you?"

Bill shoved his hand into his pocket and absent-mindedly rattled some loose change inside. "Who are they? Can't you just go to the police?"

"Rando and I both tried calling the police that night," Miller chimed in. "They already knew what was happening. The guy who answered my call even thought I was Jackson. He literally told me, 'it's under control, sir.' " Miller shook his head at the memory. "So no, that's *not* going to work."

"And the police are likely why everyone thinks Jackson Herron committed suicide," Rand added.

Bill pressed his lips together as he considered that.

"So what will you do, Rand?" Tessa asked pointedly, arms folded. She gave him the same look she used to give Libby when chastising her.

What will I do? It always comes back to that, doesn't it?

He didn't have an immediate answer, and that made him very uncomfortable. The only thing that came to mind was to lie low and wait. If—or when—someone from the Bale family came for him, then he might know how to proceed. But he *hated* the idea of waiting for his enemy to make the first move.

"You need help," Miller answered for him.

Rand already knew what Miller meant. "You're putting a lot of faith in this guy."

"Did you look at that forum I emailed you about?" Miller asked.

"I pulled it up on my computer at work, but I didn't have time to go through it."

"You really should, Rando. I know you have your walls up when it comes to supernatural experts online, but... something tells me this man is the real deal and might can help you."

"He sure wasn't willing to help when he called you the other night," Rand shot back. "Dude said we committed an *act of war* against the underworld and that we were on our own."

"Yeah, but..."

"Have you tried calling him again?"

Miller hung his head. "Yeah... a few times."

"Guess he's *really* not interested."

"I'm going to keep trying, though," Miller said. "Not planning on giving up. I'll talk to him, even if you don't want to."

There was a certain defiant edge in Miller's tone that Rand had never heard before.

Am I being too stubborn? Rand thought.

"I'm sorry, but who is this man?" Tessa asked.

Miller shifted in his chair. "I found him in an online forum about the supernatural. His posts were very detailed and accurate, and it sounds like he's helped people with haunting situations, just like Rando has. But he seems older and... possibly more experienced."

Rand clenched his jaw, but chose not to respond.

Tessa was incredulous. "You mean to tell me that the *best* idea you have for fixing this mess y'all made is some stranger online?"

"My thoughts exactly," Rand said.

"He described Akhubel perfectly." Miller's tone rose. "One of the Lords of Hell. They take on the form of the person who summoned them—their master—and do their bidding here on Earth. That's what Akhubel was! He looked *just* like Bernard Bale."

Miller was right about that. Rand remembered how undeniable their resemblance was once Akhubel and Bernard Bale were in the same room.

"This man knows things we don't," Miller went on. "And he has experience we don't have. For that reason alone, I think it's worth listening to him."

"Except he doesn't want to talk," Rand said. "And he definitely didn't like hearing that we killed one of his 'Lords of Hell.' "

Libby killed him. The Bales knew that Akhubel had died by Libby's hand. And they'd made it clear they wouldn't forget that.

Miller glared at Rand, clearly exasperated. "What else are you going to do? What other ideas do you have? Who do you have to turn to?"

Rand sighed. It always came back to that—as it should—and he still didn't have any good responses.

The one thing he definitely needed to avoid was wasting time. And it felt like a waste of time tracking down a man who didn't want to be found.

Libby's gaze was fixed to a place on the table while she chewed the inside of her cheek. She looked like she had something she wanted to say but was holding back.

Miller's right, Rand finally decided. *Trying to find any kind of help is better than just sitting around and waiting.*

"Fine," Rand said.

"What's fine?" Tessa asked, perking up at the suggestion of a decision.

"Let's see if we can get Arthur Briggs to help." Miller's eyes widened in surprise. "But as you said, Miller, the problem is he won't answer his phone. So we need another plan."

"We'll find him and meet him in person," Miller said.

Tessa's shoulders slumped. "So we're going with the stranger-from-the-internet idea."

"I've already looked into it," Miller said, ignoring Tessa. "He lives in a town called Rose Grove in Georgia, and it isn't very big. I'm sure if we asked around a bit, we could find him."

Rand blew out a slow breath. He was so exhausted that the last thing he wanted at the moment was a road trip. "Probably."

"You're leaving town?" Tessa asked. "But what about..." She gestured toward Libby.

"Just for a day or two," Rand said. "Hopefully."

"I'll be fine, Dad," Libby said. "Go see if you can find this guy. I think Miller might be on to something."

Tessa still did not seem comfortable with the situation. Rand nodded resolutely. The decision was made. Whether it was a good or bad one remained to be seen. "Are you able to leave tomorrow morning?" he asked Miller.

3

Rand was the first to leave the others. He went upstairs to Bill's guest bedroom, his new temporary residence. He opened the door and paused when he noticed the bed had been made, the white cotton sheets and navy throw blanket pulled taut over the king-sized mattress. He distinctly remembered not doing it that morning since he'd been late for work, and he highly doubted Bill himself had performed the room service.

It wouldn't surprise me if he had some hired help, Rand thought.

He removed his large duffel bag from the closet—the same one he'd packed when he'd agreed to stay at Bill's for the time being. He opened the mahogany armoire that was across from the bed and threw some clothes into the bag. Next came the supplies he'd retrieved from his office before vacating his home: a Bible and some vials of holy water. He hoisted the bag onto the side of the mattress then zipped it closed.

He went to the bedside table and opened the drawer. The only thing inside was a foot-long cross. Although it appeared simple, that was far from the case. It had been imbued with the power of Tara, the angelic being who had recently begun appearing to Rand. The cross had helped him out of several binds while in the Herron House.

Rand eyed his packed bag as he considered. Ultimately, he laid the cross on the bedside table, choosing not to bring it with him. He had other plans for it.

When he went downstairs and into the kitchen, he found Libby seated on a stool at the island in the center of the room. She had a pile of familiar-looking papers in front of her.

"What are you doing?" Rand asked.

"Grading your tests so you don't have to worry about them," she said as her eyes bounced back and forth between the answer key and the test on top of the stack.

"Right. I forgot about those."

"I know."

He usually paid Libby twenty bucks to grade the tests for him. This time, he had a feeling he was getting it for free.

Rand went to the fridge and opened it. He found a drawer filled with beer bottles, but when he picked one up and inspected it, the label proudly proclaimed it to be non-alcoholic.

Come on, Bill, you actually buy *this stuff?* Rand thought as he put the bottle back.

"Cults in the ancient Middle East were incredibly diverse and fascinating," Libby read aloud, adopting a formal tone. "They ranged from the sun-worshipping cult of Shamash to the cult of Ishtar, which focused on love and sex."

Rand closed the refrigerator and turned to face his daughter, confused. She appeared to be reading from one of his test papers. "Huh? That doesn't sound—"

"*Obviously*, Dad." Libby held up a blue book exam booklet. "It's from this."

"Oh. That belongs to Sharma. It must've gotten mixed up in the pile."

I left in such a rush that I probably took one of her tests home by accident, Rand thought.

"Sounds like her class is *way* harder than yours. Remind me not to take it when I go to college."

Rand picked up the blue book. Sure enough, "World Religions 302" had been written on the front.

"She's going to want this back sooner rather than later." That was just another thing he'd have to deal with and would distract him from what was truly important. "In fact, I bet she's already noticed."

He took his cell phone from his pocket and opened his work email. Sure enough, he had a message from Professor Sharma.

Hi Rand.

I seem to be missing an exam. I'm wondering if it got mixed in with yours by mistake. Please let me know if you spot a blue book among your tests.

Kind regards,

Dipika.

Rand typed out a quick response.

Hi Dipika.

Yes, I have it here with me. I'm taking a few days off, so I can give it to you when I get back to work.

—Rand

Rand laid his phone on the countertop. "We had to share a classroom today. There was apparently some leak —" The phone chimed with an email notification, which when he looked at his screen turned out to be a speedy reply from Professor Sharma.

Hi Rand.

Glad to hear it's with you instead of lost.

Is it possible to get it from you before your time off? I'd like to have my grades posted ASAP. The students in 302 are quite insistent.

I understand if this is inconvenient.

—D

Rand sighed.

"What's wrong?" Libby asked.

"She's asking for her test back tonight."

"Go bring it to her, then," Libby said.

Rand picked up his phone to type a response.

Sure. What's the most convenient way to get it to you?

Dipika replied quickly.

I'll be at O'Conner's later this evening. Can you swing by there?

Rand let out a curious grunt when he read what she'd sent.

"What?" Libby asked.

"She wants me to bring it to O'Conner's." Returning the test now seemed a lot less of a chore. He could have a *real* drink at O'Conner's, unlike the pointless beer in Bill's fridge.

"How does she know you like O'Conner's? Have you gone out with her before?"

"What? No. She doesn't know that."

"So it's a coincidence," Libby said. "Or, as Mom would say, a *synchronicity.* Since she's all into that new-age spirituality these days."

Libby was right. Tessa was full of different ideas and terminology lately. *But her knowledge of astrology saved my ass the other night in the Herron House,* Rand thought.

A smirk spread across Libby's face. "This lady has a workplace crush on you."

"Um... no."

"She wants her test back, but she *also* wants to have a drink with you. I like her style, killing two birds with one stone."

"I don't think so," Rand said. He remembered the disapproving look she'd given him earlier after perusing the material he'd been testing his students on.

Libby scoffed. "Right. Okay, Dad, whatever you want to believe. This is actually better. Having a drink with your hot coworker would be a good distraction for a little while."

"How do you know she's hot?" Rand shot back.

"Ah. So she *is.*"

Rand glared at his daughter. Dating was far from a top priority, and it had been that way for quite some time. A demon had harmed his last girlfriend as a roundabout way of attacking Rand. After that, Rand had sworn off women until after his life had quieted down.

And it looks like that isn't happening anytime soon. Things are only getting worse.

"I'll bring her the test back, but after I hand it over, I'm out of there."

"You can't do that," Libby chided him. "She clearly

wants to spend some time with you outside of work, so just do it."

Rand sighed again. Regardless of whether Libby was right about Dipika's intentions, Rand *did* have to return the test to her.

He picked up the phone and responded.

Sure. What time will you be there?

Her response quickly followed.

Around seven. See you then.

—D

"Okay, we're going to meet."

"Whoo-hoo," Libby said with a smile. "Dad's got a date."

4

*G*ive the test back and have only one drink, Rand thought when he arrived at O'Conner's cigar bar. He really needed to get some sleep if possible, before heading out to Rose Grove the next morning.

The bar's walls were rich wood paneling with brass accents, and the varied seating was all plush leathers. Dim lighting gave the place a sense of intimacy. Scattered around the lounge, people enjoyed their drinks as they engaged in conversation.

Rand spotted Dipika at the bar. A gentleman sat next to her, obviously chatting her up. Rand hesitated, wondering if he should interrupt.

Angie, the bartender, noticed him standing there.

"Hey, Mr. Rand. Been a while."

At hearing his name, Dipika turned. She shot him a quick smile and gestured to the barstool beside her.

"Evening, Professor Sharma," Rand said as he sidled up.

"Come on. Dipika."

The man on the other side of her sized Rand up. Rand could sense he'd been on his game, but was now thrown off by the sudden appearance.

"Whiskey neat, Mr. Rand?" Angie asked, and he nodded.

Angie was a good-looking young lady with long blonde hair and a beautiful smile. Miller had a crush on her, but more importantly, she had an excellent memory when it came to drink orders.

"I didn't know when I suggested this place that I was actually inviting a regular," Dipika said.

"I've been trying to keep away lately," Rand said. Angie placed the drink in front of Rand.

"It was great to meet you, Tim," Dipika said. "I have some business to discuss with my colleague."

"Ah, a colleague." Tim smirked. "Well, in that case, how about—"

"You seem great, but no thank you," Dipika replied before lifting her wineglass and taking a sip. The rim was lightly smudged with lipstick.

Tim's face fell slowly, as if he wasn't used to such swift rejection and his brain needed some extra seconds to process it. Finally, he gave a terse nod and slinked away.

"Don't let me get in the way of a good time," Rand said. "He seems..." He looked over his shoulder and watched Tim slump back to a trio of friends at a table in the corner. "...nice."

"That kid's like twenty-five," Dipika said.

Rand once again felt bad for interrupting. When he was twenty-five, he'd also taken his shot with women in their forties on a handful of occasions.

He couldn't blame the guy. Dipika *was* looking good that night. Which was strange, because she hardly looked different from when Rand had seen her that day at work. Maybe it was the bar's soft lighting, or something about her demeanor; she seemed much more relaxed than when he'd interacted with her earlier in class. There, she'd been rigid and stern when supervising her students taking their tests. Now, that whole vibe was gone, as if her workplace persona was just that—a rough exterior.

Focus, Rand told himself, then pulled out the blue book exam. It had a prominent crease down the middle. Dipika took it from him with a slightly disapproving look.

"Sorry about the fold. My daughter did that." That wasn't *totally* true—he'd hastily shoved it into his jacket pocket as he'd left Bill's house.

"It's Brittany Bush's test, so fold it up all you want, because the only thing she cares about is getting an A. Anything less and her world will end."

"I've had a few of those." He took another sip of whiskey as he remembered Stacy Thompson—his star student, who had gotten in trouble with a pair of demons last Halloween.

"What was your daughter doing with my test, anyway?" Dipika asked.

"She grades mine for me," Rand said. "Only costs twenty bucks. She found it in the stack, mixed in with the ones from my class."

Dipika chuckled. "Must be nice to have a grading assistant. The benefits of multiple-choice exams."

Rand detected the playful jab. He wasn't oblivious—he was well aware that Intro to Supernatural Studies would never be accepted into the pantheon of other prestigious classes in the Religious Studies department.

"I remember how much I appreciated multiple choice when I was in school," Rand said. "Just trying to pay it forward. Maybe you should try it?"

"I know what they say about my class," Dipika said. "Students never talk as quietly as they think they do."

Rand had to agree, and he'd heard the chatter as well. Professor Sharma's World Religions was dreaded among all who saw it listed as a requirement on the path to their diploma.

"These kids need to learn this stuff, though," Dipika continued. "Why sign up for a class if you don't actually want to learn the subject? And the best way to do that is study it thoroughly. And the only way to make college kids study anything thoroughly is to test the hell out of them." She spoke as if she were trying to convince herself, as if this were a debate she'd had in her head many times before.

"Well... for what it's worth," Rand began, "I've only heard them gripe about the class and tests. They all seem to like you as a teacher."

"Good. I know my course is hard, but I've never considered myself to be a terrible person," Dipika said. She shot her eyes at him. "Even though you clearly think I'm going to steal from you."

Rand furrowed his brow. He wasn't following that one. "Steal from me?"

"When you were leaving earlier." She took a sip of wine, giving Rand time to remember.

It came to him. The black cube.

"Ah." Rand shrugged in an attempt to make it seem like no big deal.

Dipika scoffed and rolled her eyes. "Come on. You fell on that thing like it was a grenade and you were trying to be a hero. What is it and how much is it worth? Can you get me one?"

Rand laughed uneasily at her joke. If he were being honest, he wasn't sure whether it was a rhetorical question, but he decided to treat it like one and avoid giving her an answer. The black cube was the last thing he wanted to talk about, or try to explain.

Dipika looked at her lap and pursed her lips. Rand detected the shift in energy from her—a slight awkwardness blooming. He figured he'd given her the impression that she'd pushed too far and had asked him a question that had been too personal.

It's better if you don't know, Rand thought, and wanted to say out loud, but knew that would only bring more questions. Or perhaps even frighten her.

To his relief, Dipika swiftly changed the subject. "I've never heard of a university that's offered a class like yours," she said. "The other teachers are curious about it. And you."

"I'm aware," Rand said.

"Do you believe in that stuff?"

Rand paused, his glass halfway to his mouth. He wasn't in the mood to have this conversation either, which he'd had perhaps a hundred times in his life. But he also wasn't in the mood to spend excess mental energy trying to dance around the topic.

"Very much so."

"Have you had... experiences?"

Experiences. A summer spent backpacking across Europe was an experience. Catching a pass for the winning touchdown was an experience. He remembered his most recent cases: Georgia Collins getting possessed; the preacher in Finnick who'd invited a demon into his own body, thinking it was an angel; the black-eyed kids who'd tormented a former student on Halloween; the harrowing night spent trapped within the Herron House, where he'd literally died and come back to life by the power of God.

"A few," he finally said.

Usually, when Rand had this discussion, this was the part where he was asked for specifics. Stories. Like a young child imploring his grandfather to regale him with tales from a faraway war, thinking it was like an action movie rather than a prolonged period of trauma and pain that the other person carried with them every single day.

But Dipika didn't press. Perhaps she picked up on his reluctance.

"Do you believe?" Rand asked.

She took a slow sip of wine, a thoughtful expression on her face, clearly searching for the right words. "I tend to spend most of my time in the realm of reality."

Rand figured as much. Dipika was precisely the kind of person you wanted teaching a class like World Religions. Someone who was able to explain each of the world's main belief systems in objective, fair detail, knowledgeable about all of them yet ascribing to none.

"I used to be the same. Until I had my first encounter with the supernatural."

"There was only one thing in my life that ever made me question if there was something else out there,"

Dipika said. A small smile crept onto her lips as she remembered. "Or one person, actually."

"Let's hear it," Rand said, only because he could tell it was a good memory for her.

"No one at work knows this, but I'm very close friends with Arun Singh."

The name she dropped was punctuated in a way that told Rand she'd expected him to recognize it.

"Who?"

Dipika gave him an incredulous look. "Arun Singh. Really? You don't know who he is?"

Rand shrugged. "My daughter gets on me all the time for not knowing celebrities."

"He isn't a celebrity. Well, not like a movie star or a singer. But he has been in the headlines lately. Search him online when you get a chance. The internet'll tell you everything."

"Okay," Rand said, now curious. "What's the deal with this guy?"

"We grew up in the same village, just outside of Nagpur, India," Dipika explained. "We were best friends. Inseparable, really. Our families thought that maybe one day we'd get married, but... it wasn't like that. He left for America first and got involved in his tech start-ups. I came over a few years later and studied to become a teacher. We stayed in touch when we could, but we were both busy.

"Anyway, Arun's very smart, but also very spiritual. Not religious, but spiritual, you know? To him, it was always clear that there was more to life and the universe. When we were young—he was eleven, I think, and I was nine—he had a book that he read over and over. Oh, what was it?" Dipika put her fingers to her temples as she seemed to dig through her memories. "*Autobiography of a Yogi*. By Paramahansa Yogananda. Have you ever heard of it?"

"I have, actually," Rand said.

"I don't know how many times Arun read it cover to cover. He'd finish it and then start it over the next day. He said every time he read it, he noticed something new that he hadn't seen before. The only time he wasn't reading it was when he lent me his copy, insisting that I go through it, too. But I was only nine, so I wasn't really interested in that stuff. When a couple of days went by and I hadn't started it, he asked for it back. I swear, that book was like a drug to him.

"One day, he confessed that he had... I can't remember how he worded it, but I guess some kind of guardian angel. A girl who only he could see."

Rand perked up, suddenly *very* curious about where this was going. Dipika didn't notice his change in rapt attention.

"He told me she'd been appearing to him off and on for several years at that point. He said that one night he was meditating and thinking about young children around the world who were being harmed by their parents or communities or the people who they thought were supposed to protect them. Then, this girl appeared in a vision and told him that in the future he'd be a great man who'd help those children."

Before Dipika had begun her story, Rand had assumed she'd been about to say she'd possibly seen a ghost out of the corner of her eye one time. Or that the electricity had flickered while playing with a Ouija board with a group of friends at a sleepover. But this tale was something else entirely. He, too, had once been saved by an entity that he could only describe as a guardian angel.

"I didn't really believe him," Dipika said. "Though I *did* believe that Arun believed what he *thought* he saw. He was never one to lie or make things up, but I figured there was some kind of rational explanation. Especially when he described this girl. He said she was surrounded by bright light and had long blonde hair." She chuckled. "I told him *of course* an eleven-year-old boy from India was going to daydream about a pretty blonde girl. But he insisted it wasn't like that at all."

There's no way it's the same entity, he thought. *Or could it...*

"What was her name?" Rand interjected.

Dipika finally realized just how invested Rand had become in her story. She looked to the side as she reflected back to her childhood.

"Tara," she said. "I think he told me her name was Tara."

5

Rand felt as if his chest had crashed into his stomach.

Tara.

Demons were timeless creatures, so that meant angels were, also. And although Rand hadn't considered it, it made sense that he wouldn't be the only one Tara had revealed herself to.

"What's wrong?" Dipika asked.

"I just wasn't expecting a story like that," Rand said. *And that's putting it lightly.*

"Well, anyway... it seems this guardian angel stayed with him over the years. She's the reason he's been in the headlines. You'll see what I mean if you look him up later."

Rand almost regretted asking her. There was so much on his mind, and the last thing he needed was another rabbit hole to dig up. A billionaire family using demons to manipulate and influence the world was enough for the time being.

But if there's someone else who has seen Tara...

"All of these memories have been coming up lately because I'll be seeing Arun soon," Dipika said. "There's an event this weekend in Washington, D.C. He's being honored for something. Can't remember if it has to do with his business or his philanthropy. Hard to keep up with all his accolades these days. Anyway, he invites me every time one of these events happen, but the timing's always been bad. I finally get to attend this time, though. That's why I wanted the test back from you tonight. I'll need to get a jump on grading them because of this trip."

Rand almost asked if he could go with her. To meet Arun and ask him about Tara. But he swallowed those words before he could vomit them out.

One thing at a time. Finding Arthur Briggs is what matters right now.

"That all sounds very intriguing," Rand said, doing his best to stifle his wonder. "I'll definitely read about him later."

"I'm interested in your thoughts when you do." She finished off her wine. "It was good to finally sit down and talk to you, Mr. Exorcist."

"You too." He drained his own glass and lifted his hand to get Angie's attention. "Both on my tab, please."

"I guess that means my story entertained you."

"More than you might realize, Dipika."

WHEN RAND RETURNED to Bill's house, everyone already gone to bed. Someone—probably Libby—had left a lamp on for him. He turned it off and went upstairs to the guest room.

Although it was late, Rand wasn't tired, despite not having gotten much sleep over the last several days. Instead of trying to pass out, he laid on his side under the covers, the light from his phone screen blinding in the darkness.

He opened his phone's internet browser and typed in a name.

Arun Singh.

As Dipika had implied, there were dozens of results, many of them recent. Most of the articles had clickbait headlines.

Tech Entrepreneur or Modern-Day Prophet? Or Both?

Who is Arun Singh and Why is Everyone Baffled?

Arun Singh: "My Guardian Angel Told Me Where Those Children Were."

Rand chose an older article first to get some context. It was called: *Twenty-Seven Missing Children Discovered Beneath Century-Old Cathedral.*

Rand scrolled through the article, which detailed how an anonymous tip had led police to discover kidnapped children in a secret basement underneath a church. Despite their initial skepticism, law enforcement had acted on the tip and, to their surprise, found exactly what had been reported.

Rand went back to the search results and found an article that was not like the others.

Skeptics Demand Police Investigate Arun Singh.

Rand clicked on it.

"Trafficking activist Katrina Richardson is calling for an investigation into Arun Singh after his startling revelation that

he was the one who provided an anonymous tip to police, leading to the breakup of a large trafficking ring operating out of the state of Wyoming.

" 'I'm not buying his story, and frankly I'm surprised anyone is,' Richardson said.

"Richardson is referring to Singh's claim that his 'guardian angel' told him the information he'd given to police, which then resulted in the arrest of six men and two women and the rescue of twenty-seven children between the ages of four and fifteen.

" 'Obviously he had prior knowledge of this group's activities and plans,' Richardson continued. 'I'm glad those children were saved, but I think law enforcement should now turn their attention to Mr. Singh to learn how he actually knew about the operation.'

"Many are pushing back against Richardson's allegations."

Interspersed in the article were screen grabs featuring social media posts about the situation.

"Trafficking activism is more than posting about it for likes and clicks. You eventually have to do something. Thank you, Arun Singh, for bringing our kids home!"

"It doesn't matter how Arun Singh knew where to find those kids. Unlike @theRealKatrinaRichardson, his track record speaks for itself."

"I don't know what drugs Arun Singh is on, but keep them coming! He's single-handedly saved more children than any politician in this country!"

Rand looked up from his phone and considered what he'd read. He found he believed every word. From what Dipika had told him, Arun Singh seemed like a spiritual man seeking answers. Tara must have appeared to him in a moment of great need and desire, just as she'd come to Rand.

The backlash from folks like Katrina Richardson made total sense to Rand. Generally speaking, the world was spiritually dead, and growing more so each year. People simply did not accept supernatural explanations for anything. It was why Rand rarely spoke about his work to anyone. Doing so invited both ridicule and mockery. He again remembered the look on Dipika's face when she'd snuck a glimpse at his student's test.

Rand felt a heavy conviction—almost shame. Arun Singh could've kept his relationship with his guardian angel a secret. He could've avoided the skeptics and their criticisms, which came from them refusing to entertain for one second that there was more to life than the mere three-dimensional reality they saw in front of their noses.

But he didn't. He'd spoken out in faith, and as a result, children had been saved from evil people. He'd made the world a better place. He'd done what Rand strived to do every time he accepted a new case.

Arun Singh. Arthur Briggs, Rand thought as he set his phone down and rolled over in bed. *They're the real deal. I assumed I was doing good things too, but lately it seems like I'm just making everything worse.*

6

The sky was just beginning to turn purple with the rising sun. The winter morning was like ice. Rand started up his Jeep to let the windshield begin defrosting, then tossed his heavy-duty black bag that he'd packed the night before into the trunk.

"When are you coming back?"

Rand hadn't noticed that Libby had joined him outside. She wore thin pajama pants and an oversized sweatshirt, arms folded over her torso to ward off the early-morning chill.

"I'm not sure yet," he said.

Libby frowned. "I don't like you leaving."

"I know." Rand scooped her up into a hug. "But I'll be back as soon as I can."

He didn't want to be gone long, either. He and Miller planned on making the drive to Rose Grove in a single day, so hopefully they could track down Arthur Briggs that evening.

"Here." Rand reached into his jacket pocket and took

out the cross that was imbued with Tara's essence—the one that had brought him back from the dead and that his daughter had used to kill Akhubel. He held it out to Libby.

She stared at it without taking it. "What?"

"It'll keep you safe while I'm gone."

"But what about you?"

"I'll feel a lot better if you have it."

Libby reluctantly took the cross.

Besides, it doesn't respond to me anymore, Rand thought. It hadn't ever since he'd touched the black cube. Whatever corrupting power was inside that thing seemed to overpower the cross.

"Thanks," Libby said flatly. Rand could tell she was still apprehensive about him letting her keep what had so far been their most powerful weapon against the demonic.

"School and home only while I'm gone." Rand gave his tone a slight sternness. "Remember what we talked about yesterday. We don't know what these people are capable of."

"I understand," Libby said. His heart broke. Although his daughter tried to hide it, he could still detect a hint of fear behind her eyes.

Rand checked his watch. He was late in picking up Miller. "I have to go."

"Okay."

He paused before getting inside the car as something else popped into his mind.

"Have you ever heard of Arun Singh?" Rand asked Libby.

"Yeah. He's like super famous right now. Because of

that whole thing with the kids." She cocked her head. "Why?"

He realized he didn't have the time to go into everything Dipika had told him the night before. "I'll tell you about it later, but it's important." Libby nodded, still confused.

Rand got into the car and pulled out of Bill's driveway. In his mirror, he saw how his daughter lingered and watched him until she disappeared from view.

7

Janet Yardley was worn out, but that was nothing new.

Even though her plain black shoes had promised arch support, that had turned out to be a lie cleverly peddled by some marketing department. A familiar dull ache had settled into her lower back and knees. The mental fatigue was considerable as well. The constant focus she'd given the last couple of hours had taken its toll, and now her brain seemed to wallow in a fog.

It was exhausting being one of the few employees of Elite Eats Catering Company who *actually* pulled their own weight on the job.

You got this, she told herself. *It's almost over.*

Janet had overheard more than a few people making the rounds and saying their goodbyes. Empty champagne flutes had begun to congregate on the tables, most of which had been abandoned.

At the end of each event, she still had to clean.

Majestic oaks lined the perimeter of the mansion's backyard. Strung-up fairy lights illuminated the lawn from above. Circular tables had been set up outside, each seating six. The centerpiece of the outdoor area was a fountain of stone cherubs, water cascading down from the jars they held.

Nearby was a bar, where her colleagues Grant and Stu mixed drinks. They were her favorite pair to work with. Janet enjoyed the quips they offered when she passed by the bar. Little things like that really helped pass the time.

The events jumbled together in her mind. This was for some old guy named Dunmore. His sprawling mansion, while impressive, didn't awe her at all. Janet had seen too many similar homes in the course of her work. Whatever celebration Elite Eats had been brought in for, she had no idea. When she'd first started working for the catering company, she used to ask. Not anymore. It wasn't relevant.

Janet spotted a man sitting alone at a circular table. Plates containing scraps of food remained. The man's attention was locked onto his phone.

"Excuse me, sir. Can I start clearing some of this away?" Without waiting for a response, Janet started stacking the plates and glasses on her tray, some of which contained a surprising amount of neglected hors d'oeuvres.

The people at these kinds of events can be so wasteful sometimes, she thought.

The man looked up from his phone and scanned the table, as if realizing for the first time that he'd been alone there for quite a while. "Sure. I don't think any of them are coming back." He then gave her a wide smile. Curiously, it seemed genuine.

As she worked, she felt the man's eyes remain on her.

"Or how about you take a break instead?" the man asked.

Here we go, Janet thought. She'd quickly learned that being waitstaff had somehow magically made her into a magnet for unwanted advances.

"Wish I could, but there's a lot to do." Janet forced a polite smile.

"Ned Lofthouse is your boss, isn't he?"

A slick glass almost slipped through Janet's fingers. Her mind worked to decipher the meaning behind the man's question.

Is he threatening to report me if I don't sit and "take a break" with him?

"He's an asshole," the man continued.

Janet gave a nervous chuckle. "No comment."

"Look, I'm part owner of your company. You don't know me, but it's true. I've known Ned for a while. If you're sitting with me, he won't get onto you for slacking off, I promise. Besides, he can't retain staff to save his life, and it looks like you actually do your job, so I don't think there's any risk if you take a short break." He sat back in his chair, one ankle crossed over the other knee, and continued smiling at her.

Janet stopped what she was doing and appraised the man. *Who is this guy?* He was quite handsome, that was for sure. Her eyes quickly went to the wedding band on his ring finger.

Janet sensed this situation was more complex than she'd first thought. While the job was grueling, there *was* a reason she'd chosen to work for Elite Eats, the high-end option as far as catering companies were concerned: only those willing to spend a lot on their parties could afford them.

Janet Yardley had big plans for a small-town girl. She'd had her eye on an MBA and was striving to make that happen. Each and every paycheck was dutifully stashed away into her saving account. By her calculations, she was about sixty-five percent of the way there.

But the degree wasn't her only goal—this job was her covert classroom. Mingling with one-percenters was just as much a part of her strategy as enrolling in college. Her father had taught her that *who* you knew was often more important than *what* you knew.

Assuming this guy wasn't simply trying to hit on her, she wasn't at all opposed to sitting down and chatting for a bit. Especially if he was telling the truth and could shield her from Ned Lofthouse's ire.

"Fine." Janet set her tray on the table and sat in the seat nearest to the man. Nothing about this smile or demeanor changed after he'd convinced her—as if he known Janet was going to comply all along.

As soon as her butt hit the chair, it felt like a wall of pressure had come off her feet. She let out a long breath.

"That's better," he said. "I could tell you needed it." His eyes went to the name tag pinned to the front of her shirt. "So. Janet."

It was almost strange to hear her own name. Their name tags were kept in a single bin, and she usually snatched up a random one in a hurry at the start of her shift, heedless of who it actually belonged to. At events like this, it rarely mattered what her name was—people generally opted to call her "Hey!" and "Ma'am" while waving their hands to get her attention.

"Yes."

The man leaned forward and offered his hand. "I'm Nathan."

"Nice to meet you," she replied, shaking it.

"You and your team did a great job this evening."

Even more rare than hearing her own name was someone complimenting their work. If they did well, no one said anything. But if they did less than what had been expected, the complaints came, and they'd hear about it the next morning from Ned.

And he called us a team, Janet thought. Usually, she and her colleagues were only called that by the performance-improvement consultants Ned brought in once a year and forced them to listen to—almost always on their day off.

"Do you like this job, Janet?" Nathan asked.

"It's a job." She shrugged.

"Let me guess," Nathan said. "Lots of people just stop showing up for work without any notice."

"Yes. It's actually very common." It surprised her that Nathan would be aware of the challenges of working for Elite Eats. When coworkers flaked on their shifts and vanished, Janet had to fill in for them. It happened so often that Ned usually didn't even bother calling them to see if they were planning on continuing to work for him.

"I don't blame them," Nathan said. "Like I said, Ned's kind of a jackass. I want to swap him out with someone who knows what they're doing, but I'm still trying to convince the other owners."

Janet felt more at ease. Like Grant and Stu, she appreciated anyone who was willing to talk shit about Ned. She also found it amusing that Nathan was technically getting paid to party—he got to show his face at Dunmore's *and* score some business for his catering company at the same time.

"What do you do?" Janet asked. "Besides own part of Elite Eats?"

"This and that," he replied with a smile.

Janet had read somewhere that wealthy people usually had multiple streams of income. Various businesses, investments, and interest that paid out on a recurring basis. She figured that maybe it was hard for Nathan to sum it up simply.

"Sounds... interesting," Janet said, an attempt at a mild joke. To her relief, Nathan actually laughed.

"Janet," someone barked her name over her shoulder, startling her.

Oh no, she thought. It was time to see if Nathan was the real deal or all talk.

Ned appeared. "I need you on shell duty." He then dropped a brown leather sack onto the table in front of her—and then did a double take when he saw who Janet was sitting with. Janet noticed his tension, and she relished it.

"Evening, Ned." Nathan still smiled.

Ned nodded at him. "Nathan." He turned back to Janet and regarded her more gently than before. "Just... whenever you get the chance. Thanks." He left them as quickly as he'd come.

"So you *were* telling the truth," Janet said.

"What's shell duty?" Nathan asked, seeming genuinely curious.

"Oh. Because there were oysters for dinner, I have to

go through all the trash and separate the shells for composting."

She eyed the brown leather sack Ned had dropped on the table. Everyone who worked for Elite Eats knew what that sack meant—fill it with the shells.

"Sounds like a dirty job." Nathan frowned.

"But someone's gotta do it. Though it seems like it's me every time." More often than not, that sack seemed to find its way to Janet, simply because she'd proven herself reliable in the past. The shells stunk, and she almost always cut her fingertip when handling them—especially when she was rushing to finish faster so she could go home. "I guess that makes me the bag woman."

Nathan laughed again. "Very clever. I like that."

Janet eyed the leather sack. Even though she'd begun to enjoy Nathan's company, she knew it was better to begin her hunt for every oyster shell on Dunmore's property. The sooner she started, the sooner she'd be done.

"I can tell you want more from this," Nathan said, gesturing to their surroundings, the party, and the people. "You're here for a reason."

"Of course. This is all a means to an end," Janet said.

"Isn't everything?" Nathan briefly checking the screen of his phone. "What does your family think?"

"I lost my parents a long time ago," Janet said. "But I like to think they'd be proud of where I'm heading."

Nathan nodded slowly. He seemed to be considering something. "Married? Kids?"

"Neither." It sucked to admit that she was all alone in the world, but she'd come to terms with that a few years back.

"Did you see the lake Dunmore has on his property?" Nathan asked.

The abrupt subject change caught Janet off guard. She hadn't even known there was a lake nearby. "No."

"Let's go. I'll show you real quick, and then you can get back to work."

Janet thought it was an odd request, but it felt wrong to decline. She wasn't sure why yet, but she liked Nathan. She'd appreciated both the small talk and the chance to give her feet a break for a few minutes—while being protected from Ned. "Okay. Why not?"

Nathan took the leather sack with him when they went, which Janet found a bit odd. *Maybe he'll throw it in the lake,* Janet mused.

The voices of the party grew fainter as they walked away. The cobblestone pathways that weaved through Dunmore's backyard gave way to an earthy trail.

They didn't have to go far; Dunmore's property backed up to the lake. It was simple, yet still nice. Tall reeds lined the perimeter. A wooden gazebo was near the edge. A plain dock extended a few feet into the water. Janet could imagine Dunmore's young children, if he had any, spending countless hours jumping off of it in the summer.

"I like it," Janet said, letting the tranquility wash over her. It was as if Nathan knew that such a sight would help her recover a bit of energy to carry her through the rest of her shift. *Maybe one day I'll be able to afford a house with a lake.*

She realized that Nathan hadn't responded. Nor was he standing beside her anymore.

Her world went black when a coarse material covered

her head—the oyster shell sack. The rough leather scratched against Janet's cheeks and nose. Something tightened around her neck, choking off her air, and she couldn't even scream. Janet tried to fight back, but her assailant was too strong.

There was a voice in her ear, muffled by the sack—Nathan's, speaking some strange language, the words indecipherable and ominous.

It was the last thing she heard.

8

The windshield wipers swiped left to right in a hypnotic rhythm as rain pattered down, which was the only sound besides the soft thrum of the car engine. Outside, the world was a wet blur of dark shapes and muted colors. They were currently driving on a narrow, two-lane state highway. On either side, Georgia farmland became visible only when lit up by the frequent flashes of lightning.

"Rose Grove should only be half an hour away," Miller said, checking his phone.

The sky's grayish hue had followed them for the past ten hours. Only when they were nearing their destination did the rain finally decide to come.

The trip should've taken less time, but Rand had known from the beginning that Miller would slow them down. His tolerance for a full bladder wasn't as refined as Rand's, so they hit more than a few rest stops along the way.

"You're worse than Tessa and Libby," Rand had quipped.

Lunch at a roadside diner had stretched out longer than either of them had anticipated. The "Now Hiring All Positions" sign out front should've been the first clue that the service would be slow.

The sun set early, as it always did on cold January days. That left Rand and Miller arriving in town under the cover of night. The Jeep's headlights seemed to be swallowed by the darkness, even with the brights on, and the rain certainly didn't make things any easier. Periodically, the highway made sharp curves through the farmland that flanked the road on either side. Rand slowed considerably during the sections; the last thing they needed was to get tangled up in some sugar cane.

Headlights appeared in the distance behind them. It was the first pair since they'd seen while on the long, winding state highway that would lead them to Rose Grove.

"They're flying," Miller said, eyes locked on the passenger-side mirror.

He was right. The headlights had gained on them.

The car caught up quickly, its lights nearly blinding Rand as they grew brighter in the rearview. The driver slammed on their brakes mere inches from Rand's rear bumper, then began blaring their horn.

"The hell is this dude's problem?" The other driver's unnecessary road rage sent anger coiling through Rand's limbs. He gripped his steering wheel.

"Rando, just let him pass." Miller's body stiffened.

"There's no shoulder." Rand eased his foot off the gas and drifted to the side of the highway. The Jeep tipped as they teetered over the slightly sloping edge of the asphalt.

The car behind made sharp swerves left and right as if preparing to pass Rand in the other lane, but they never did. They just continued tailgating and laying on the horn.

"What do we do?" Miller held onto the center console and the bar above of his window.

More headlights appeared in the distance in front of them.

"Damn it," Rand whispered.

The car behind started flashing their lights as well, adding to Rand's distractions.

A baritone horn sounded—the coming eighteen-wheeler truck must've seen the erratic driving ahead of him.

The car still occupied both lanes, as if unafraid of the oncoming truck. Finally, it shifted into the right lane a split second before the big rig passed on the left, nearly causing a head-on collision.

"This guy's crazy," Miller said. "I think—"

Rand and Miller lurched forward as the car rammed into the back of the Jeep. Miller let out a yelp.

"What the *fuck?*" Rand barked.

The black car slowed and then sped up again, giving Rand's Jeep a second pounding, this one stronger than the first. Now that the left lane was clear, Rand swerved over to get out from in front of the attacking vehicle.

But it only followed him.

Rand jerked the wheel back to the right, but the front bumper of the other car, like a magnet, stayed behind them. Whoever was driving seemed to have more skill and control on the slick roads than a Hollywood stunt driver.

He's trying *to run us off the road,* Rand realized.

The car sped up and slammed into the Jeep a third time. The tires lost their grip on the wet asphalt. Rand didn't have a chance to react, or to even swear again. They careened across the other lane and off the edge. The world spun. Rand smelled burning rubber. His body pressed against the locked seatbelt. His neck and head whipped around while his stomach lurched like it did when an airplane hit turbulence. Pain shot through his forehead. Airbags deployed with a loud *pop.*

Then blackness.

9

Rand opened his eyes. Blinked a couple times. His vision and focus slowly returned. At first, he saw the lights on the center console and the dashboard. Then he noticed the smear of blood on the deployed airbag. His memories cascaded back.

Miller slumped forward against his seatbelt, head dangling.

"Miller," Rand said.

The man didn't move.

An onslaught of worst-case scenarios flashed through his mind.

"Miller!"

Rand tried to lift his arm to shake his friend's shoulder, to wake him up, but his limbs were like lead.

He remembered the other car—they'd been run off the road.

Rand looked to his left and out the passenger window. Raindrops streaked the glass, obstructing his view. Even if it hadn't been raining, he still would've struggled to see anything in the dark night. A jagged slice of lightning flashed through the sky. The black sedan was gone.

"Miller, come on, wake up."

Rand found his strength as his fingers desperately searched for the button that would release his seatbelt.

The lightning came again. Its brief illumination revealed that someone now stood about fifteen paces away from the Jeep. Rand thought he saw bare feet.

Who the hell was that?

His fingertips brushed against what they'd been searching for. He pushed the button and the seatbelt released with a *click*. But he couldn't feel his legs.

Are they broken? Am I paralyzed?

The sky lit up once again. The figure standing in the rain appeared to be a woman. Her pale flesh and faded, simple dress were soaking wet, and she was indeed barefoot. Rand couldn't see her face because of a brown sack that covered her head. A rope cinched the opening around her throat.

A fearfulness spread through Rand's body.

Despite the bag over her head, the woman seemed to still know where they were. She lumbered toward the crashed Jeep, her frame waddling from side to side as if she struggled to walk. The lightning faded, and the night hid the woman from view again.

A second later, the window shattered as a thick, milky forearm burst through. A long-fingered hand wrapped around Rand's neck, clenching, instantly cutting off his breath.

He reached up and tried to pull the strong hand away,

but the grip was iron. The only way he'd be free—the only way he'd be able to gasp for air—was if this woman decided to spare him.

Then he heard his name.

10

"Rand!"

He snapped awake.

"Rand, are you okay?"

His vision was hazy. After a moment he realized Miller was peering at him, face stricken with worried fear.

Remembering what had happened, Rand jerked his gaze in the opposite direction. The window was intact.

Lightning flashed. There was no woman with a bag over her head.

"That bastard ran us off the road," Miller said. "Are you all right? You have a cut on your forehead."

Rand's heart pounded. He still felt the residual fear from his miniature nightmare. Somehow, Rand knew it had been more real than he cared to admit. Those long fingers and the powerful grip closing off his windpipe...

I've had some terrible dreams before, but nothing like that, he thought.

He found his strength faster than he had in the dream

and unfastened the seatbelt. "Get the flashlight from the glove box."

Miller opened the compartment and rifled through the manuals, paperwork, and gas receipts that were years old.

Rand threw open the car door and slid out from behind the deployed air bag. The heavy rain immediately soaked his clothes.

His friend came around the back of the Jeep and handed him the flashlight. Rand turned it on and used it to survey the vicinity for any trace of the entity. Although he no longer saw her, he still sensed a distant, looming menace somewhere in the surrounding darkness.

"What are you looking for?" Miller asked.

Rand knew Miller would believe him if he shared the harrowing, lifelike dream. However, he didn't want to worry Miller unnecessarily at that moment. "Nothing." He went to inspect the front of his car, which had been torpedoed into a rainwater-filled ditch. "We can probably get this out. You get behind the wheel and I'll push." He hadn't done much off-roading since he'd gotten the Jeep, but he knew it was built for that kind of terrain.

Miller slid into the driver's seat and shifted into neutral.

Rand worked to find solid footing, but his feet only slipped around on the rain-soaked ground. Still, he had to try. "Go now." He pushed while Miller tried to reverse, but Rand saw that with every engine rev and tire spin, the Jeep only dug itself deeper into its muddy grave.

"Stop!" Rand shouted, and Miller let off the gas.

"I don't think it moved at all," Miller said.

"Shit, we're stuck." Rand interlaced his fingers at the

back of his head as he thought about their options. "We'll need to call someone to help us."

"Or maybe not," Miller said, looking at something in the distance.

Headlights were approaching.

11

The headlights were high and moving pretty slowly, so Rand assumed it was another eighteen-wheeler. He went to stand on the side of the road and started waving his hands, hoping he was visible through the rain. The truck slowed, then stopped.

The cab opened and out plopped a stocky man, silhouetted against the bright light of his truck's headlights.

"Holy cow. What happened here?" he said in a thick southern accent. He approached Rand and Miller, and in the short distance from his truck to where they stood, he'd already gotten soaked, but didn't seem to mind.

"Someone ran us off the road," Rand said.

The man grimaced in a way that almost seemed exaggerated. "Sorry to hear that, folks. Y'all okay?"

"Yeah." Rand's fingertips absent-mindedly went to his forehead.

"You get a good look at the car?"

"Unfortunately not," Rand replied. He hated to lie, but he wanted to spare this guy the details.

The truck driver shook his head. "Damn shame. Where y'all headed?"

"Rose Grove."

The man's brow crinkled as he thought. "That's right up the way from here. The next town, if I'm not mistaken."

"That's the place."

"I gotta tell you, I've been driving trucks for twenty-two years, and what they say is true. The worst accidents always happen close to home or close to where you're going."

This man might've believed he was making conversation, but what he said triggered something in Rand—their trip had gone without issue *until* they were within miles of their destination.

Maybe they didn't want us to get there, Rand thought.

"Well, come on. I'll give y'all a ride into town." The man checked his watch. "It's a bit late now, so the towing companies'll be closed. But I'm sure you can find someone to pull your Jeep out in the morning. Name's Dale, by the way." He extended his hand.

"Rand." He clasped the man's wet palm.

"That's a nasty cut on your face, Rand. You might want to have that looked at when you get a chance."

Rand took their bags from the trunk while Miller gathered up the cell phones and chargers from the front. Once done, Rand used his key fob to lock his Jeep—as ridiculous as it felt.

Rand and Miller went to the passenger side of the truck's cab. Miller struggled to climb inside, so Rand had

66

to give him a boost up by hoisting the back of his jeans. Once Miller was in, Rand leapt up and closed the door. Despite being completely soaked, it was still a relief to be out of the rain.

The truck cab was cramped and cluttered, the seat's upholstery ripped and stained. It smelled of diesel fuel and sweat. Dust and grime covered the dashboard. The steering wheel was twice the size of what Rand was used to, and its leather covering was peeling in places. Rainwater did little to wash away the dirt that streaked the windshield's glass.

"Here," Dale said as he twisted a knob, and the warm air that was already blowing through the vents doubled. The heater was a welcome relief to Rand, who shivered in his soaked clothes. Now that they'd been saved from immediate danger, his body was beginning to feel the full effects of the cold night and the even-colder rain. Miller raised his palms toward the vent that was directly in front of him.

"Well, the important thing is that y'all weren't hurt," Dale said as they set off. "Minus that cut on your forehead, but you know what I mean. It could've been much worse."

Rand glanced in the truck's rearview mirror—a large reflective rectangle. Lightning lit up the night, and in that brief flash Rand made out a figure standing in the middle of the road.

A woman with a bag over her head, watching them drive away while the rain continued to soak her dress and mottled flesh.

12

W hite floodlights triumphantly angled their beams at a sign that read, "Welcome to Rose Grove." To Rand's relief, it had only taken fifteen minutes to get there from where they'd crashed.

"I really appreciate you helping us out," Rand said.

"Not a problem," Dale said. "Is this home, or are y'all just passing through?"

"We don't live here," Rand replied, glancing at Miller. As usual, it had been Miller's job to sort out the accommodation for their trip.

Miller didn't react or respond, so Rand figured his mind was wandering. Rand nudged Miller with his elbow to get his attention. "What's the name of where we're staying?"

"Oh, it's called..." He closed his eyes as his memory worked. "The Grove Retreat."

"Don't know it, but it sounds nice," Dale said. "Do they have free breakfast?"

"I *never* book a place that doesn't include breakfast," Miller said gravely. He had many strong opinions when it came to hotels.

"You and me both, brother," Dale agreed. "Do you know where it's located?"

"I can check." Miller lifted his butt off the seat to fish his phone from his pocket. He tapped it a few times. "It's actually only a couple of minutes from here."

"Let me see." Dale took a pair of glasses from where they were folded onto his shirt's collar. Dried rainwater had covered the lenses with grey smudges. Miller passed his phone to Dale, who studied the map, every so often casting a glance at the road in front of them.

"So here's the thing," Dale said, handing the phone back. "This place is downtown, and those roads don't allow trucks like mine. I can let y'all off close, but y'all are going to have to walk some of the way."

"Anything's better than what we would've been doing if you hadn't come along," Rand said.

Dale slowed down his truck about a minute later, and then came to a complete stop. "The place on your map should be right down there." He pointed through the passenger-side window. The only visible thing was a row of streetlights with glowing, white orbs. "Again, I hope y'all don't think I'm just tossing y'all out."

"Really, you've been a huge help," Rand said. "And it's not like we can get any wetter than we already are."

Dale barked a laugh. "You got that right. Y'all be careful."

Rand opened the truck's door, grabbed his bag resting on the ground between his feet, and leapt down. A puddle splashed up around his ankles. His clothes and wet skin seemed to instantly freeze now that he was out of the warm cab. Luckily, the rain had slowed to a very light drizzle.

Miller followed Rand out, nearly tumbling when he slipped on the sidebar.

"Whoa, easy there, bud," Dale called from inside the cab.

After Rand shut the truck's door, Dale drove away, his truck leaving behind diesel fumes.

"All right," Rand said. "You still have your map open?"

Miller checked his phone. "Straight ahead."

The narrow downtown road was lined with stores that had long since closed for the night. As far as Rand could tell, they were the only people around. The street-lamps were the sole source of illumination, casting small circles of light in the darkness. A handful of cars were parked on the shoulder.

As they walked, Rand glanced behind them. He couldn't quite shake the feeling that they weren't as alone as they seemed to be.

They passed a seafood restaurant, a liquor store, and a post office. Rand's breath frosted in front of his face with every step. His wet clothes clung to his numb skin, as if trying to become a permanent part of him. A dog barked somewhere in the distance.

Rand glanced behind them again.

"Here," Miller said. He pointed toward the left side of the road—at a building that had no lights on whatsoever.

"You sure?" But when Rand got closer, he spotted a sign out front that proclaimed it to be the Grove Retreat. A pot of bright red flowers dangled from the bottom of the wooden frame, though they were wet and flattened from the storm.

Rand checked his watch. It was only half past nine—not nearly late enough for a hotel to be closed.

"This doesn't make sense," Miller said. "When I called them yesterday evening to book the room, they told me they had twenty-four-hour reception."

Rand frowned and shivered. *Something's off,* he thought. He believed Miller—there was a reason his friend was always in charge of booking a place whenever he and Rand went out of town for a case. His strict standards and preferences for hotels never led them astray.

And it wasn't just the hotel—Rand realized how strange it was that the entire downtown area was eerily empty.

Miller peered through the darkened windows at the front of the building, then made his way to a narrow alleyway alongside the hotel to look for any sign of life inside. Rand waited, predicting that Miller wouldn't find any.

A prickling coursed through Rand. Now he knew for sure they were being watched. He turned. By the light from the nearby streetlamp, Rand saw her.

The woman with the bag tied over her head.

13

"Fuck." The word escaped Rand's mouth unbidden, a frosty whisper.

He heard Miller coming back from around the side of the hotel. "Not a soul. Not a single—" His footsteps halted. "Who's that?"

Miller can see her too, Rand thought. *This isn't another dream.*

The woman started toward them.

Her body lurched from side to side, as if her legs weighed more than they should. Somehow, though, she quickly gained speed. Her shoulders hunched forward, heavy arms swinging like she was using them to help her gain momentum. Despite the sack over her head, cinched closed around her throat, it was obvious she could still see, since she was walking straight toward them.

"Rando, who the hell is that?"

Rand slung the bag from his shoulder, fumbled for the zipper. He needed something sanctified—his Bible or some of the holy water he'd brought with him.

The woman was now more than halfway to them.

He couldn't find the zipper.

"Rando!"

"What's going on here?" Another voice, this time not Miller's. It boomed from Rand's left, startling him so badly he leapt to the side.

An elderly man had appeared from seemingly nowhere, glowering at them.

Rand turned again. The woman had vanished. He straightened and exchanged a glance with Miller, who was wide-eyed and tense.

"Hey," the man pressed.

"Sorry, hi, good evening," Rand stammered, giving his attention back to the man who'd inadvertently saved them. "We're uh..." He took a steadying breath after being startled twice now. He pointed toward the hotel. "We have a reservation, but..."

"That ain't right," the man replied before spitting on the street. "I'm the owner, and I've cleared the calendar for the next six weeks for renovations." Despite the winter night, he wore short sleeves and pajama pants, and his papery skin seemed immune to the chill.

Miller stepped forward. "I called and spoke with someone on the phone. They charged my card."

"When was this?"

"Yesterday evening."

The man shook his head. "Must've been somewheres else. Because I wouldn't have taken your booking."

Miller took out his phone and started tapping on the screen, searching for evidence of his claim.

"So, what are you doing here now?" Rand asked, trying to keep the skepticism out of his voice.

"I live right across the way." He gestured vaguely to a building on the other side of the road. Some second-story residences were above a bakery. "Saw y'all from the window and it looked to me like y'all were up to no good."

"That's not the case," Rand said. "We were just looking for our hotel."

"Well, you found *a* hotel, but not *your* hotel."

"Look." Miller showed the man his call history on his phone. The owner squinted and held the screen at arm's length so he could see.

"Hmm. That *is* the hotel's number." He shrugged and handed the phone back. "Maybe the signals got crossed? Can that still happen with these cell phones?"

Rand was already piecing together what had likely happened, and it wasn't "crossed signals." The woman with the bag over her head had given it away.

Eerie events often started happening to Rand in the days leading up to him getting entangled in a supernatural situation—usually on new cases. It was a demonic entity's way of trying to scare him, warning him to not get involved. One of the common things was strange and unexplained phone calls. He'd answer and only hear static, or his own voice mimicked back to him.

It seemed that it had happened to Miller this time.

Rand didn't know who Miller had spoken to when he *thought* he was booking the hotel, but it definitely hadn't been this guy. Someone—or something—was very interested in impeding their journey, whether that meant intercepting their phone calls or running them off the road.

Rand sighed heavily. He felt his frustration rising, but kept a lid on it.

"Where y'all from?" the man asked. He'd seemed to soften now that he recognized they were in a bit of a pickle due to the misunderstanding.

"Louisiana."

"What brings y'all here to the Grove?"

"Passing through," Rand said.

"We don't have many visitors here, especially during the winter. That's why I chose January to close up—to get the work done before spring."

Rand had no patience for small talk at the moment. "Look, we apologize for the mix up. Is there maybe another hotel nearby where we could stay?"

The man examined Rand from head to toe; he gave Miller a once-over as well. "Y'all got caught in the storm earlier?" By then, even the drizzling had stopped, which Rand was thankful for.

"Yes," Rand said. "Car accident. Had to walk the rest of the way into town."

The man's stern, skeptical expression softened. "Tell you what. I'll let y'all stay here for the night, since there's one room the workers haven't touched yet." He extended his index finger in front of his face, long and straight, to emphasize his next point. "But not a *word* about this to anyone in town. Got it? If the construction company or the insurance guys hear about this..."

"We can keep quiet," Rand said.

"I mean it, now. People talk 'round here. You go on about staying here tonight while having a drink down at the Country Corner, word'll move faster than a NASCAR race."

"I promise we won't say anything."

The man's body was stiff and unmoving except for his eyes, which ping-ponged back and forth between Rand and Miller, appraising them to see if he could probe deeply enough into their souls to figure out if they were truly able to keep a secret.

The man took some keys from the pocket of his pajama pants and went up the hotel porch steps. He unlocked the front door.

"I *swear* I booked the place," Miller whispered to Rand. The man clicked on a light, instantly making the building look like it had come back to life.

"I know you did," Rand said. "I think your call got intercepted by something... unfriendly."

Miller's eyes widened at the thought. "Oh."

"Let's go. If we get inside now, we might actually thaw out by morning."

14

Rand stepped into a red-carpeted lobby. A chandelier hung overhead, pieces of fine glass dangling from the fixture. A desk to the right of the entrance was clearly a late addition to a building that had almost definitely been something else in the distant past—perhaps a private residence.

Nicer than I was expecting, Rand thought. To him, that essentially proved Miller had, in fact, booked their stay, given how picky he was about hotels.

Rand couldn't help but note, disappointed, that it wasn't much warmer inside than it was outside. *Makes sense that he'd keep the heat off while closed for renovations. I'm going to turn that room into a furnace, first thing.*

The man went behind the desk and took a key from a drawer. "Room seven's upstairs." He held it in his hand as a mask of concentration fell over his face. "As for payment... since this is off the books—"

"We can pay cash," Rand said.

The man smirked. "Old is gold, I always say. All this

technology slows everything down. I had a young couple pass through here before we shut down who paid by scanning their phone? I didn't even know my credit card machine could *do* that."

"Wild stuff." Rand pulled out his wallet. "You offered us one night before, but could we get two?"

Just in case things something else goes sideways and we need more time, Rand thought.

The man seemed to consider how far he wanted to push his luck, given the risk he was taking by letting them stay there. His eyes lingered for a moment on Rand's wallet before he replied. "Okay."

"How much?"

After Rand paid for the room, the owner gave him directions:

"Go toward the back, then up the stairs. Don't knock over any of the stuff left behind by the crew, please. Y'all need anything before I head across the street?"

"Actually," Rand said, "as I mentioned earlier, we were in a car wreck. On the highway leading into town, about fifteen or twenty minutes away. Do you know anyone who can help tow my Jeep out of a ditch?"

"You're talking to the right guy." A smile spread across the man's face. "Well, almost the right guy. My cousin Tucker owns a towing company, so when you need vehicle-relocation services in and around Rose Grove, he's who you call."

"Great. Can you give me his number?"

"I'll do you one better and call him for you." The man picked up a nearby phone from the receiver and punched in some numbers from memory.

"Hey, Tucker. Sorry to call so late." Cousin Tucker

said something on the other line that Rand couldn't make out. "Listen, I have a couple of fellas here at the hotel, and —" He paused as Tucker interrupted him. "Yeah, it's closed, but these guys—well, that's a long story, but they got into a wreck earlier on Highway Forty. They walked the rest of the way here. Could you give their car a tow back into town? It's a Jeep."

"It's orange," Rand said.

"An orange Jeep." The man listened for a bit, then turned to Rand.. "And your name?"

"Rand Casey."

"Rand Casey," he told his cousin. "All right." He hung up. "Tuck says he'll get your car first thing in the morning. Swing by his place tomorrow and pick it up." He used a nearby pencil to scribble something on a piece of paper and handed it to Rand. *Grove Towing Co.* "You can look that up on your phone, can't you?"

"Yes," Rand said. "Thank you."

"Anything else?" the man asked.

"I think we're good." Rand slung his bag from one shoulder to the other. It wasn't heavy, but after carrying it for so long, the weight had started dragging him down. "Thanks again for accommodating us."

A door on the far end of the lobby led to a narrow hallway lined with doors. A ladder in the hall blocked the way forward, and thick plastic crumpled underfoot as Rand and Miller walked over it. Most of the floral wallpaper had been ripped off. They went upstairs and encountered more similar work. Room seven, just as the man had said, seemed to be the only one that the construction hadn't yet touched.

The room was simple inside. There was a double bed

within a black iron frame. Red curtains with copper trim were pulled apart on either side of a window, which overlooked the road in front of the hotel where Rand and Miller had stood just a few minutes before. The wallpaper featured a repeating pattern of three birds. It looked old, and Rand had a feeling the birds wouldn't survive the renovation. A chandelier, similar to the one in the lobby, only smaller, was the main source of light.

Rand dropped his bag by the door with a loud *thunk,* then went to the window unit on the far side of the room. He twisted the dial all the way to the left, making it point toward a red sticker on the panel. It clanged to life, and the first hints of heat rose to Rand's face.

"Rando. Who *was* that out there?" Miller joined Rand by the heater.

The woman who looked like a reanimated drowned corpse with a bag wrapped over her head. *The Bagged Woman,* he thought.

"I saw her... or I *thought* I saw her after we crashed," he replied. "In a weird dream state when I was knocked out."

"Why didn't you say anything?"

"I didn't want to mention it in the truck in front of Dale. Besides... I hoped that it was just a dream, that maybe I'd hit my head harder than I remembered." For the first time, he brought his fingertips to his forehead. The blood had washed away in the rain, but the sore spot still stung when he touched it.

Miller seemed to accept that. "Is it a demonic entity?"

"That's my guess."

"Sent by them?"

Them. The Bale family.

"I don't know," Rand said. "But it wouldn't surprise me if that were the case."

"Do you think she was driving the car behind us? How would she even see?"

"Seems unlikely." Although it was clear the Bagged Woman was fully aware of her surroundings, despite the sack over her head.

"So someone else ran us off the road. Maybe so that woman could come finish us off."

Rand peered through the window. He could see the precise spot they'd been standing when the Bagged Woman had appeared. With that vantage point, he felt like a sentry on watch.

"I wonder who she is." Miller rubbed his hands together over the heater. "If she's demonic and we knew her name, then we could send her away instead of running." He paused. "Maybe Arthur Briggs will know."

Rand could hear the hopefulness in his friend's tone. Little by little, Miller seemed to be letting himself believe that once they located Arthur, it would solve all of their problems. Rand felt it was a long shot.

"So we're here. What's the plan to find this guy?" Rand walked away from the heater, finally feeling sufficiently thawed.

"One of the main contributors to that forum I sent you was a man named Trevor," Miller explained. "Trevor apparently lives here in Rose Grove, in a house that used to be haunted—until Arthur Briggs helped him remove the demon that was inside."

"Why do we need Trevor's help to find Arthur?"

"Because I'm not sure exactly where Arthur lives," Miller said, "but I know where Trevor does. His house and its haunting have been written about online, so it was easy to track down. It's called the Decker House. Since Arthur was the one who helped him, I figured he could tell us where the guy is."

To Rand, that seemed a lot faster than going door to door. "So tomorrow we drop in on Trevor, who'll point us in the right direction."

"That's what I'm thinking," Miller said.

It seems *simple,* Rand thought, *and after what happened tonight, I hope it is.*

15

Mr. Neeson, the history teacher, droned on in his usual dry style. Libby was only half-listening. Her mind was elsewhere.

Libby hadn't wanted her dad to leave town yesterday. She preferred him to be close, especially since she'd already lost him once. But she reluctantly agreed that he and Miller had to push forward.

It was a memory that kept Libby up at night—her father's bled-out corpse sprawled in the middle of the room. If it hadn't been for the power of the imbued cross, she'd be at his funeral instead of class.

The same people who'd killed her father were still out there, and were likely going to try again. That was why she hated to see him leave. She tried to remind herself that he wasn't any safer in town with her, but somehow it just felt better to have him near.

Libby's eyes wandered to the window beside her desk. It looked out to the front of the school. Yellow buses had begun to line up, as they always did at the end of the day, and the drivers had convened in the parking lot for some friendly chit-chat before the final bell rang.

Someone among the drivers caught Libby's attention. He was separate from the group, not participating in the conversation. To Libby, he stood out from the others because of his oversized, dark brown suit—and because he was staring right at her through the window.

Libby focused on the man, wondering if he was actually locking eyes with her, or if she was imagining it.

Then she realized the man's strange appearance was more than just his clothes. His flesh appeared an unnatural grey color, and even at that distance Libby could tell that his eyes were completely black—the telltale sign of a demonic entity.

Icy tingles broke out over her body.

Libby clenched her eyelids shut. *Go away. Leave me alone,* she thought. She opened her eyes, but the man hadn't moved, continuing to watch her.

Although he stood near the other drivers, none of them acknowledged his presence, or even seemed aware that he was even there. Libby knew she was the only who could see him.

Heart thumping, Libby tore her gaze away and forced herself to look down at her desk. Her breaths came sharp and quick, so she tried to get them under control before someone around her noticed.

Relax, she told herself. *Dad sees demons all the time. It's almost normal.*

But just because her dad saw them didn't mean she did. Until now.

SLAYER OF AKHUBEL.

She remembered the words scrawled on her bedroom

wall at her dad's house. She strongly suspected this entity appearing to her all of a sudden had something to do with that. Besides her father laying in his own blood, that was the other thing that lingered with Libby late at night as she tried to fall asleep.

Libby cast another nervous glance out the window. The man in the old suit had not moved.

She nearly fell out of her desk when the sharp trill of the final bell rang, startling her. Libby quickly gathered up her things and shoved them into her backpack.

Normally, when she weaved her way through the student-packed halls at the end of the day, she would think about what homework she had for each class so she could grab the necessary books from her locker. That afternoon, however, the demon sighting had blocked any other thoughts from her mind. She just wanted to go home. Focused on that, she walked right past her locker.

"Libby!"

Hearing her name so suddenly made her flinch.

"Whoa. Jumpy." Her friend Bailey approached, backpack slung over her shoulder.

"Sorry," Libby said.

"Are we still studying tonight?"

"For what?"

Bailey gave her an incredulous look. "We have that big history test tomorrow? We planned to meet up with Terrance, since he seems to absorb this stuff somehow and could probably help us."

"Oh. I thought that was... not tomorrow." Honestly, she couldn't remember when she thought the test was.

"Didn't you just come from that class?"

Mr. Neeson had likely mentioned it, but there was no

way Libby's preoccupied mind had registered anything he'd said.

"Right. Sure. What time?" Maybe having Bailey over would help distract her from everything that was going on with her dad.

"Seven? Do you think your mom and Bill let us study at their house?"

"Yeah. And seven sounds fine."

They walked outside, falling in line with the rivers of other students. Most headed toward the buses. Libby again looked to the spot where the demon had stood, but he wasn't there anymore. In that moment, she wasn't sure if that was a good or bad thing. She nervously scanned the school grounds, checking to see if he was still there.

But someone else caught her eye—someone she recognized. A blonde woman sat on one of the benches near the flagpole, legs crossed casually, peering down at her phone through large sunglasses. A short distance behind her, a black sedan was parked in the bus lane, violating the nearby sign's warnings of being towed.

Miranda Herron.

"What's wrong?" Bailey asked. "What are you looking at?" She tried to follow Libby's gaze to see what had captured her friend's attention.

"Nothing."

She's here for me, she thought. There was no other reason for the woman to show up at Denton High. Given their last encounter in the Herron House, Libby had a feeling Miranda Herron wasn't finished with her yet.

"Libby, are you okay?" Bailey asked. She gave Libby a soft, concerned look.

"I'll be fine," Libby said, her tone unconvincing,

even to her own ears. Two nights ago, she'd told Bailey that something had happened with her dad, but hadn't gone into details. Bailey had a vague understanding of what her father did in his spare time. Occasionally, she'd asked Libby to tell her more, only to stop her abruptly as soon as she got to some of the more chilling aspects.

"If you say so." Bailey seemed unconvinced. "See you at seven?"

"Sure."

Bailey left her there, and only after she was gone did Libby realize that may have come across as brushing her friend off.

I'll apologize when she comes over later, Libby thought.

She turned her attention back to Miranda Herron and clenched her jaw. *What do you want?*

As Libby approached the woman, she felt a strong, bitter revulsion bubble up inside her chest. She could never forget—or forgive—what Miranda and her family had planned to do with their daughter Carmen that night in the Herron House.

Libby came to a halt a few paces from the bench, yet Miranda continued texting on her phone, seeming oblivious that Libby was there.

Miranda seemed so normal in her jeans and a simple yellow blouse that matched her blonde hair. Based on her appearance, there was nothing that would indicate how dangerous and twisted she really was. It was like she was hiding in plain sight.

Miranda finally paused her texting and turned her attention to Libby. She studied her for a few seconds. "I appreciate you not making me look for you." The woman removed her sunglasses, revealing a deep purple bruise around her left eye, marring her pretty face.

"That suits you," Libby said. She'd given it to her during their tussle a few nights before.

Miranda seemed amused by that. "You're going to want to be nice to me, Libby."

"Where is she?" Libby said through clenched teeth.

"Who?"

"You know who I mean."

Miranda frowned. "Trust me. That'll be the least of your worries soon."

"Tell me where she is," Libby demanded again.

Miranda rolled her eyes as if Libby was nothing more to her than a nagging child. "Look, Libby, I get it. What you saw made you very uncomfortable. But you need to understand it's all *very* over your head. And you have bigger issues to worry about now."

"You planned to sacrifice your own daughter to a demon," Libby said, keeping her voice just above a whisper in case anyone in the crowded bus area could overhear them. "What kind of sick—"

"And you killed that demon. That very *high-ranking* one."

"He attacked me first." Libby instantly wished she could take the words back. Only after she said did she realize it made her sound quite childish.

"This isn't some courthouse where you can plead self-defense," Miranda said. "It was *your* hand that committed the act, so that is what is now written into the fabric of reality for the rest of time."

Fabric of reality?

"There are many people who are very, *very* unhappy

with you," Miranda continued. "That's why you'll want to be nice to me. I might be able to help you."

Libby scoffed. "I don't need your help."

Miranda seemed to find that amusing. "You're a smart girl. You'll figure it out sooner than most. But until you do... you see him, right?"

"Who?"

Only then did Libby become aware of a presence a few feet beyond the bench where Miranda sat. The grey man in the brown suit, eyes like dark portals. Staring directly at her.

"That's who I mean," Miranda said. "He's behind you too."

Libby looked over her shoulder. The demon had seemingly teleported in an instant to beside a tree near the faculty parking lot.

"Check on top of the school."

Libby turned the other direction. The demon stood straight as a rod on the roof, gaze boring into her from above.

"What's the point of—" When Libby turned back, the creature now sat on the bench next to Miranda. He still watched her. Libby took a step away, not wanting to be so close to the entity. His pitch-black eyes seemed ready to absorb her.

"He's been called many things over the centuries," Miranda said, "but we know him as Ulvareth. He'll be keeping an eye on you from now on."

Libby couldn't tear her gaze from Ulvareth's affixed stare. He reminded her of a painting that watched you no matter where you stood in the room.

"He's nowhere near as strong as Akhubel, but he was

very loyal to his master, and he isn't pleased with what you did. And as long as he's keeping an eye on you, it's only fair that you also keep an eye on him."

Libby finally managed to look away from Ulvareth and back to Miranda. In that same split second, Ulvareth reappeared over Miranda's shoulder, near the front of the black car that Libby assumed belonged to her.

That was when Libby realized that Ulvareth was going to appear and reappear no matter where she looked. He'd always be in her visual field.

"Is that it? He jumps around and stares at me?" Libby tried to bolster her voice to make herself sound strong and unaffected. In reality, she was wary about the implications of having this demon following her.

"That's cute," Miranda said. "And yes, you're right. You'll be able to tolerate him for a while, but trust me, this is going to get insufferable really quick."

Libby glanced over toward the buses. Ulvareth stood in front of one like he had some sort of teleportation superpower.

And Libby understood that Miranda was correct. It wouldn't take long for this to make her crazy.

And that's the point, Libby realized. *It'll slowly drive me insane, won't it?*

"I wanted to be here to personally introduce the two of you," Miranda said, putting her sunglasses back on. "Since you and him will be spending a *lot* of time together from now on."

She stood from the bench and walked toward the car. A second later, her driver got out and quickly scrambled to open the backseat door for her.

"I'm going to find Carmen, you know," Libby called after Miranda.

Miranda turned to Libby, and just then Libby wanted nothing more than to knock the self-satisfied look off her face. Give her a second black eye to match the first.

"Have a good day, Libby. I'll see you soon."

16

Grove Towing Co. was housed in a white clapboard building located a few blocks' walk away from the hotel. The weathered walls were full of cracks and covered with chipped paint, but was still standing proudly despite their age.

"Well, would you look at that," Rand said as they approached. Beside the main building, a chain-link fence enclosed an asphalt lot with a handful of cars, with Rand's orange Jeep immediately catching his eye among the others. "The cousin came through." It was about eight in the morning, so he must've woken up quite early to retrieve it.

The cramped office had barely enough room for the chair and the two folding card tables pushed together to act as a desk. A coffee mug was dangerously close to one of the edges. Maps and posters of cars and trucks covered the walls. Other knick knacks adorned the shelves—trinkets from fishing trips or objects purchased from cheesy souvenir shops. A calendar on the wall had dates crossed off in red marker, but was four days behind.

The man sitting at the card tables rose. He was tall and looked to be in his fifties. Rand could see the resemblance to the hotel owner in his lightly wrinkled face. "You must be Rand Casey."

"That's me."

"You were pretty stuck, but we got you out. You'll want to address the damage on the front bumper, but it shouldn't be too big of a ballache."

Tucker led the way through a second door on the side of the office that granted access to the gated outdoor area.

"I really appreciate you helping us out," Rand said.

"You're far from the first to fly off that highway," Tucker said. "Some folks crash when it isn't even storming. I have half a mind to complain to the city council about it, but then the devil on my shoulder reminds me that one road sends me a *lot* of business."

When they reached the Jeep, Rand circled around to the front to inspect the damage. The bumper was bent and dented, and there were a few remaining specks of dried mud, but Tucker had generously wiped away the worst of it. The back bumper was also damaged from when the car had repeatedly rammed them.

It looked ugly, but Rand was relieved. It could've been worse—there was no way he could fit car repairs into his budget right now. His desecrated house was first and foremost on his mind, and he still had no idea how much that was going to cost.

Rand climbed into the driver's seat. He started the engine, and it fired up as normal. No unusual sounds, clicks, or clangs.

"Cosmetic damage only," Tucker said, nodding resolutely. "I've printed up your invoice. It's in the office. I'll make you a copy."

Rand and Miller tossed their bags in the trunk, and Rand was happy to be free of them. They'd walked from the hotel to Tucker's place with their gear slung over their shoulders like a couple of vagabonding nomads. Tucker headed back inside and they followed him; once in the building, he sat down at his card table and started hunting and pecking on his keyboard, squinting at the computer screen.

"Mr. Tucker, do you know a man named Arthur Briggs?" Miller asked.

Tucker looked away from the screen for a moment as he thought about it. "No. Don't believe I do."

Rand frowned. In his experience, people who lived in small southern towns all knew each other.

"What about a place called the Decker House?"

Tucker didn't have to think about that one—a dark expression immediately came over him. "What about it?"

"It's here in town, isn't it?"

Tucker turned back to the computer screen, as if trying to avoid answering the question. Rand could've sworn Tucker started typing faster, as if he'd suddenly wanted them to leave.

"Look, I'm not sure what y'all are up to, but don't go bothering those people. Not everyone believes what happened to them, but I do. That poor family has been through enough." He loudly jabbed a final key and a printer on the floor beside the card table roared to life.

Rand was happy to hear that Tucker believed in supernatural phenomena—and also seemed to take seriously. Under normal circumstances, he would've agreed with Tucker. He didn't appreciate it when random paranormal enthusiasts visited the locations of famous hauntings just to get pictures or videos to post on their social-media accounts. Rand liked it even less when the victims of these hauntings were harassed for interviews where they'd have to relive the trauma.

And while Rand hated to do precisely what Tucker had asked him not to do, they didn't have a choice.

17

"We're here," Miller said, eyeing his phone where it rested on his thigh.

They'd left Rose Grove and had come to a residential area on the edge of town. The houses there were larger and more spread out on their sizable plots of land.

The Decker House was a two-story home with a wraparound porch, painted white, and looked like a peaceful, idyllic family abode. At first glance, Rand would not have suspected that the place had ever been haunted. But if there was one thing he'd learned over the years, it was that a house being run down and decrepit was *not* a prerequisite for paranormal activity. All it needed was a dose of negative energy from a traumatic event.

And according to Miller—who'd done his research as always—the old Decker House fit that description perfectly.

"A banker named Tom Decker built the place in the 1800s," Miller had told him on the way over. "Story goes that Decker's wife ran off with their son after he'd beaten the kid pretty badly. Somehow, Decker got it in his head that this other guy named Benjamin knew where the wife had gone to, and Decker was *also* convinced that Benjamin and the wife were having an affair. Decker ends up killing Benjamin in a barroom fight. The rest of the people in the bar followed Decker back to his house, where, um... a little mob justice went down. Apparently, the tree where he was hanged is still in the backyard. It's the usual story for the next hundred years or so—families come and go, but no one stays for long. Local legends say Decker roams the halls, searching for his wife and son. Well... till recently, when Arthur Briggs helped the current owner remove the demon inside."

The house had no clear driveway. It was set on a massive piece of property, and it seemed the front yard served as the general parking area, indicated by a bright red truck near the porch. Behind it was a trail of tire-tread marks in the grass, brown and wet from the storm the night before. Even if the yard already had ruts, Rand didn't want to create any new ones—especially since he was about to ask for information—so he parked a respectful distance from the home.

"All right," Rand said. "Let's hope the small-town southern hospitality continues in our favor."

Dale the trucker had helped them; the owner of The Grove Retreat had let them in when he shouldn't have; Tucker from the towing company had retrieved his car. If good things came in threes, then that meant he'd used up all his luck for a while.

Rand trudged across the wet grass, which squelched

underfoot as he walked carefully toward the house, keeping an eye out for slick mud or water-filled holes.

The porch steps creaked as they climbed, the wooden planks sounding hollow under their footsteps. They left behind muddy shoe prints.

The home, like so many in the south, had two doors. The inner front door was open while the clear screen door was closed. Miller hung back while Rand stepped up and rapped loudly on the screen.

A few seconds later, a young boy appeared from a room off to the side of the door. For several moments, his eyes darted between Rand and Miller, saying nothing, as if trying to decide how to react.

Rand cleared his throat. "Hi there." He raised his palm in a stiff wave.

The boy didn't respond. He only turned and walked down the hallway that passed beside the staircase and disappeared into another room.

Rand looked over his shoulder at Miller, who shrugged. After a long stretch of silence and stillness, Rand considered knocking again. Just before he did, a tall, broad-shouldered figure appeared and approached the screen door, his heavy footsteps loud on the hardwood.

As he neared, Rand was better able to make the man out. He wore a light blue, collared shirt with a hem that hung low beyond his waist, like something from the "big and tall" store. His jeans were generic and the overly long hems bunched up around his white sneakers.

"That's Trevor," Miller whispered from behind Rand. "The articles I read had his picture."

"Can I help you?" Trevor asked through the screen door.

His tone was very guarded and suspicious, and Rand felt his hope for small-town hospitality sinking. He cleared his throat again and put on his best friendly smile. "My name is Randolph Casey. Friends call me Rand. This is my friend and colleague, Miller Landingham."

Trevor's eyes darted back and forth between Rand and Miller, just as the young boy's had done. "Okay." He made no move to open the screen door.

"I was... wondering if you could help us," Rand continued.

"Are you here because of the house?"

That question told Rand all he needed to know to empathize with the man. Paranormal enthusiasts had probably bombarded him with visits. Paranormal sight-seers, so to speak. Miller had found information about the Decker House online, so that meant others could as well. Having people trespass onto your property to take a selfie with your family home could be annoying, but the more bold and reckless paranormal nuts might've even knocked on this same door and requested to spend the night, just so they could conduct their own investigation.

"In a way, but it's not what you think," Rand said. "We *did* read about your house online. On a forum about supernatural activity and demonic hauntings, but—"

"My house is not haunted anymore," Trevor cut in tersely. "That problem was solved years ago. There's nothing of interest for you here now."

That all but confirmed Rand's suspicions that the man had had problems with people wanting to treat his family home like a Halloween haunted attraction. "I'm happy you no longer have issues. And that's why I'm here, actually. I'm looking for a friend of yours. Or... maybe he's not a friend, but either way... I'm sure you know him."

Trevor scowled. "Who might that be?"

Rand had a feeling the man already knew. "Someone named Arthur Briggs."

Trevor stared at Rand for a long while through the window, his expression unreadable. He abruptly shoved open the screen door, so Rand took a large step back to avoid getting swatted in the face. It fell closed with a loud *clack*.

Now that Trevor stood closer, Rand saw how much taller the other man was than him. He wasn't necessarily muscular, just big. He scrutinized Rand, eyes boring into him as if trying to extract the truth.

"Why do you need to find him?"

"So you know him?" Rand asked, even though he already knew the answer. He didn't want to press the man too hard, too fast; he wanted this to be a conversation, not an interrogation. Rand sensed Trevor was waiting for him to elaborate.

Before he could, Miller stepped up. "Rando is a paranormal investigator and a demonologist as well. During the last case we worked on together, we encountered an entity that sounds like something Arthur Briggs might know of. We want to find him and speak with him about it."

Trevor seemed to soften as he considered Miller's explanation. Rand figured at least part of Trevor was relieved that they weren't there just to take some pictures of the house. He took a step back from Rand, as if now realizing he didn't need to put in such an effort to come across as imposing. "You've encountered these things too?"

"More than just encountered," Rand said, sensing that they were making some headway. "I fight them for clients."

"I'm sorry to hear that."

Rand rarely received that reaction when he told others what he did. "Why?"

"A police officer or a firefighter would've been a far less dangerous job, don't you think?"

The cautionary tone in Trevor's voice was apparent. People had warned Rand away from the supernatural plenty of times. It was the primary reason he'd decided to teach his class at the university—to educate his students about the dark side of the spiritual world just enough to convince them to avoid it. Rand may have once heeded that advice, but as things stood now, he was stuck.

"I appreciate your concern," Rand said. He'd lost much because of his work with the supernatural and paranormal. But someone needed to do it. "That's actually why we've come here to meet with Arthur. He might be the only one who can help us out of a... little situation we're in."

Trevor watched him levelly, as if trying to divine whether or not Rand was being honest. After several long moments, he finally said, "I can't help you."

Rand was stunned. He'd felt they'd been getting somewhere with Trevor. "Sorry?"

"I can't tell you where to find Arthur Briggs."

"Can't or won't?" Rand pressed.

"Both. Can't, because I don't know. And even if I knew, I wouldn't tell you."

"I thought he lived here in town?" Rand asked.

"He *did*, but I'm not sure if he does anymore. I haven't seen him in about two years. He might still have a home here, but he travels a lot."

"You don't keep up with him?" Rand had a feeling Trevor wasn't telling him the entire story.

"After what my family went through in this house... I prefer to leave as many aspects of it in the past as I can. I'm grateful for what Arthur did for us—he saved my life, quite literally—but seeing him reminds me of it all. I told him I didn't want him coming around, and why. He understood."

Begrudgingly, Rand could relate. He didn't keep in touch with his clients after he'd resolved their situations, either. After the pain and trauma people endured during a haunting, the best thing for everyone to do after it was over was to move on.

"Could you tell us where he lived when you worked with him?" Miller interjected hopefully.

"No," Trevor said sharply. He turned to Rand. He seemed frightened again. "Playing with these demonic forces might seem fun and interesting to you currently. I'm sure you feel like a hero and that you're contributing some good to the world. But Arthur Briggs is an old man. He's been doing it twice as long as you have, easy. The toll this stuff has taken on him... it's too much. No amount of feeling heroic is worth what this eventually does to you. I would know." He gestured toward the front door. "You read about this house online, right? I moved my family into this place even though I *knew* it was haunted. It nearly destroyed us all." Trevor shook his head, face filled with shame, as if he were confessing his darkest secret.

It very well could be, Rand thought. Trevor's guilt at having brought his wife and son into a haunted house was apparent, yet the man must've felt strongly enough about it to share it with Rand.

"You can remove the spirit from the home and be victorious, so to speak," Trevor continued. "But the demons *always* win. They leave a mark. My family and I are doing well today, but we will never be the same. Especially my son."

Rand remembered the young boy who'd come to the door when they'd first arrived. He'd regarded them with deep suspicion, something he'd probably picked up from his father. Rand could only imagine what the kid must have gone through.

Trevor fell silent, and a distant expression came across his face. He seemed to be falling back into those memories, to a time that he wished had never happened —or that he could forget forever, but couldn't.

"I'm sorry you went through all of that," Rand said. He chose his next words carefully. "I hear you and understand. You're right about all of it. I've seen how my clients and their families were affected in all the ways you describe. But we *can't* go back. This is more than just haunted houses. There are things far beyond that, and that's why we're asking you for help."

"I already told you that I don't want any part of it," Trevor said.

"And you won't have any part of it," Rand implored him. "I'm only here to ask you for one thing—where I can find Arthur Briggs. After that, you'll never see or hear from me again." Trevor considered the question for a moment as he eyed Rand with a hard glare. "Because this time, it's not about a client. It's about me and my family. We've pissed off the wrong people *and* the wrong demons. We're in a lot of danger, and I don't know what else to do... except look for help."

After an extended silence, Trevor slowly shook his head. "I'm sorry. I refuse to be the one to get more people wrapped up in this insanity. You both need to leave now."

Rand swallowed heavily, searching for anything he could say that would turn Trevor around. But Rand knew the man had dug his heels in. Pushing Trevor any further could cause trouble.

And I have to admit, I completely understand why he's refusing, Rand thought, as frustrating as it was.

Rand dropped his gaze, sighed, and started down the front porch steps. He sensed Miller's dejected energy.

When he stepped onto the wet grass, he heard the screen door give a final *clack* behind him.

18

Rand paused before getting back inside the Jeep and once again turned to the Decker House. He wasn't sure why, but it seemed *different* from before. When they'd arrived, his first impression had been that it looked like a pleasant home. Now it came across as a bit more foreboding. Maybe it was because the morning sky had gotten grayer with a second storm rolling in. Despite the external appearances, it was still the home of a family who'd been touched by the demonic. Rand could tell. They were suspicious and mistrustful, and it was hard for Rand to fault them for it.

Miller broke their silence. "That went... poorly."

"You know what's frustrating? If I'd been the one who worked on their case, after it was over, I would've told Trevor to do *exactly* what he just did. Send away anyone who showed up looking to drudge up the past."

"So what now?" Miller asked.

"We've come too far to give up," Rand said. "This is a small town. That guy isn't the only person who knows

Arthur Briggs and if he still lives here. I'll go door to door if I have to."

Another car drove by them, though Rand hadn't seen or heard it approaching. It was a simple, grey sedan and the woman behind the wheel eyed them through the window as she passed them. She parked next to the red truck in front of the house, and when she got out, she kept her eyes fixed on them from afar while she used her key fob to open the trunk, revealing brown bags of groceries.

"Must be the wife," Rand said. "Come on."

He once again trudged through the muddy yard. He knew this was a long shot, but he had to take a swing.

The woman had been about to pick up some bags, but let them be so she could turn her full attention to Rand. She was short with a round body and wore a floral-pattered dress. Her straight brown hair hung above her shoulders and had several strands of grey.

"Morning," he said, smiling. "I'm sorry to bother you, but—"

"We don't do tours, pictures, or interviews." The words sounded like lines she'd memorized and had said a hundred times before.

"I understand." Rand kept his smile in place. "We're not here for any of those things. My name is Randolph Casey. Friends call me Rand." The woman shook his hand limply and hesitantly. "This is my friend Miller Landingham."

Miller, who stood just behind Rand's right shoulder, gave an awkward wave.

"I'm Linda Nolan. We don't really like when the para-normal people come by." Again, she sounded as if she were reading off a script—one that her husband had likely given her.

"That isn't why we're here," Rand said, shooting a quick glance toward the front door. He wondered if Trevor had heard the car pull up. If Linda took too long coming inside, he might come out to check on her, so Rand knew he had to get straight to the point. "We're looking for Arthur Briggs."

Linda's face tightened at the name. "Maybe you should speak to my husband."

"Honestly, ma'am, I already did, just before you got here. And he was very hesitant to help me."

"You really shouldn't be involved with this kind of stuff." Linda let out a short groan. "I *told* Trevor to stop posting about us online. I knew this would happen." Her face contorted as she fought her internal dilemma. "If my husband didn't want to say anything to you, then I'm sure he has his reasons."

"A little bit of information is all we need," Rand said.

Linda scooped up the grocery bags, the material crinkling as they all mashed together in her arms. It impressed Rand how she'd gathered them all at once and then expertly balanced them on her hip just long enough to free up a hand so she could close the trunk.

"I don't know where Arthur is these days. It could be he's no longer in Rose Grove. But I *have* heard he became quite the alcoholic..."

"If Arthur's left town, then there's no harm in telling us where he lived when he was here," Rand said, rushing to get the words out. Linda shifted uncomfortably under the weight of the grocery bags in her arms. She sighed, and Rand could sense her resolve slipping.

"Grove Gardens Cemetery," she finally said.

Rand was taken aback. "You mean... he's dead?"

"No," Linda said sharply, as if Rand's assumption was the dumbest thing she'd heard in a while. "His house was next door to the local graveyard. Maybe that's fitting, as strange as it sounds."

"I appreciate that very much, ma'am."

Linda gave a terse nod before turning away and climbing the porch steps. Her car chirped twice when she pressed the lock button on her key fob.

As they got back into the Jeep, Rand spotted Trevor's hulking figure watching them go through the screen door, likely making sure that they were *actually* leaving this time.

19

Grove Gardens Cemetery on the other side of Rose Grove, but since the town wasn't that large, it would only take them about fifteen minutes to get there.

Before long, the wrought-iron fence that delineated the cemetery came into view. Magnificent oak trees grew along the grounds, standing like guardians of the dead, their branches extending over the tops of the bars. Gnarled roots had spread out and upended some sections of the gate. The fence culminated into an arched entrance that faced the road.

As they drove farther, they came upon a solitary house in the plot of land next to the graveyard. It was very simple—a single story and primarily made of wood. The roof had flattened over time and looked like it was about to cave in at any moment. The grass surrounding the home was tall and unkempt. There was no driveway, nor a car parked outside.

"Who on Earth would want to live next to a grave-yard?" Miller asked.

"I'm guessing the location makes it more affordable," Rand said. "At least the front door faces *away* from the cemetery."

"So what do you think, Rando?" Miller eyed the house with skepticism.

"It could go either way. It kind of looks abandoned, but maybe Arthur just doesn't keep up with the maintenance." Rand had to admit, the current state of Arthur's home was better than his own. "Let's find out." He took off his seatbelt.

Rand trampled the tall, brown grass with every stride as he headed to the porch. The wooden steps creaked, the planks loose beneath his feet.

He knocked on the door and waited. Silence. He went to a nearby window and cupped his hands over his eyes as he tried to peer through the glass.

"You see anything?" Miller asked.

"It's too dark," Rand said.

Miller folded his arms around his chest and shivered. "Do we just wait here for him to come back?"

"If he's moved away, or is currently out of town, then waiting here won't help."

Miller considered something for a few moments. "If you were an old man who'd spent his life fighting demons and that work had taken its toll on you, like Trevor said, where you would be and what you do?"

"I'd need a fucking drink," Rand muttered as he checked another window farther along the porch. Once again, it was too dark to make out anything inside.

Only when Rand noticed Miller's silence did he realize what he'd just instinctively said.

"Linda Nolan mentioned that Arthur had become an alcoholic," Miller said. "Do you think..."

Rand glanced at his watch. "It's eleven in the morning."

"From what I've heard, alcoholics don't care about the time." Miller took out his phone again and tapped the screen with his thumbs. "Looks like the most popular bar in town is a place called the Country Corner." That rang a bell to Rand. The owner of the Grove Retreat had mentioned it the night before as they were checking in. "He might not be there so early, but if he drinks a lot, then maybe someone there will know more."

Rand sighed. It was a fine idea, but he was quickly growing weary of the search. He felt like he was chasing shadows. "All right, then. Let's take a look."

20

The Country Corner was a simple establishment atop an elevated frame to protect it from floods. A line of motorcycles was parked out front, completely disregarding the handicapped parking sign. A sloping boardwalk wrapped around the side of the building, leading to both the entrance and a raised porch that overlooked a small lake.

Inside was dark and dingy. Under neon signs, the bar made an L-shape in the back corner of the room. Crowded shelves bent under the weight of hundreds of bottles. A handful of drinkers were spread out along the bar, leaving a couple of stools in between each other. Classic rock played from a touch-screen jukebox near the entrance.

There were also two long, high tables. A pair of older gentlemen sat at the end of one of them, a chessboard between them. Across the room, in a raised section, was a pool table. Four burly guys dressed in jeans and leather crowded around, focused hard on their game. Rand assumed the motorcycles belonged to them.

The bartender was a young blonde girl. She wore jean shorts and a black t-shirt with "Country Corner" written on the top. The same shirt was affixed to the wall behind the bar, a price tag of $35 pinned to the fabric.

"Whiskey, neat," Rand told her. "And whatever he wants."

The girl looked at Miller expectantly, but was met with silence; Miller's attention had been captured elsewhere. Rand followed his gaze to the bikers playing pool.

"I'll have a Coke." He patted Rand on the shoulder, left him at the bar, and walked over to the pool table.

Rand pulled up a stool, and a few seconds later the bartender set the two glasses down in front of him.

Across the room at the pool table, the four men in leather stared at Miller as he spoke to them. They exchanged glances with each other as if they couldn't believe what they were hearing. Then they started digging into their pockets, pulling out cash.

Rand already knew how this was going to end. "Those guys over there won't beat my friend's ass for winning all their money, will they?" he asked the bartender, who had started stacking freshly washed glasses. That was the last thing they needed.

The girl glanced over and shook her head. "They act tough, but they're nice."

"Good," Rand said, taking his first sip of whiskey. He had a feeling Miller wouldn't be back for his Coke anytime soon—he knew how his friend got when there was a pool table around. He'd seen it several times before. To Miller, it was a quick way to win some easy cash.

The bills were stacked on the edge of the pool table—the bets were on. Miller chose a stick from the mounted wall rack and twisted blue chalk over the tip while the biggest of the bikers racked the balls in the triangle. Half a minute later, the first loud *crack* of the cue ball breaking up the other balls sounded through the entire bar, cutting through the hard rock song grinding out from the jukebox.

"By any chance," Rand continued, "do you know a man named Arthur Briggs?"

The girl stared at him for several long, silent moments, and her knowing expression was its own answer. "What about him?"

"I take it he's been known to come here?"

"That's the nice way to say it. Stick around and you're bound to bump into him."

As the playlist on the jukebox went on, the bar started to fill up. When someone new came in, a cold burst of wind blew through the place for a few moments before the door closed again. Each time, Rand checked over his shoulder. Now that he was waiting, he realized that he had no idea what Arthur Briggs looked like. He wasn't sure why, but he had a feeling he'd just *know* when he saw the man.

Rand finished his first drink. The girl behind the bar noticed he was empty. "You want another one?"

"Please."

Uproars came from across the room. It seemed the bikers were figuring out that Miller had grown up in a house with a pool table *and* with a dad who'd competed in tournaments.

She upended the bottle into this glass, eyeballing the

volume. When she was done, Rand could see she'd actually given him a bit more than a normal pour.

"Hey, don't go too far with that bottle," came a gruff voice from the other end of the bar.

Rand looked over and saw a man who'd just sat down. His face was old, haggard, and weathered, and his skin was tan and leathery, as if he spent a lot of time working outside. What little hair remained on his head was grey and short. Sharp stubble covered his cheeks and angular jawline and he had a fierce, intense look about him.

The bartender made no move to pour him a drink. "Russel says no more till you settle your tab."

The man didn't reply. Only glared at the girl, holding her gaze. Rand's eyes shifted between the two of them, wondering who was going to win this standoff. She then snatched a whiskey glass from the shelf beneath the bar, set it in front of the old man, and filled it halfway—even more than she'd given Rand.

Without a word, he scooped it up and took a long sip.

The bartender caught Rand's eye and signaled with a head nod toward the guy. Rand knew what that meant.

That's him.

21

Rand forced his gaze away and looked into his drink. Behind him, a pool ball clacked loudly against another, followed by the *thunk* of one of the balls falling into a corner pocket.

Rand twisted on his stool. He hoped to catch Miller's eye and let him know that Arthur was here... but of course his friend wasn't paying attention. He was too engrossed in his game. Miller leaned over the table, bent at the waist and stiff at the back, his pool stick resting on his propped-up thumb as he lined up his next shot. He jerked the stick and sent the cue ball flying, clacking loudly against a stripe, and sinking it into a corner pocket.

Miller's large, leather-clad opponent groaned in despair. "He's a fucking prodigy."

Rand turned away from the game. *Let him do his thing. I'll move in first.*

It'd been a while since he'd walked up to a stranger in a bar. Before, it had always been a woman. This time, however, he sensed the stakes were a bit higher. *Say the wrong thing and he might refuse to talk to me, just like Trevor did.*

Without knowing what exactly he was going to say, Rand took his whiskey glass and stood. He claimed the second stool over, leaving an empty one between the two of them. The man either hadn't noticed Rand changing seats to get closer to him, or if he had, he didn't react.

Rand had the idea to just reuse the same conversation he'd already had with the bartender, so he went for it: "Those bikers look tough, but how scary are they, really?"

Arthur only stared into his glass as if he were trying to divine the future in the alcohol. Either he hadn't heard Rand, or he was ignoring him.

"Only reason I ask is because my friend over there has a bad habit. He gets into pool games with people who completely underestimate him, then ends up winning all their cash."

Across the room, Miller blasted another ball into the pocket with a snake-like strike.

Still no response. Rand took a sip of whiskey as he watched Miller. "It's just that if I'm going to end up in a fight, I'd prefer to find out now, rather than be surprised later."

Arthur finally gave Rand his attention, looking up and glowering. "*Why* are you talking to me?"

Rand suddenly admired the bartender a lot more for not wilting underneath the man's disapproving glare. There was something powerful behind his dark eyes. "Just making sure my friend isn't headed for the ass kicking of the century. I figured you were from around here and would know if those guys shouldn't be messed with or if they're all show."

Arthur's face remained like stone. He almost seemed confused and angry that someone had dared intrude on his space. "Over there with the chessboard is Donald Tilby. If you want to talk, go talk to him." His rough tone suggested this wasn't merely a friendly suggestion. "He'll tell you all about how he lost everything in the recession and how he's allegedly a descendent of Henry the Eighth. And here's a tip—he always opens with the Queen's Gambit." He turned back to his drink. His body rotated just enough to show Rand the backside of his shoulder. The leather jacket he wore hung loose on him, like he'd bought it before losing a bunch of weight.

Rand caught the bartender listening in. When she realized Rand had noticed her eavesdropping, she hurriedly buried her face in her phone.

"I didn't mean to bother you. Just thought I'd make friendly conversation."

"I'm not your friend," Arthur said. "And I don't like conversation."

"Fair enough. My ex used to get annoyed at me for the same thing. She said it's weird to talk to strangers in public out of nowhere, and that times are different now and people don't trust each other anymore, but I'm not sure I agree with her.."

"You're really going to make me take my whiskey to go," Arthur muttered. "Can't find a peaceful spot *anywhere* in this world." He drained the rest of his glass and slammed it down so hard that Rand was surprised it didn't break. Arthur then reached over the bar, snatched up the bottle the bartender had poured from, and helped himself to a generous second serving.

No charming this guy, Rand thought. *I'll just have to go for it.*

"I killed one of the Lords of Hell," Rand said, "and I need your help."

22

Arthur's glass froze halfway to his mouth. He slowly turned his stony gaze to Rand once again. Although Rand hated the old cliché, he couldn't help but think Arthur looked as if he'd seen a ghost.

"What the *hell* did you just say?"

Rand shifted in his stool and faced Arthur with his entire body. "You heard me."

Arthur's eyes flicked up and down, taking Rand in. "Who are you? How did you find me here?"

However, Arthur didn't wait for a response. He shot up off the stool, moving quicker than Rand would've thought he'd been able to.

Rand stood and blocked the man's path. Now that they were face to face, Rand realized he was nearly five or six inches taller than Arthur, and much broader. He glanced around the bar to check if anyone was watching them. From afar, it might look like he was pinning a senior citizen in a corner.

"Get out of my way," Arthur growled.

"Please sit, Mr. Briggs," Rand said. The man's eyes hardened when he heard his name come from a stranger's mouth. "I just want to talk to you."

"It's you. *You're* the one who called me a couple of nights ago."

"Actually, it was my friend." Rand pointed toward the pool table.

Arthur never took his glare off Rand. "So then who are *you?*"

"Randolph Casey. Friends call me Rand. I'm a para-normal investigator and a demonologist."

"Is that so? You sound so *proud* when you say it." He practically spat the words. "Like one of those idiots on TV running around with night-vision goggles on."

"I'm nothing like them," Rand said. "I don't take the supernatural lightly. Like I said, I killed one of the Lords of Hell. That's what you call them, right?"

"I don't call them anything anymore."

"Well, whatever your name for them is, there's one less of them now."

"Yes, you've mentioned that a few times already." Arthur's eyes manically darted around the room as he if he were afraid of who might overhear. "You sound pleased with yourself over that little accomplishment. And, it's clear you have no idea what you've done."

Out of the corner of his eye, Rand caught the bartender shooting them a wary look. She'd probably sensed the tension between them.

"Then tell me what I've done," Rand whispered. "Please, just talk to me for five minutes."

Arthur settled onto his stool, like an eyewitness to a

crime who'd finally been convinced to talk about what he'd seen.

Rand sat back down as well. "Is what my friend read about you true? Do you also fight the supernatural?"

"I've been doing it for far too long," Arthur muttered as he took another sip of the drink he'd nearly abandoned moments before. He eyed Rand up and down once again. "You seem young enough. You should give it up while you still can."

"I think I've passed the point of no return," Rand said. "When I killed Akhubel."

Technically, it had been Libby. But Rand figured there was no need to complicate an already-delicate conversation.

Arthur choked on his drink and coughed. He wiped his lips with the back of his trembling hand. "I... haven't heard that name in quite some time."

"But you *have* heard it."

"Yes."

"Do you know the names of the other Lords of Hell?"

"Only one," Arthur said, as if admitting to something that he shouldn't have done.

Rand could feel Arthur now giving off a different energy. Before, the man was merely closed off from the rest of the bar. Now, the rigidness he'd come in with was gone. In a way, he seemed... sad.

"There are other reasons why I can't walk away from it all," Rand said.

"Why?"

"I'm not the only one who's in danger. My daughter is also a target."

"So?"

Rand paused. He figured what he'd said was self-explanatory. "*So* I want to protect her."

"Maybe you can't. Maybe it's too late. Maybe you'll lose her just like I lost—" Arthur cut himself short, eyes going dark.

Rand let the silence linger for a few moments. He pushed away the thought of potentially losing Libby to these entities. It seemed Arthur had been through a similar situation. As Miller had said, Arthur had clearly waged his own battle against the supernatural—but twice as long as Rand had. That meant he'd likely endured twice the amount of suffering.

"I came here looking for you because I'm on a similar trajectory as you. And I want to learn how to keep my family from getting hurt. I need help."

"I stopped helping people," Arthur said. "It's no longer worth the effort." The words were like a guilty confession.

Rand frowned. "Please. There must be something I can do."

"If I knew anything that could actually help," Arthur muttered, "then I would've done it a long time ago."

"I'm sure if we put our heads together, we could find a way to fight back against these people and their demons."

Arthur's eyes went wide, digging even more wrinkles into his forehead. "Wait, *what* people?" His words came out as an exhaled breath.

Rand suspected that Arthur already knew who he meant.

"Tell me!" Arthur lashed out and shoved Rand's shoulder with surprising strength.

Rand swallowed. "A man named Bernard Bale and his family."

Something shifted in Arthur's face. He now looked at Rand as if he were the scariest person Arthur had ever seen.

"You've led them here," he finally whispered.

Rand balked at the accusation. "No, of course not."

"There's only one way you would know that man's name, and that's if he *wanted* you to know. That means he's watching you. Following you. You brought him right to me."

Rand's first instinct was to deny it... but the words caught in his throat. He remembered the black car that had run them off the road. And the Bagged Woman.

Arthur moved fast again. He reached over the bar and snatched up the bottle of whiskey he'd used to serve himself earlier. Then he was off the stool and hustling toward the exit with a powerful gait for someone his age. He burst through the door as if trying to break it down.

Arthur's abrupt departure caught Miller's attention. Miller turned to Rand, a questioning look on his face. Besides the cue ball and eight ball, the only other ones on the table were stripes. Miller, as usual, was dominating.

Rand slid off the stool and bolted after the Arthur.

Outside, the freezing air hit him like a wall of needles. The Country Corner's gravel parking lot had more cars than before, and Arthur was weaving in and out between them as he hurried away.

Rand burst into a light jog to catch up, his breath frosting. "Arthur, wait!"

Arthur only quickened his pace, now doing a little

limp-leap instead of actually running, suggesting he'd suffered a leg injury at some point.

It wasn't hard for Rand to close the distance between them. He passed Arthur, then turned and stood in his path. "Who is Bernard, really?" he asked.

"You ought to know," Arthur barked. "You're the one who brought him up. And if you don't know now, then you will soon."

Arthur tried to walk around Rand, but Rand only stepped to the side, blocking him again.

"These are the kinds of things I need to learn if I'm going to save my family."

"And you led them straight to me." The flickering floodlight overhead cast a blinking shadow across half of Arthur's face. The grey storm clouds had rolled in so thick that the darkness had likely triggered its sensor, causing it to turn on. "That's the worst part."

He twisted the cap off the whiskey bottle and brought it to his mouth so quickly the bottom nearly clipped Rand's chin. The man took a long pull before letting the bottle fall to his side, the liquid inside sloshing around.

Rand wanted to insist that he'd led no one to Arthur, that he hadn't been followed, but wasn't sure if that was true.

"Leave me alone and don't come near me ever again," Arthur said, voice low and breath smelling of whiskey. "I worked hard to get away from those people. On a good day when I have enough of this"—he shook the bottle in Rand's face—"I can almost convince myself they've forgotten about me. But now you've put everything at risk."

Arthur maneuvered around Rand again, and this time

Rand let him go. He stomped toward an old pickup truck, taking yet another long sip from the bottle.

Arthur Briggs got behind the wheel and fired up the engine, its loud roar suggesting that it didn't have too many cranks left. The back tires kicked up a plume of dust as Arthur tore out of the gravel lot.

As Rand watched him go, he heard the crunch of approaching footsteps.

"You all right, Rando?" Miller asked.

"That was Arthur Briggs." Rand let out a deep sigh. "I think that means we're on our own."

23

"Lib!"

Libby snapped out of her trance. Both Bailey and Terrance were looking at her expectantly.

"Sorry." She had no idea how long they'd been speaking to her.

"Do we need to take a break?" Bailey asked.

"No, I'm good."

The open notebook in her lap reminded her that they were supposed to be studying. She and her two friends were in Bill's living room. Bill had built a fire in the fireplace, which gave off a cozy warmth. It should've been comforting on that chilly January night, but her surroundings were currently the last thing on Libby's mind.

"You've been in outer space this whole time," Terrance said, studying her through his glasses, as if trying to deduce why she was so distracted.

"I know. Sorry."

Bailey frowned at her. Libby knew that look—Bailey wanted to ask what was troubling her, but was hesitant. Which might have been a good thing in that moment, given the dark nature of the thoughts tumbling through Libby's head.

The demon Akhubel consuming Carmen Herron's life energy.

Her fight with Miranda.

The night Dad died.

Something in her periphery caught her eye—a form in the corner. The flickering apparition came in and out: the vague shape of an old man with rotten, mottled flesh, his tattered brown suit looking like he'd been wearing it when he was interred.

Libby hated giving the entity her attention. He was always there, always around. When she really focused, she could make herself refuse to look at the demon. But even when she was successful, she still knew he was there, intruding.

Her brief victory never lasted. The mental energy it took to ignore the demon compounded throughout the course of the day. Ultimately, her resolve always gave out, her willpower depleted. Her eyes were then drawn to whatever corner of the room the demon lingered in.

I can't keep doing this, Libby thought.

The simplicity of Miranda's plan made it even more insidious. The demon's constant, stalking presence would eventually drive her insane.

Bailey twisted where she sat in Bill's recliner, following Libby's gaze. When she didn't see anything, she turned back. "What are you looking at?"

"Nothing." Libby tore her eyes away from the demon in the corner.

"I feel like someone's about to sneak up on me."

Don't worry. He's only here for me, Libby thought.

Bailey checked over her shoulder one more time, just to be sure.

"We can leave if you need us to," Terrance offered. "If you're not feeling well."

"No," Libby said quickly. She didn't want to be alone. Terrance and Bailey were a decent distraction from the ever-present phantom.

"Then I say we each read the first part of chapter fifteen, and then quiz each other," Terrance suggested. "Mr. Neeson told us there would be a lot of stuff from this section on the test."

"Sounds good to me," Bailey replied as she adjusted herself in Bill's recliner into a more comfortable reading position.

Libby flipped to the page, but only got through the first paragraph before an idea suddenly flashed in her mind.

Arun Singh.

That guy who'd found the missing kids. Her dad had mentioned him just before leaving town.

If he figured out where they *were, then maybe he could help find Carmen,* Libby thought.

Libby laid her phone on top of the open textbook in her lap. She glanced at both Bailey and Terrance, but both were reading and not paying attention to her, so she used the opportunity to search for Arun on social media. His profile came right up. He had hundreds of thousands of followers. Despite that, he hadn't deactivated the option of sending him a direct message.

This is crazy, Libby thought. She figured his fans and supporters bombarded him with messages that he probably never looked at. *There's no way he'd see mine among all the rest.*

But she decided it was still worth a try.

She started typing.

Hi Arun,

I'm sure you get these kinds of messages all the time, but I feel like I have to give it a shot, so here it goes. I know a girl who has gone missing. Her name is Carmen Herron, and she's nine years old. Is there anything you can do to help me find her?

She reread what she'd written over and over again. It seemed wrong to describe such a terrible and complex situation in only a few words—like she was minimizing it. But it also felt unnecessary to waste time crafting a message that would likely never be seen.

Libby clicked the "send" button and her message was delivered into Arun's inbox, probably falling in among hundreds, perhaps thousands of others from desperate people begging for his help.

She sighed at the hopelessness of it all.

"Okay, so I have *no* idea what I just read," Bailey announced, looking up from her textbook.

Terrance shrugged. "It's not that hard, actually."

"Explain it to me, then."

Libby's attention bounced between Terrance and Bailey as they went back and forth. With each glance, Ulvareth appeared behind Terrance, then behind Bailey, and then again behind Terrance. It almost seemed like there were two of them.

She closed her eyes for a couple of seconds, as if that would reset things. She opened them and looked around the room. Ulvareth was gone. A moment later... Libby felt drawn to look up. Ulvareth hung onto the ceiling like a fly, his head craned to peer down at her with his perpetual, maddeningly neutral expression.

Even when the demon *hadn't* been in her line of sight for a few seconds, she'd somehow been compelled to find him.

"Libby?" Bailey asked.

She'd been busted again.

Screw this, she thought as she set her textbook aside. "Give me a minute."

This couldn't go on. It was immensely frustrating how quickly Miranda's plan was working. She decided to handle this the way that seemed most obvious to her.

By doing the same thing she'd done to Akhubel.

LIBBY CLIMBED THE STAIRS, then went down the hallway to her bedroom. She turned on the lamp that was on her desk near the door. Across the room was a window that overlooked the backyard and pool area behind Bill's house. Ulvareth peered at her from the other side of the glass. He hovered like a balloon with just enough helium to keep it floating in one place. The tips of his black shoes pointed to the ground.

Libby crossed the room while keeping her gaze on the demon, knowing that if she blinked or looked away, then he would relocate. She gripped the bottom of the window and pulled it open. The cold air blew in, though Ulvareth stayed where he was.

Her bed was beside the window, made up neatly with all her many pillows arranged at the headboard. Slowly, Libby reached to her right and slipped her hand underneath the nearest pillow.

Her fingers brushed against wood. She gripped the cross that her father had given her before he'd left. The same one she'd thrust into Akhubel's chest, killing him instantly.

SLAYER OF AKHUBEL.

She tightened her grip around it. To her surprise, Ulvareth once again didn't react—reaching for a weapon didn't elicit even a flinch. He kept his black eyes fixated on her all the while, as if genuinely curious about what she would do next.

There were several feet of open air between her and where Ulvareth floated. He was out of reach. But Libby knew his tendencies. Simply looking somewhere else would cause Ulvareth to reappear—likely closer.

Libby took a breath to steady herself, then whirled away from the window. As expected, Ulvareth now stood in the corner of her room, behind her open door. He peered out from around it with one eye while keeping the other half of his face obscured.

She rushed toward him, raising the cross like a knife.

The lamplight flickered and went out and she lost sight of Ulvareth in the darkness. Still, Libby slashed the cross downward in the general area where he'd been standing. Her attack connected with nothing but air.

No! I missed!

She cried out and swiped around in the dark, desperate to strike—afraid of what retaliation might come.

A strong force lifted Libby off her feet and sent her spiraling backward. She landed on her bed and tumbled over the other side, her body slamming into the opposite wall.

Groaning, she curled into a ball, head and back aching.

Frantic footsteps came from outside her bedroom. The door flung open.

"Libby?" came her mother's voice. "What was that noise?" The light clicked on, and a moment later Tessa rushed to Libby's side. "What happened? Are you okay?"

"I'm fine." Libby pushed herself upright, refusing to let the pain keep her down.

Tessa's eyes landed on the cross that Libby still gripped and her lips pressed into a thin line. "I'm calling your father."

"No," Libby grabbed Tessa's arm. "I thought I could find it without turning out the light, but I tripped." She held up the cross.

"Why do you need that?"

"It makes me feel safe." Which actually wasn't a lie.

Tessa furrowed her brow. Libby could tell her mom suspected otherwise, but the story was plausible enough.

"Maybe be careful about carrying that around," Tessa said. "You don't want to freak out your friends." She helped Libby to her feet. Her first step was a limp, and Tessa appraised her with a concerned, skeptical look. "Are you sure you're okay?"

"Yeah. Just tripped, like I said."

They went back downstairs together. By the time Libby got halfway down the stairs, she'd walked off most of the pain.

Well, that didn't work, she thought. *Like at all.* She had a feeling that the demon could've hurt her way more than he actually had. *Maybe throwing me across my own bedroom was just a warning shot.*

Even worse, she now wondered if she'd merely gotten lucky in her brief encounter with Akhubel. Perhaps she was less capable of dealing with demonic entities than she'd thought.

Once again, Libby sensed a presence behind her, and she looked over her shoulder. Ulvareth stood at the top of the stairs, watching her descend.

He still wore his blank-faced stare, not seeming at all angry about what she'd tried. Instead of looking away, Libby gazed back into his deep black eyes. She might have imagined it, but she thought she spotted the first hint of emotion on the demon's stony face. Now, he seemed ever so slightly amused.

24

From the Country Corner, Rand and Miller headed to a nearby local restaurant.

Rand had lost all track of time while waiting for Arthur to wander into the bar—it was four-thirty in the afternoon, although it seemed much later due to the overcast sky and early-setting winter sun.

The whiskey had made Rand a little tipsy, so he ordered a massive chicken fried steak. Miller went for a basket of buffalo wings—his go-to at most places.

"So," Miller said after the waitress left to put their order in, "Arthur stormed off because he thinks Bernard Bale followed us here to Rose Grove and now knows where he's been hiding?"

Rand had filled Miller in on the short drive to the restaurant. "Yes."

"Do you think... we actually *did* do that? By accident?"

"It's very strongly possible." Rand wasn't yet ready to admit that he'd done exactly what Arthur feared. But he also couldn't deny it.

"If that's the case, I wouldn't necessarily blame him for not wanting to talk to us." Miller idly picked at a loose thread on the red-and-white-checkered tablecloth. "Are we considering him a lost cause?"

"Of course not," Rand replied, looking out the window near their table. A couple walked by, bundled up in heavy jackets that seemed a bit overkill. It was cold, but not *that* cold.

"So then what?"

"I don't know yet." Rand was almost embarrassed to admit it. "For starters, we'll head back to the bar tonight. And tomorrow night as well."

"What makes you think he'll be back after what happened between you two?"

"His drinking habit."

Miller grunted. "Fair enough."

Their food arrived a few minutes later, and they ate. Rand rarely ordered dessert, but they did that evening, hoping it would give Arthur even more time to decide he wanted—or needed—to return to the Country Corner.

Long after their plates had been cleared, Rand finally noticed the waitress giving them an impatient side eye. "Alright, Miller, I think we overstayed our welcome. Let's go."

They paid and headed back to the bar.

"You see his truck?" Miller asked when they arrived, scanning the parking lot.

"No, but that doesn't mean he won't be here." Rand did note, however, that the line of motorcycles that had been there earlier was gone.

The Country Corner was much fuller now that it was

evening. Donald Tilby was still in the same spot, facing off with a different opponent.

Miller joined Rand at the bar this time, since there didn't seem to be any money to be won from playing pool. The heavy dinner had helped Rand's fuzzy head, but if they were going to linger around, it meant he'd have to have another whiskey or two. *I'll drink slower,* he thought. Miller went for a Coke again.

As the evening wore on, the place got even busier. Rand kept his eye on the door, waiting for Arthur to arrive, but the man never did. In fact, now that Rand had met Arthur, he had the feeling nighttime at the Country Corner wouldn't be his scene. It was much more crowded than it had been in the mid-afternoon, and louder. Rand could see Arthur not being a fan of the ruckus.

"What're you thinking?" Miller asked.

Rand finished his drink. "I'm guessing that Arthur prefers this place when there's fewer people."

"So we should come back tomorrow?"

"That… might be our best bet."

"We know where he lives now. What if we paid him a visit?"

Rand had considered it while they'd been waiting. "I don't want to spook him even more. The last thing we need is for him to shut us out completely."

Which might've happened already, he thought.

———

BACK AT THE Grove Retreat hotel, Rand went straight for the heater again and let the warm blast wash over him. Despite the warmth, he still shivered.

Miller changed into pajama pants. He turned his jeans over and over, fishing into the pockets until he found his wad of cash, which was pretty thick and looked to be mostly twenties.

"I think you make more money hustling people at pool than you do owning a bookstore," Rand said.

"Don't tell me that. You'll tempt me to actually turn it into a career."

"You might even make more than I do as a college instructor." Which wouldn't have been hard—it was why they always had to share rooms whenever they were out of town.

After Rand had sufficiently warmed up, he got underneath the thick comforter. Miller wasn't long behind him in doing the same. It was just after nine o'clock, but Rand welcomed an early night given how poorly he'd been sleeping lately. Within five minutes, Miller was snoring softly.

Despite his tiredness, Rand laid on his back and stared up at the ceiling. The heater clanked as it worked hard. The white light from the moon streamed in through the window.

"I can almost convince myself they've forgotten about me. But now you've put everything at risk."

Arthur's words still rattled around in his head, stuck like the annoying pop songs his daughter listened to.

Rand had a sinking feeling Arthur was right.

———————

RAND'S EYES POPPED OPEN.

He didn't remember falling asleep. His brain had

been running even harder than the ancient heater, filling with thoughts that were loud enough to keep him awake all night. *Did I really put Arthur Briggs in danger by coming here? Do I have any chance at all of saving my daughter?*

An icy breeze drifted across his room, and his flesh prickled.

Rand cocked his head, wondering if the heater had shut off. It hadn't. But no matter how hard it tried, it would never keep up as long as the window was open.

But we... didn't open the window.

He turned. Miller lay with his back to him, his large frame rising and falling with heavy, rhythmic breathing.

Rand next scanned the room. The moonlight streaming in wasn't enough to illuminate the corners. Those remained in shadow.

Stop being paranoid, he thought. The gap in the window was too narrow for someone to fit through. Besides, their room was on the second story.

Rand threw off the comforter and sat up. His feet, when they touched the wooden floor, felt like he'd stepped onto an ice rink. The bed springs squeaked with each of his movements.

He crossed the room and went over to the open window. Warm air rose from the machine at his waist while the cold wind blew in, creating a very uneven sensation around his torso.

He reached to slide the window closed, but movement outside on the street below caught his eye.

Although Rand couldn't make out the shape clearly, he already knew what it was.

The Bagged Woman trudged down the road toward

the hotel. The cold seemed to have no effect on the milky flesh of her arms and legs.

Rand stiffened at the sight of her, and a surge of dread wrapped around his stomach.

She dragged something behind her. Although it looked heavy, it was weightless to her.

Rand forced his slightly trembling hands to open the window all the way in order to get a better view.

The Bagged Woman came to a halt. She then shifted her head to look up at Rand, somehow able to see despite the dirty sack that covered her face.

Is that...

Yes, it was. Now that the woman was closer, Rand could barely make out what she'd brought with her.

A body. Limp and motionless. She held it by the throat.

She turned the body's face toward Rand, giving him a clear view of her victim.

Arthur Briggs.

The man's terrified expression was frozen in place by death, as if his final moments had been filled with abject fear.

The Bagged Woman presented him to Rand like a cat proud of the bird it had killed.

"No..."

The next thing Rand knew, he shot up in bed. The room was uncomfortably warm from the heater, and he was pouring sweat. The window was closed.

"Fuck," he whispered as he wiped at his face. His palms came away slick.

Another dream.

Or was it? Maybe it was a threat.

"I can almost convince myself they've forgotten about me. But now you've put everything at risk."

Arthur had been very concerned that Rand had led the Bales to him. What if the Bagged Woman was giving him a preview of Arthur's fate?

Ideas like that ensured Rand wouldn't be getting any more sleep. He threw the covers off and went to the nearby chair where he'd draped the clothes he'd worn earlier and started putting them on.

"Where are you going?" Miller's voice was thick with sleep.

"Back to Arthur's house."

Miller sat up. He wiped at his groggy eyes. "What for?"

"I had a dream that something terrible happened to him."

Miller took a few seconds to process the words, then threw his legs over the side of the bed. "Give me a minute and I'll be ready."

"You can stay," Rand said. "It might've *actually* been just a dream." Regardless, he appreciated his friend not trying to convince him otherwise. In supernatural situations, dreams and reality often mixed.

Miller gave an indignant grunt, suggesting that his remaining behind was out of the question.

Rand took his watch from the bedside table and fastened it to his wrist—it read half-past one o'clock in the morning. He unplugged his phone from the charger and slid it into his pocket.

Miller zipped up a softshell jacket, pulled the hood over his head, and put his glasses on. "Ready when you are."

25

Rand sped down narrow small-town lanes that were barely illuminated by the streetlights. Apprehension clawed at him more and more with each mile that passed.

What if we get there and find exactly what I already saw?

Miller said nothing as they drove. He seemed to sense Rand's uneasiness.

When they arrived, the inside of Arthur's house was completely dark, making it seem as if he wasn't home. But unlike the previous day, Arthur's truck was parked out front.

"At least he made it back without flipping his truck," Miller said. "Didn't you say he drank a lot before he drove away?"

"Yeah, he was hammering the whiskey." Once again, Rand remembered the sight of the Bagged Woman dragging Arthur's corpse. He unfastened his seat belt and got out of the car, closing the Jeep's door quietly behind him.

"What if he whips out a shotgun?" Miller asked. "He seemed like the type to have one."

Rand nodded. He and Arthur hadn't parted on great terms, so showing up on his property at two in the morning wouldn't mend any bridges, no matter how many nightmares about him Rand claimed to have had.

Still. Something's off, Rand thought. *I can sense it.*

Rand used his cell phone flashlight as he approached Arthur's house. The tall, untended grass in the yard swayed in the chilly wind.

The first porch step creaked loudly the moment Rand put his weight on it. Miller lunged over it and started with the second, which was significantly quieter.

Rand suddenly noticed Arthur's front door was slightly ajar.

"Look at this," Rand whispered, aiming his light at the door. The inside of Arthur's house was pitch black.

"He came home drunk," Miller said. "Probably forgot to close it behind him."

"And let the cold in? Even if he forgot, he'd notice eventually, right?"

"Unless he was so far gone that—wait, what's that?" Miller pointed.

Rand shifted his light. Someone had etched a pentagram into the door. The lines were unnaturally straight, as if done by a machine rather than by hand. "That *definitely* wasn't there before." Rand's gut churned as he realized his premonition might have been correct.

"It looks unfinished," Miller said. He stepped up beside Rand and traced his finger along the bottom part of the pentagram. The downward point of the star lacked a final connecting line that would've completed the symbol. "Maybe they were interrupted?" Miller took out his own phone light and inspected the nearby wall for anything else out of place.

"We have to check inside," Rand said.

Miller didn't answer. He was too busy hunting around, making his way to where the porch turned at a right-angle corner toward the side of the house.

Rand was just about to go in when something caught Miller's attention and he said, "Rando."

Rand went to the corner of the porch and followed Miller's gaze. A small fire burned in the backyard, and a figure was standing beside it.

"That's him, isn't it?" Miller asked.

Rand descended the porch steps and walked toward the fire, Miller on his heels. Rand wondered if Arthur, who sat hunched and unmoving, was asleep.

How can someone sleep out here when it's so cold? Then that made him wonder if something worse had happened.

The dead leaves and grass crunched underfoot. Yet if the old man heard them approaching, he didn't react.

"Arthur?"

Rand was relieved to see that his eyes were open. The fire's reflection danced in his pupils. The whiskey bottle from the bar rested at his feet as he sat on an overturned mop bucket.

Just beyond Arthur was the black, wrought-iron fence of the neighboring Grove Gardens Cemetery. Gravestones jutted up from the grass near the bars.

"The fuck are *you* doing here?" Arthur muttered without taking his gaze away from the fire. If he was angry that they'd shown up, he wasn't showing it—yet.

He still wore the same thing from the bar—a dirty t-shirt with his old jacket. He seemed entirely unaffected by the cold.

Rand went with the truth. "I saw you in a dream. A demonic entity murdered you."

Arthur gave off a mirthless chuckle. "Is that so? I have that same dream damn near every night. Why do you think I drink?"

He picked up the whiskey bottle and took a sip. It had been mostly full earlier at the bar, but now only a small amount remained.

He's been hitting it pretty hard since then, Rand thought.

Arthur wiped his mouth with the back of his hand. "If you're worried about demonic entities showing up here, then go stand in the graveyard."

Rand glanced at Miller, who only shrugged.

"Why?" Rand asked.

"It's hallowed ground. Demons can't tread there."

"I never knew that," Rand replied.

"And you call yourself a demonologist?" Arthur took another sip. "Look at my house. Why do you think I live in that shit hole? Because it's close to *here*." He pointed a thumb toward the headstones beyond the iron fence. "When I want to cleanse the negative energy, I go walk through the cemetery for hours."

Rand was very familiar with the need to remove negative energy. He did so after every case. "I usually just pray."

But I haven't done that since leaving the Herron House, Rand remembered. *I've been too preoccupied.* Realizing that brought him a stab of guilt.

"I stopped praying a long time ago. The graveyard is far more welcoming these days," Arthur said.

He's a real grim bastard, but I can't blame him.

"Arthur," Rand said. "I came because I think you're in danger. And there's something on your door that—"

"Of course I'm in danger. I told you earlier, you led the Bales straight to me." The same accusation, except this time he said it without fury. Now, he almost seemed resolved. "I was pissed before, but then after thinking about it—and drinking some more—I realized this is a good thing. Finally... it can end."

"Arthur—"

"No more running. No more hiding. No more finding peace in graveyards."

Rand and Miller exchanged a heavy look.

"I don't think that's the right way to go about this," Rand said.

"Why wouldn't it be?"

"I... think I can help you."

Arthur chuckled, this time sounding genuinely amused. "You've done quite enough already."

Rand sat down in the cold grass closer to the fire. Miller remained standing just behind him. "If you want to die so badly, then I guess it's your right to choose that. It isn't so bad, actually. I would know—I died the other night."

Arthur truly looked at Rand for the first time since he'd arrived. He had a feeling that would catch the man's attention.

"You don't seem very dead."

"I came back."

"Jesus."

"Not quite. An angel named Tara sent me back. At least, I'm pretty sure she's an angel."

"How nice. You have a guardian angel. I've always said the newer generation doesn't know how good they have it."

Despite the sarcasm, Rand was glad that Arthur was actually listening to him without storming off or getting angry.

Progress. Although it's a weird *progress, I'll take what I can get.*

"A couple of nights ago, I was lured to a mansion called the Herron House. This guy named Jackson fed me some bullshit about needing me to clear out the demon that haunted the place. He was actually bringing me there *for* this demon, Akhubel. Remember who we talked about earlier at the bar?" Arthur watched Rand carefully as he recounted his story, the lines in his face deep crevices. "The whole point of it was some kind of... ritual. Jackson was married to a woman named Miranda, who's Bernard Bale's daughter." At the mention of the name, Arthur sat up a few inches straighter on his bucket. "From what I could tell... he was trying to earn his position in the family. Marrying Miranda wasn't enough. He ultimately agreed to sacrifice their daughter to Akhubel. But I stopped them."

Rand paused as he let the story sink in with Arthur.

"Everything is a ritual," Arthur finally said.

Rand perked up. "I'm pretty sure Jackson Herron told me the same thing right before he killed me that night."

"He wasn't wrong. It might as well be the Bale family motto." Arthur took a sip of whiskey. He extended the nearly empty bottle to Rand, but Rand shook his head. "And Akhubel. You're sure you got him?"

"Yes."

"One less of those bastards."

"What more can you tell me about them?"

"Not much."

Miller cleared his throat. "I read your message board post, where you talked about traveling to Iraq and Iran last year to research the Lords of Hell."

Arthur let out a low groan. "I knew I should've left that website alone."

"What did you learn?" Rand asked.

"Not much. But I can at least tell you about what happened there."

Now we're finally getting somewhere, Rand thought. "Please do."

Miller sat down next to Rand by the fire. Arthur was silent for a long time, and Rand started to wonder if he'd changed his mind about telling them. His frown seemed to pull his entire face toward the ground.

Then Arthur began to speak.

26

Southern Iraq
One Year Ago

"Don't let the appearance trick you," Rashed explained as Arthur followed. "This place is very nice."

Rashed turned out to be right. Despite the guest house's plain exterior, Arthur was pleasantly surprised by the inside.

The smell of strong coffee intermingled with a hint of perfume and spice. A Persian rug was near the entrance, intricate colors contrasting with the walls decorated with multicolored tiles. Arthur almost felt guilty trampling it with his dusty boots. A narrow, old, wooden staircase spiraled from the first floor to the next. Its antique appearance gave Arthur the impression that it would never pass inspection if this place had been located in a western country.

The only apparent drawback was that the inside was only a few degrees cooler than the arid desert air he'd just come in from. Two fans helped circulate the stuffiness through the open windows, but they didn't make much of a difference.

He couldn't be picky. Comfort was the last thing he'd expected on this particular journey—both physical and mental.

A lone young woman sat at a table on the far side of the room. When Arthur and Rashed entered, she lifted her sheila and haphazardly covered her jet-black hair.

Rashed spoke to her in Arabic, which was mostly foreign to Arthur's ears. The girl opened a large leger book to a bookmarked page and started penciling in information on the narrow, lined rows, writing in elegant Arabic script right to left.

She asked a question and Rashed responded, "*Wahed, bes.*"

Arthur happened to understand that particular phrase. *One only.* He'd come to Iraq speaking no Arabic— that was one reason he'd hired Rashed—but during their journey he'd inevitably picked up on a few key words and phrases.

He looked at Rashed with a questioning look. Rashed pressed all five of his fingertips together, a hand gesture that indicated for Arthur to wait.

His guide produced cash from his pocket and paid for the room for the night. The woman counted it quickly, placed it into a nearby drawer with more bills, and took a key from the next drawer over, which she handed to Rashed. Rashed then passed it to Arthur.

"You're not staying?" Arthur asked.

Rashed held Arthur by the shoulder and drew him away from the woman, as if he didn't want her to hear what he was about to say. "Listen, *akhee.*" *My brother.* The word technically referred to two men who shared the Islamic faith, but Arthur had quickly garnered that cordial locals were willing to extend the term to friends of any belief system.

Rashed's voice was hushed and conspiratorial as he said, "There's a lady who lives near to this town." The way he said it made it sound like an embarrassing admission. "It's just that I don't often get the chance to come this far south, and—"

"Okay, okay," Arthur didn't want to hear any more. "Do you what you need to do."

"*Wallah,* I'll be back at sunrise."

"Sure."

Let him take a break, Arthur thought. He was paying Rashed well to be his guide through the region, and so far the man had gone above and beyond.

"You'll be okay here without me for the rest of the day?"

"Yes."

Rashed seemed unsure. "You will still ask the local Imam about..."

"Yes."

Imam was the title given to the prayer leaders at each and every mosque. It was these men Arthur had been speaking to throughout the country with the help of Rashed's translating.

"*Tamam.*" *Okay.* "If he does not speak English, *ma fi moushkala, khalas.*" *No problem, forget about it.* "In that case, I'll speak with him when I return."

"That'll work."

Rashed broke out into a wide smile, as if he'd been expecting Arthur to deny his request. "I will go there now, *akhee.* Call me if you need me. But... try not to need me."

"Sure."

Rashed moved as if he couldn't get out of there fast enough. "Oh," he called over his shoulder just as he was about to walk out. "Your room is upstairs. Number five."

"*Shukran,*" Arthur said, and started up the stairs. *Thank you.* He held tight to the railing as he climbed the steep steps—his bad leg had made stairs more difficult in recent years.

The rooms were very close together in the narrow hallway. Someone had taped pieces of paper on each door and written the room numbers in Arabic script. Arthur remembered what the number five looked like— it often appeared on speed limit signs.

The room was small and simple, just as Arthur had come to expect. The bed rested on a wooden frame, adorned with a crisp white sheet, a hand-woven blanket, and a single flat pillow. There was an adjoining bathroom no bigger than a closet, and it consisted of nothing more than a squat toilet, a faucet meant for showering, and a plastic bucket filled with water.

Arthur tossed his rucksack onto the bed, the sight of which reminded him of his exhaustion, but resting would have to wait. His stomach rumbled.

Food first, then work, he decided.

He opened his rucksack and removed a smaller backpack. He stuffed his leather-bound notebook inside, then slung the bag's strap over his shoulder and went back downstairs.

Once in front of the guesthouse, he surveyed the area. It didn't take him long to spot the tallest structure in town —a minaret that denoted the location of the local mosque. It was a tall, obelisk-like tower.

Bingo. He'd head there after he ate.

Arthur wandered into the first restaurant he found. The outdoor patio had mismatched plastic tables and chairs. There were a fair bit of people already there, all of whom peered at him as he sat down. He guessed the locals weren't accustomed to seeing foreigners this far south—or in their country at all.

A young boy of about twelve brought a menu, which was nothing more than a laminated sheet of paper. He also set a foggy glass on the table and poured water out of a plastic bottle. Everything on the menu was written in Arabic, but there were a handful of pictures, one of which Arthur recognized but couldn't remember what it was called. Rashed had ordered it for them once. It was chicken cooked in a tomato-based stew. Arthur pointed to the picture, and the boy nodded before hustling back to the inside section of the restaurant, likely where his mother or father was doing all the cooking.

Arthur sipped his water and felt the staring eyes of the man at the next table over. He was broad-shouldered with thinning black hair and a bulbous nose. He sucked on the end of a shisha pipe and let the smoke escape from the side of his mouth. Arthur smelled the apple-flavored scent.

When their eyes met, the man smiled and said, "*Ahlan.*" *Welcome.*

Arthur nodded. "*Shukran.*"

"*Inta min wayn?*" *Where are you from?*

"United States."

"Ah." The man inhaled his pipe again and looked away, likely assuming that was about as far as he'd get in a conversation with a foreigner.

The young boy returned, carrying a tray over his head in one hand and two metal baskets in the other. He set the tray in front of Arthur, which contained bread and three different sauces. Next, he went to the local man. He lifted off the top of the shisha pipe and dumped the grey and flaky coals into one of his baskets. He put the piece back, and then used tongs to pick up fresh, red-hot coals from his basket before arranging them precisely in the receptacle.

"*Shukran,*" the man told the boy.

The soup arrived about five minutes later, and only when it was in front of him did Arthur realize how hungry he actually was. It went down quick, and it didn't take him long to decide it was the best he'd had since starting his travels through the country with Rashed.

When he was done, Arthur paid with a single large note that he figured should cover the bill. The boy brought him his change—some tattered, smaller bills and coins. Arthur left the coins on the table as a tip.

The sun was setting by the time Arthur departed from the restaurant. *Time to head to the mosque,* he thought as he checked his watch and frowned at the time. *And I bet it's about to get busy there...*

As if someone had read his mind, the call to prayer began resonating through the town a few seconds later, projected from the minaret Arthur had spotted earlier. The male voice sang passages from the Quran—the pleasant, now-familiar sound had quickly grown on Arthur. In ancient times, the tower's height allowed the call to be heard throughout the village. In the modern era, that was still the case, but they also had some help from speakers and microphones.

He fell in with the townspeople and followed them to the mosque. They left their shoes outside before entering, men going one way and the women the other.

I'll give it some time, Arthur thought. *The Imam will be busy now.* The good thing about praying five times a day was that each session didn't take long.

It wasn't long before the townspeople started filing out of the mosque, sliding their feet back into their shoes and sandals before leaving again.

Arthur caught someone studying him—it was the boy who'd served him at the restaurant.

"*Tehki Inglizi?*" Arthur asked. *Do you speak English?* The boy nodded. "I'd like to talk with the Imam, *min fadlak.*" *Please.*

The boy seemed confused, yet at the same time excited about the prospect of helping the rare foreigner that had traveled to his town. He pressed his fingers together the same way Rashed had earlier. *Wait.*

He rushed back to the mosque, kicking off his plastic blue flip-flops before he reached the door. A few minutes later, he returned with an older man wearing a white kandora. The boy pointed at Arthur.

The Imam approached Arthur, a kind smile on his lips and in his eyes.

"*Tehki Inglizi?*" Arthur asked.

"*Shwaya*," the Imam said. *A little.* "But enough, I think. I am Ibrahim." He held out his hand, and Arthur clasped it.

"Arthur."

Ibrahim smiled. "Welcome to my town."

"*Shukran.*"

"What can I help you with, Arthur?"

So far, it seemed to Arthur that Ibrahim spoke enough English to converse with him. *No need to wait on Rashed this time.* Most of the Imams they'd met with had spoken no English.

Arthur unslung his backpack from his shoulder and took out his notebook, then opened it to a random page; it didn't matter which one, because they all contained a similar writing.

"Do you recognize this script?"

He turned the page toward Ibrahim, and as Arthur had expected, the Imam's face lost all sense of goodwill. A harrowing expression came over the man as he looked at the jagged, demonic scrawl that filled the notebook. He even took a step back.

Ibrahim stared for several long, silent seconds, as if unable to look away. "*Shoo bidak?*" he finally asked. *What do you want?*

Arthur mercifully closed the notebook. The poor man had seen enough.

"Only to talk. And to learn from you."

"Where did you find this... this..." He gestured toward the notebook, but failed to come up with an English word that accurately portrayed his disgust.

"From other Imams such as yourself. Most of this came from someone named Abdul, in Basra. Do you know him?"

"I do."

Good, Arthur thought. *If one of his brothers trusts me enough, then maybe he will too.*

"Can we speak?"

Ibrahim seemed to consider that long and hard, almost visibly weighing the pros and cons. Finally, he said, "Come."

He led Arthur to a small building that looked like a home. There, they went to an even smaller structure in the back, consisting of a single, unadorned room. Inside was a simple table and a floor fan circling warm air through the open windows. Arthur got the feeling Ibrahim was bringing him here to avoid being seen speaking with him.

Not that it offends me, Arthur thought. *I don't blame him one bit.*

"Sit, please." Ibrahim said. "*Mai?*"

"Sure."

Ibrahim pulled a bottle of water from a half-empty pallet wrapped in plastic. He placed it on the table in front of Arthur, then sat across from him.

"This writing that you showed me," Ibrahim said. "It's *haram.* Very *haram.*"

"I know."

"It's from the djinn." The word dropped heavily from Ibrahim's mouth.

Arthur nodded. *Djinn* was an Arabic word that literally translated to *genie*, but generally referred to what people in the west called demons.

"I fight these entities," Arthur said.

Or at least I used to. He'd more or less given up the supernatural battles. He'd simply gotten too old, too feeble, worn down over time. Still, there was a part of him that had always wanted to learn more.

"So, why have you come?" Ibrahim asked.

"I'm here researching a specific type of djinn. From what I've learned so far, they seem to be closely associated with an ancient child-sacrifice cult that was prominent in this region over the centuries."

Ibrahim looked away, and Arthur immediately knew this wasn't the first time the Imam had heard of such atrocities. "That is all in the past."

Wishful thinking, Arthur thought. "The cult has *mostly* faded, yes, but the demons they worked with are eternal."

"Right..."

If someone was going to refuse to speak to Arthur further about the subject, this was usually the point where they made that clear. Many in the region believed whole-heartedly in the djinn and, as a result, refrained from talking about them. In Arthur's opinion, that was far better than most of the people in his own country who foolishly didn't believe in demons at all. They often still refused to admit their existence, even when being directly oppressed.

"Have you had any recent supernatural experiences?" Arthur pressed.

"I have not."

"What about anyone else in the town?"

This was why Arthur was specifically seeking out Imams. If someone encountered what they believed to be a djinn, it was likely the first person they'd inform was their local Imam.

"The... children." Ibrahim seemed hesitant to admit it.

Arthur straightened in. "What do they say?"

Ibrahim took a deep, steadying breath. "They tell me he comes from the desert, and that he travels with the wind. He taunts them at night."

"How so?"

"His appearance, and his eyes. He frightens them. When the children come, I pray for them and assure them Allah will keep them safe. But sometimes, I wonder if that is true. I feel shame for having a weak faith in this matter."

"Does he hurt the kids?" Arthur asked.

"So far, no. It seems he only wants to scare them. But I'm afraid that soon he will want more."

"Do you know this djinn's name?"

Ibrahim met Arthur's gaze. "He speaks his name to these children, and they tell me. I have warned them to never say it aloud."

That was good advice. There was power in a demon's name. Using it correctly could send them away, if you knew what you were doing, but uttering it carelessly could inadvertently summon them.

"Tell me." Arthur asked.

Ibrahim's eyes bored into his. "I shouldn't."

Arthur opened his notebook to a blank page, then set it down in front of Ibrahim. He took a pen from his pocket and laid it on top of the page.

Ibrahim still hesitated. "How do I know you're not one of them?"

"Them?"

"One of the ones who conjures these djinn."

Seems like he knows remnants of the child-sacrifice cult are still around, Arthur thought. Ibrahim had said the stories were all in the past, but they both knew that was merely wishful thinking.

Arthur unbuttoned the top half of his shirt and pulled it aside. Three jagged gashes marred the flesh over his heart—scars from a particularly nasty encounter many years before.

Ibrahim's gaze lingered on the old wounds.

"You know what this is?" Arthur asked.

He nodded gravely. "Sometimes they appear on the children."

Arthur buttoned his shirt back up. "As you can see, they don't care for me too much."

Ibrahim visibly swallowed as he picked up the pen. He clicked the top and started to write. When he was done, he pushed the notebook back to Arthur. He'd written the demon's name in Arabic script, which Arthur couldn't read, so he'd have to show it to Rashed when the man returned.

"Do you know the names of any others?"

"No."

"So the town's children don't talk about any other djinn?"

"Only this one." Ibrahim nodded to the notebook.

It wasn't much, but it was something. Since many of the Imams so far had refused to speak to him, Arthur could count this interaction as a win.

"*Shukran.* I appreciate this."

"*Afwan.*" Ibrahim merely whispered the word with a heavy heart. *You're welcome.*

———

ARTHUR LEFT the mosque feeling victorious.

He'd learned a name of one of the Lords of Hell. It was the first he'd received since coming to the Iraq. Abdul had been helpful in giving him copies of demonic writing that he'd collected, but even he had been unable to give Arthur specific names for any of the entities.

And now it's time to take the edge off, Arthur thought.

He found a small shop with only one shelf inside, which was crammed with snacks, canned drinks, and bottles of water. Behind the counter near the door was a man in his early twenties. He was kicked back in a chair watching something on his phone, the rapidly spoken Arabic underpinned by a laugh track.

Arthur didn't bother checking the shelves—he knew what he'd come for wouldn't be there.

"*Salaam Aleikum,*" Arthur said.

The young man returned his greeting. "*Walaikum, salam.*"

"*Kahul, min fadlak.*" *Alcohol, please.* It had been one of the first words Arthur had learned from Rashed.

"*Ma andee, akhee. Haram.*" *I don't have any.*

Arthur expected such a response. He reached into his pocket and laid a wad of bills on the counter. The boy studied the money for a long time and Arthur could almost hear the internal battle happening within him. Finally, he relented, as Arthur had known he would. He took his feet down, put his phone aside, and opened a cabinet. Bottles clinked, and then the young man set them on the counter side by side. Whiskey, vodka, and some red wine. None of them were unopened; someone had been helping themselves.

Arthur place his hand over the bottle of whiskey. "*Kam?*" *How much?*

The man shifted through Arthur's stack of cash and took what he needed and probably a generous bonus for himself. He seemed quite displeased about parting with the whiskey.

With the essentials handled, Arthur returned to the guest house. The woman at the desk smiled at him when he came in, this time not bothering to cover her hair. He went upstairs to his room and sat on the bed. The only sound was the fan in the corner, which continued blowing a jet of warm air at him. Arthur kicked off his boots and leaned his back against the bed's headboard. It wasn't comfortable, but that wouldn't matter soon. He took his first pull of whiskey straight from the bottle.

ARTHUR AWOKE SUDDENLY with no memory of dozing off. He was in the same position as before—reclined with his back against the headboard. The bottle of whiskey rested in the crook of his elbow, like a sleeping baby.

The room was dark. Night had fallen. Arthur's head swirled from the alcohol, but it was a sensation he was accustomed to—he'd feel lost without it.

The silence was cut by the sound of the doorknob

twisting, then the door opening with a long and sustained *creak.*

"Who's there?" Arthur called out.

The door opened the entire way on its own, showing nothing but the dark hallway outside. No one was there. At least, it *looked* like no one was there. The air in the room had become dense, as if an overbearing presence coursed through the place.

I'm not alone, Arthur realized.

Arthur stood from the bed and set the whiskey bottle down. He made sure to always be on his feet when the demons came.

"Don't hide, you fucking coward," Arthur called to the open door.

No response. No movement.

Arthur went into the hallway and looked both left and right. Still nothing.

He tread downstairs, stepping carefully to keep from tumbling forward in the dark. The guesthouse lobby was vacant.

Arthur went outside and to the dusty road that passed through town. The surrounding buildings and homes were dark as the families inside slept. There wasn't much light pollution in the region, so Arthur was afforded a look at the millions of stars and galaxies overhead. The moon hung low, casting a spectral glow over him. Normally it would've awed him, but his focus was currently on other things.

Arthur shivered. Despite the oppressive heat of the day, after sunset the desert air always felt like ice. He was the only one outside.

A single sharp, cold gust of wind blew in Arthur's

face, seeming to rush past him. He knew at once that it wasn't natural. A miniature tornado of dust and sand swirled about ten paces away from him.

"He travels with the wind," the Imam had said.

Where the swirling air touched down, an arm-shaped shadow burst from beneath the road, then a second. The head appeared, followed by the body. The elbows bent as the entity crawled the rest of the way out of the earth, as if emerging from a trap. The shadowy form straightened as the dusty gale rapidly orbited around his body. His eyes were two brilliant orbs of ethereal light.

Arthur fought the urge to take a step back. He'd confronted many demons before, but the encounters never got easier. He strengthened his resolve now that he was in the presence of evil. "Who are you? Tell me your name," he demanded, keeping his tone was steady and firm.

He was sure this was the entity that Ibrahim had told him about, but since the man had written his name in Arabic, Arthur didn't yet know it.

'You've been asking about me,' a dark voice emerged from the shadow within the whirlwind.

"I have. I want to learn more about the Lords of Hell."

'An amusing title.' While hovering in one spot, the demon's amorphous body undulated and shifted like a desert mirage.

"Then let's start there. Tell me what they are actually called." Even if he spoke with every Imam in the country, still the best way to get the knowledge he sought was to inquire right at the source.

'We have been known by many names.'

"We? So you're one of the Lords of Hell?"

'Yes.'

Arthur almost wanted to smirk. Demons lied. One thing they most often lied about was their true potential. "Is that so? You seem quite... small." It was a calculated attack on the demon's ego. Demons were fiercely prideful creatures and rarely tolerated someone questioning their capability.

It wasn't just a blatant insult, though. Arthur had come to learn that a demon's power and ranking in hell usually correlated with his size. The shadow before him was of a similar size to him, and Arthur was an old man, and in some ways, frail.

The two glowing eyes seemed to narrow. '*You mock me.*' Arthur didn't respond, only held the demon's bright gaze. '*You should not be seeking me. That is a grave mistake. You must be punished twice for your transgression.*'

That was a new one to Arthur. "Twice?"

'*Tonight, and again in the future.*'

The apparition vanished, and the small tornado encircling his body dissipated.

A speck of fear bloomed in the pit of Arthur's stomach. He suddenly had the feeling that he might've made a mistake in challenging the demon.

A distant roar rolled in from somewhere far away. Arthur turned to face the direction the sound had come from. He wasn't sure, but he thought he felt the ground give a near-imperceptible tremble.

Another whirlwind rose up in the distance, this one becoming the size of a skyscraper. Arthur craned his neck upward as he watched it continue to grow toward the sky. Gusts of powerful wind whipped at his clothes, almost blowing him off his feet. They rushed past his ears with a deafening roar, like he was hanging his head out the window of a speeding car.

Sand twisted up from the ground and into the massive tornado. Thousands of grains came together and morphed into an unmistakable face that dominated the night sky.

Arthur shielded his eyes from the particles of sand that blew past him, scraping his cheeks and forehead.

A light switched on in the building to his right. The noise had woken someone up.

The tornado began to move, heading straight toward Arthur. The demonic face in the sand opened its mouth, gaping wide, ready to consume.

"No," Arthur whispered.

The storm reached the edge of the town, ripping the buildings from their foundations, wood and brick spiraling in the wind. The deafening sound of destruction filled Arthur's ears. Amidst it all, however, the screams cut through.

He didn't have time to react. The sand and wind surged directly toward him, too large and all-consuming to escape. All he could do was shield his face and squeeze his eyes closed.

He felt himself lifted from his feet. A split second later, everything went black.

ARTHUR OPENED HIS EYES. They were immediately filled with sharp, prickling pain. He sat up, frantically brushing at them as sand fell off his face and chest.

He finally managed to blink away the sand, his tears helping. He saw that he was outside, laying on the ground in the middle of the road. His legs were covered in debris and dirt, as if someone had attempted to bury him alive.

The sun was purple with the beginnings of sunrise, so there was just enough light to see the destruction.

Not a single building remained standing. Everything had been leveled into piles of splintered wood and bricks. The only sound was the faint whistling of the wind around him.

Arthur pushed against the ground, willing himself to stand. He was hindered by his bad leg and his age. *I'll be stuck like one of those nursing-home geezers who fell in the bathtub.*

The mere thought was unbearable and wound up forcing some extra resolve into his muscles. Finally, he was able to plant both his feet and straighten. His legs wobbled, so he took it slow. More sand fell from his clothes and pants as he rose. He spat, but his mouth and throat were still coated.

Then he saw the bodies.

He could make out the remains of the townspeople among the debris, crushed by their houses falling on top of them as they slept.

Killed by a demon, simply because Arthur had inquired about him. If he hadn't come here, this never would have happened.

This is my fault.

The strength in Arthur's legs gave out, and he fell back to his knees.

He just as easily could have been swept up in the

demon's sandstorm. The demon had chosen to spare him so he could witness what he'd caused.

Arthur's chest heaved. The first several breaths expelled dust from his mouth. An extreme and oppressive guilt settled on his shoulders, threatening to crush him into the ground. All his thoughts seemed to leave his head, giving him plenty of space to fully feel what he'd done.

He didn't know how long he knelt there. At some point, a sound finally brought him back into awareness—an approaching car.

Arthur turned. A familiar truck kicked up dust as it neared. It braked hard and suddenly close to Arthur. Rashed got out and looked around at the remains of the town, eyes wide and mouth open. Then he met Arthur's gaze, his expression filled with questions and fear.

"*Akhee...*"

Arthur didn't respond. He couldn't think of anything to say.

Rashed rushed over him, wrapped his hand beneath Arthur's armpit, and helped him stand. "What happened, *akhee?*"

Arthur remained silent. He felt as if telling Rashed the story was admitting his guilt.

Something on the ground caught Rashed's eye—Arthur's notebook. It had landed face down and was open. Rashed picked it up and used his palm to dust the sand off the page, revealing the name the Imam had written. He stared at it for a long time.

In that moment, Arthur no longer wanted to know what it said, wished he'd never spoken with the Imam. Or had come to Iraq at all.

What was I thinking? I'm in over my head.

"*Vyraxus,*" Rashed finally said.

The man then reached into his pocket and took out the prayer beads that he'd kept close to him throughout their journey. "Allah," he whispered as he began to pray.

27

Arthur fell silent.

Rand could see the pain behind his eyes. The weariness and the guilt. He would've also felt responsible for what had happened to the village.

And that's how these demons work, isn't it? Rand thought. *They're willing to harm everyone around you just to break you.*

The silence stretched on for a long time before Rand said something. "I'm sorry that—"

"I'm cold," Arthur blurted. He snatched up his whiskey bottle by the neck and rocked back and forth three times to get to the momentum to stand up from the mop bucket on which he sat. He froze and started struggling halfway up, and Rand thought he should help him, but eventually Arthur straightened with a grunt and a loud *pop* coming from one of his hips.

As Rand and Miller followed Arthur back to his house, they shared a silent look. Rand could tell that Miller was also horrified by what he'd heard.

As they approached the porch, Rand suddenly remembered.

"Wait."

Arthur stopped and turned to face him.

"There was something on your door..." He almost said, 'that wasn't there before,' but caught himself.

"What?"

"A pentagram."

Arthur's gaze hardened. He whirled and walked faster back to the house as best he could with his limp. When he got to the door, he glowered at what was etched into the wood.

"It's a Bale symbol," Arthur said. He didn't sound displeased, or even afraid. Now that it was more or less confirmed, he seemed to have accepted his fate.

Rand's stomach hollowed out. *He's going to tell us to leave.*

"I know it's theirs because it's incomplete." Arthur pointed to the detail Miller had referred to earlier—the missing line that would have completed the symbol.

Arthur went inside, and although he hadn't specifically invited them in, Rand sensed that him not shutting the door in their faces was his way of permitting them to enter.

"How do you know?" Rand asked, following after Arthur. "Aren't pentagrams a common demonic symbol?"

They stepped into a cluttered living room. It appeared as if Arthur had checked out an entire section from the library and stacked all the books in various piles—and had returned none of them. Tables and shelves were filled with clocks and gadgets. The furniture was sparse, and dark stains marred the rug.

He's an old recluse, Rand thought as he looked around. He felt like he was intruding on a tomb that was never meant to be opened.

"As I said, because it's incomplete." Arthur busied himself at the fireplace. He took logs from a nearby stack and tossed them in. He then twisted a knob on the side of the fireplace and the smell of gas filled the room. "As you know, a pentagram is actually an ancient *positive* symbol representing the importance of spirit over the material world. The symbol is corrupted when you invert it, placing the material world over spirit. That's precisely what you do when you summon a demon and sell your soul—you trade your spiritual core to gain all the material things of the world," he said, then paused for a moment to strike a match and drop it on top of the logs. The flames roared to life.

He straightened again with some effort and went to the back of the living room and examined a stack of books. He took a leather-bound notebook from between two other books and flipped through the old pages as he walked over to Rand. Grunting, he lowered himself onto the torn sofa and laid the notebook flat on the nearby coffee table. Rand and Miller got closer to look over his shoulder. On the page was a hand-drawn pentagram, each point of the star labeled with what looked like Hebrew letters. Arthur's small and messy handwriting was scrawled around the drawing.

He's finally going to talk to us, Rand thought, elated. *And Miller was right—he knows his shit.* He wondered if this was the same notebook that Arthur had mentioned in his story.

"Each point represents one of the four elements that

make up the material world," Arthur explained. "Fire, water, earth, and air." Arthur tapped each corner of the star. His index finger then went to the uppermost point. "Spirit is at the top."

He flipped the notebook upside down, inverting the pentagram. The simple movement put "spirit" at the bottom of the symbol.

"The Bales took it a step further and distorted the shape entirely by making the connecting lines uneven. A correct pentagram's measurements reflect the Golden Ratio, which is found everywhere in nature. By distorting the lengths, you create a symbol that spits in the face of nature. And by not completing the pentagram, breaking out one of the sides, you also degrade and destroy nature. The Bales have done both with their symbol."

Arthur's explanation drudged up a memory within Rand. "I saw uneven and inverted pentagrams inside the Herron House," he said. "They were drawn on the walls. No two were the same."

"Now you know," Arthur replied.

Rand's mind whirled. Despite the darkness of it all, he was beginning to see that perhaps Miller had been correct about coming here all along. This man—if they could keep him talking—had things to teach them. Rand sat down in an old chair that was at a right angle to the couch Arthur occupied. As long as Arthur was in a teaching mood, Rand had more to ask him.

The star-shaped symbol rang another bell for Rand.

Stars.

"Arthur... why or how does astrology affect demons?"

He'd remembered his final confrontation with Akhubel. As the demon had fed off of Carmen Herron,

Rand had tried to send him away by commanding him with the name of Jesus Christ—a technique he'd used in all his previous cases. But that time, it hadn't worked. At the last minute, Rand had realized why Jackson's father had included astrological references throughout his home: because some demons were apparently susceptible to it. Akhubel had been.

"I don't know," Arthur said as his eyes settled on Rand, studying him for a long time. He didn't seem confused by the question. "Why are you asking me that?"

"Because Akhubel didn't respond when I tried to command him in Jesus's name. It was only when I invoked the signs of the zodiac that he got defensive."

"And how did you figure out to do that?"

"Because of the guy who built the mansion. He'd included astrological references in the architecture." He remembered the cylindrical room in the center of the home that was entirely dedicated to the zodiacal wheel.

Arthur gave a contemplative nod. "I've also determined that there's something more to astrology and how it relates to demons. Though I'm not entirely sure."

Although Rand hadn't gotten an answer, there was something else beneath Arthur's tone that Rand struggled to decipher—maybe the first hint of respect since he'd come to a similar conclusion.

He probably didn't expect me to know there was a connection.

There was only one other question he had that was more burning than that.

Rand reached into his jacket pocket and his fingers touched the cool, glass-like material. "Arthur. What is this?"

He withdrew the black cube and displayed it on his flattened palm.

Arthur stared, seeming unable to tear his gaze away from it. His eyes narrowed as if his arch nemesis had just shown up to his house in person. Despite the darkness that had come over the old man, Rand could see Arthur recognized what he held.

"Why the *hell* would you bring that into my home?"

"I'd have preferred if I didn't, but every time I try to get rid of it, it comes back to me somehow, like magic."

"I'm sure it does."

"What is it? I found it the same night I killed Akhubel, and it seemed important to him." He remembered the little altar where the cube had been displayed, inside a dedicated throne room built for the demon. "I took it so that I could study it later, but I... regret doing that now."

"Regret." Arthur gave a mirthless chuckle. "We regret not taking more chances in life. We regret letting the right woman slip away. You should feel something more than regret after touching a *tesseract*."

"A what?" Rand leaned in toward Arthur; Miller, who was standing behind Rand, did the same.

Arthur sighed and took a swig from his whiskey bottle. He was well-practiced at always keeping it close. "This is the problem with people. This is why evil still runs rampant in our world." He seemed to speak more to himself than to Rand and Miller. "People think they can just *shove* themselves into the world of the occult. You exorcise one demon and you feel like a hero, so you think that's what it's all about. No. No one *knows* anything. No one has any true *knowledge* anymore. Fuck what you believe. All that matters is what you know. There needs to be research. Learning. Gathering information from ancient history, religion, symbolism, and science, because all of those are connected." Arthur threw up his hands as if Rand was some kind of lost cause. "Without *knowledge* of those crucial things, then *of course* you'll pick up a tesseract the first time you stumble across one."

Rand felt hollow as Arthur chastised him. He *did* know a lot. He *had* read and researched. Hell, he taught a damn class about the supernatural. Yet he didn't defend himself.

Could it be that after everything I've been through, I've still only barely scratched the surface?

"A tesseract," Rand repeated, clearing his throat. He turned to Miller. "Have you ever come across this in your research?"

"Research?" Arthur switched his hard gaze to Miller, and Miller immediately began to squirm. Rand could tell his friend didn't enjoy being the subject of Arthur's crotchety attention. "So you're the brains behind the operation while he's the brawn. Please tell us, then. What *have* you learned about tesseracts in all of your 'research'?"

Rand knew it was a rhetorical question. Arthur had spoken like a lawyer developing a line of questioning—never asking questions he didn't already know the answer to.

"I think I've heard it mentioned in movies," Miller managed to squeak out.

Rand... hadn't been expecting that response. *Movies? What movies?*

"You've learned nothing. You won't find any freely

available information about tesseracts because it's all deeply occulted." Arthur took another sip of his whiskey. "I'm going to assume you don't know what *occult* means, either. It simply means hidden. Not evil, and not Satanic, like so many people think. It just means hidden."

Arthur leaned forward and turned to a blank page in his notebook. From his jacket pocket, he pulled out a fountain pen that looked nicer than anything else in the home. He paused, pen poised over the paper, and clenched his eyes then opened them. Perhaps it was the first sign that the alcohol might finally be affecting him. Once he'd refocused, he drew a square. "What's this?"

Another rhetorical question. "A square," Rand replied. He settled in, sensing that Arthur was one of those people who, when questioned about a subject they knew well, would put on a little show, as if he'd been waiting years for someone to ask him questions.

Libby had once accused Rand of something similar.

Arthur drew another square, a portion of which over-laid the first. He then added some connecting lines, which turned the two squares into a cube.

"And now what's this?"

"A cube," Rand said.

"What's the difference between a square and a cube?"

It had been a long time since Rand had taken geome-try. "Uh..."

Miller chimed in, "A square is two dimensional, and a cube is three dimensional."

"Maybe you have learned a thing or two in your *research*," Arthur muttered as he pressed the tip of his fountain pen to the paper again. This time, he drew squares and lines over and under each other. Rand cocked his head and tried to focus, but he'd lost the sense of what Arthur was drawing.

He leaned back as he examined his work. "What's this?" he asked again.

"Looks like some kind of optical illusion," Rand said.

"That's because a four-dimensional shape can't be drawn well on a two-dimensional surface, like paper. But that's what this is—a cube within a cube. A tesseract."

"So a tesseract is a four-dimensional shape," Rand said. "There's a square, a cube, and then a tesseract."

"Take a closer look at your toy and you'll see it," Arthur said.

Rand lifted the black cube to eye level so that the fire in the fireplace was behind it. The yellow light was barely able to penetrate through the clear, glass-like material. Rand felt Miller's breath on his neck as the other man leaned in to get a better look as well.

Rand had noticed it before when he'd found it. If he looked close enough, and in the right lighting, there was a smaller cube inside the first. He shifted it around in his hand, and when he glanced down at the picture that Arthur had drawn, he could see the resemblance.

"So it's a cube within a cube," Rand said. "But what does it *mean*?"

"It's deeply symbolic," Arthur said. "Circles, spheres, and spirals occur in nature. Cubes do not. For that reason, evil occult practitioners adopt the cube in a lot of their symbolism. Remember the uneven, broken, and inverted pentagram of the Bale family? Dark symbols can always be taken a step further to enhance their power. A tesseract is a cube within another cube and represents all things unnatural in the fourth dimension—the dimension that we cannot perceive through our five senses, but very much exists."

"The spiritual world," Rand said. "Where ghosts, angels, and demons are."

"Exactly."

That was why psychics and mediums had always been so valuable to Rand in his cases. They were better able to discern the fourth dimension—to see and communicate with entities that were not visible to the naked human eye, but were still very much present.

And the tesseract represents the darkest presences that occupy that space, Rand thought. He wouldn't be surprised if it also attracted them.

"How do I get rid of it?" Rand asked.

"Hell if I know," Arthur said. "That's *your* problem."

So maybe I won't *get all the answers tonight,* Rand thought. He remembered what Miller had mentioned earlier. "What were you saying about movies and tesseracts?"

But Miller wasn't behind him anymore. He was peering out the window near the front door.

"What's wrong?" Rand asked. Miller squinted as he focused on something outside. "Miller?"

Then Miller's eyes widened. He turned to Rand. "It's her. She's here."

Rand shot up, putting the tesseract back into his jacket pocket. He went over to the window, and when he looked through it, could barely make out the burly shape of the Bagged Woman in the distance. "Arthur... it's the demon from my dream."

"About fucking time," Arthur said, forcing himself up from the couch and draining the last of his whiskey.

"She's here to hurt—"

Arthur brushed past Rand and threw open his front door so hard it banged against the outside wall. He strode onto the porch and stood stiff, chest out, as if ready for a bar fight. "They sent a female demon after me. That's a new one."

Arthur stared ahead at the woman. She didn't move. It was a standoff.

Rand's mouth went dry as he remembered Arthur's words from earlier. *"Finally... it can end."*

He was watching the old man meet his fate with the last bit of pride he could muster. Welcoming his demise.

"Arthur, please don't—"

"Do you have anything you can use to ward her off?" Arthur said, keeping his eyes on the woman.

"No," Rand replied with a sinking feeling—he'd left all his supplies back at the hotel.

"That's what I thought. Get in my truck."

Rand was taken aback. "What?"

"Get in my truck so we can get the hell away from her."

Arthur started walking briskly in the direction of where his old truck was parked in the yard. As soon as he moved, the Bagged Woman did as well, hustling in long strides toward him.

At least he's changed his mind about dying tonight, Rand thought as he followed on Arthur's heels. Miller was just behind him.

The Bagged Woman was closer to the truck than them. Hew knew they wouldn't beat her to it.

Arthur picked up his pace, pushing through his limp. Mid-stride, he drew back and launched the empty whiskey bottle with surprising strength. It took the Bagged Woman squarely in the face and shattered, halting her for a few valuable seconds.

Arthur threw open the driver's door of his truck and Rand jumped in the passenger side with Miller right behind him. It was a tight squeeze for all three of them.

Arthur started the ignition with a key from his pocket. His foot pressed on the gas pedal. The engine roared and the tires spun... but the truck didn't move.

Rand turned. They weren't moving because the Bagged Woman clasped the truck's tailgate. Her brute strength was keeping them in place.

"She's too strong," Rand said.

"No, she isn't." Arthur smashed on the gas again, turning the wheel back and forth as if trying to twist the truck out of the demon's grasp. With a loud sound of rending metal, they finally lurched forward.

They sped away. The Bagged Woman grew smaller in the distance, the truck's tailgate door still in her hands.

28

R and fished around for something—anything —to hold on to as they sped through the night. The cab shook wildly, as if the shocks on Arthur's truck had blown out long ago and he'd forgotten—or hadn't cared enough—to replace them.

The headlights only illuminated the street a few feet ahead of them. Everything else was pure darkness, since the part of town where Arthur lived had no streetlights. The old man maintained his speed, driving faster than Rand would've preferred on the narrow, winding road. A sharp curve came and Arthur jerked the wheel. They all leaned precariously, and a moment later Arthur straightened just as abruptly as he'd made the turn, causing them all to rock back and forth. Rand truly felt like he was on a roller-coaster ride.

"I think she's far enough behind," Rand said. "We can slow down now."

Arthur didn't respond, nor did he let off the gas. Rand and Miller exchanged a nervous glance.

Arthur steered with one hand as he peered through the windshield. Although he seemed to have good control over the truck, Rand remembered how much he'd seen the man drink over the course of the night. They were riding in a car through the dead of night with someone who was likely more drunk than sober.

"The symbol on my door, that demon showing up," Arthur said. "Still want to pretend like you didn't lead the Bales here?"

"We're doing the best we can with what we know," Miller said. Rand sensed his friend was getting tired of hearing about how they'd doomed Arthur by their mere presence.

"And that's the issue," Arthur muttered. "With the supernatural, what you don't know can kill you—and others. As I told you before, a lack of knowledge is the most dangerous thing when it comes to these entities."

"Which is why we came looking for *you*," Miller said, voice rising.

Whoa, now, Rand thought, shooting Miller a warning look. Rand sensed this discussion wasn't heading to a productive place, and he was still grateful for the progress they'd made in getting Arthur to speak to them at all. He quickly jumped in, deciding to change the subject. "What happened to you giving up and being glad it was all over with?" he asked Arthur.

Miller fell silent, clearly eager to hear the response to that too.

Arthur contemplated for a long time as he drove, but eventually replied, "there might be a thing or two I can teach you. Maybe there's still hope for you."

Rand didn't know Arthur Briggs well, but from what he *did* know, that seemed like a breakthrough.

After driving for another few minutes, they arrived in a more condensed part of town. The area had streetlights, and Rand felt a lot better now that he could see their surroundings. Arthur finally let off the gas, allowing the truck to slow.

"Where are we heading?" Rand asked. *Are we just driving around in circles before going back to the house, hoping that the demon will be gone?* he thought.

Suddenly, red and blue lights flashed behind them.

"Shit," Arthur said, looking into his rearview mirror.

Rand sighed and massaged his temples. This was the last thing they needed right now. "Come on. You'd already slowed down."

"This isn't about speeding." Arthur eased onto the shoulder and the cruiser followed.

There was a single streetlight that illuminated the police car. Rand watched in the mirror as the driver's door opened and a man in a tan uniform strolled toward Arthur's side of the truck.

"So much for giving myself a second chance," Arthur muttered, though it was more to himself than the others. "Now I definitely won't make it through the night."

29

"What's that supposed to mean?" Rand asked.

Before the other man could answer, the officer appeared at the truck's side and tapped twice on the glass. Arthur lowered the window.

"Evening, Arthur."

"Brannon," Arthur said.

Officer Brannon was a heavyset man, looking very ill-prepared for having to chase a suspect if he had to. His beige uniform fit snugly against his protruding belly and coarse back hair covered his thick forearms. He had full cheeks and a fleshy neck, but the bill of the black cap that was pulled low over his eyes obscured much of his face and sported the police department's logo.

Officer Brannon bent down a bit to get a more level look into the truck's cab. "I see you've got some company tonight. You start driving for Uber to earn some extra whiskey money?"

Rand realized what this was about. Arthur hadn't

been speeding, but Brannon had recognized Arthur's truck. Everyone knew what everyone drove in a small town like Rose Grove, and Brannon was likely aware of Arthur's drinking habit. Pulling Arthur over was possibly a matter of routine. More often than not, Arthur was probably driving while under the influence. Just like tonight.

"Very funny." Arthur seemed resigned to his fate. Rand had a feeling that these two men had danced this dance before.

"Out of the truck, Arthur." He didn't sound hostile, but rather like a parent who reluctantly had to discipline their child, but not before saying, "This is going to hurt me more than it'll hurt you."

Arthur threw open the door and stepped out. Brannon shone his flashlight in Arthur's eyes. He blinked and seemed unable to focus.

"Mm hmm," Brannon said. "Try to walk a straight line for me, Arthur."

Arthur attempted to do so, putting in a decent effort —as if he'd had plenty of practice. Despite that, he wobbled.

"You *know* I have a bad leg," Arthur protested.

"What have I told you about this? You can't drink and drive."

"You act like I'm the only one in this town who does," Arthur said, turning and facing Brannon in a way that, to Rand, almost seemed confrontational.

Please don't start something, Arthur, he thought. Some of the worse experiences of Rand's life had been when law enforcement had gotten tangled up with the super-natural. Just last Halloween, he'd been pulled over with a pair of black-eyed kids in his backseat. You couldn't easily explain that to the cops.

"I'll be the first to admit that Rose Grove ain't a perfect postcard town, but I don't think that little vice is as widespread as you claim." Brannon was remarkably calm, despite Arthur's hint at hostility. "You know I've got to take you in."

"Why can't we let it slide this one time?" Arthur said, tone flat, almost sounding sarcastic.

"We've cut you plenty of slack already. Come on, turn around."

Arthur wobbled toward Brannon and turned, offering his wrists behind his back. Brannon took his handcuffs from his belt and fastened them into place with a series of loud clicks.

"Sorry, fellas," Brannon said to Rand and Miller. "You're going to have to find another ride." He reached underneath the steering wheel and twisted the key to turn off the truck's engine, pocketed it, and led Arthur back to his police cruiser.

Then, like a flash of thunder, it occurred to Rand what Arthur had meant when he said he wouldn't make it through the night.

The drunk tank. That demon's going to come for him there. He won't be able to get away.

Rand slid over and got out of the truck through the driver's door. He caught up with Brannon and Arthur. "Officer, I'll drive him home and keep an eye on him until he sobers up."

"Sorry, my friend." Brannon guided Arthur into the backseat of the cruiser. "If you really want to help your buddy, check him into rehab or something."

"Sir, please—"

But Brannon only got back behind the wheel and closed his door on Rand. Without another word, he cut off his flashing lights and drove away. He made a left and disappeared from view.

Miller stood beside Arthur's truck, watching the police car leave them. "Well," he said, "that took a turn."

Rand didn't want to waste any time. "Come on. We're going to the station."

And hopefully getting there before she *does...*

30

The streets were empty. As Rand pressed on, he wrapped his arms around his chest in a vain attempt to ward off the chill. It was past four in the morning and the night had grown the coldest it was likely to get before the sun eventually rose. While it wasn't cold enough for snow, the frigid air made both Rand and Miller very uncomfortable. Southerners were often ill-prepared for wintry temperatures.

"Should be up here and on the left," Miller said, a couple of paces behind Rand. He was tracking their route on his phone's GPS. Rand was glad Rose Grove was such a small town—the police station was walkable from where Arthur had been pulled over.

Rand knew they'd arrived before Miller confirmed it, since it was the only place on the block that had any signs of life. Yellow light streamed from the windows on the first floor while the upper stories were dark. The street-lights provided just enough of a glow to illuminate the station against the inky night sky with pinpoints of starlight.

The building looked old, as if it had been present since the town had been incorporated a hundred years ago, and only later been turned into a police station. Some trees grew up from the sidewalk in front, the paving having been worked around their trunks to preserve them. Steps led up to the entrance. Windows from a basement section were half visible at the street level. Three cruisers were parked along the shoulder. Rand was sure one of them was what Officer Brannon had been driving.

"What now?" Miller asked.

"I'm going in there to talk to Brannon again," Rand said.

"He didn't want to listen to you earlier."

"Yeah, well, now he can't drive away. Maybe if I have more time, I can convince him to let Arthur go."

Even as the words came out of his mouth, frosted in the cold air, he realized that it hardly sounded convincing.

Hey, excuse me, I know my buddy was driving drunk—and not for the first time—but would you please let him out? I need to pick his brain about demons.

Miller didn't say anything, but Rand could see from his expression that his friend shared his thoughts.

"Look, I didn't plan on any of this happening, so I don't exactly have a playbook."

"Can you bail people out of a drunk tank?" Miller asked. His hand went into his pocket and came out with the wad of bills he'd won from the bikers in the bar.

"I'm not sure, but bringing in a handful of cash seems closer to a bribe than bail money."

Miller only shrugged.

A welcome blast of warmth enveloped Rand when he stepped inside. His footsteps on the hardwood floor rang hollow, sounding like there was only a thin support over the basement levels below that Rand had seen from the outside.

Dotted around the room were mismatched wooden desks, each looking like something a schoolteacher from the 70s would occupy. A musty staleness lingered in the air, which dated the building almost as much as its appearance.

Only one fluorescent light was on over a desk at the far side of the room. At first, Rand didn't see Officer Brannon sitting underneath the light, and when Brannon noticed he had visitors, he seemed annoyed by their intrusion. All the other desks were empty.

"Evening," Rand said, lifting his hand in a stiff wave.

Brannon was like a statue as Rand went toward him. Once they were near, he finally made his first move, which was to lean back in a chair that looked like it belonged in an antique store. It squeaked beneath Brannon's weight.

"Listen, fellas... I'll tell you like I tell my son. You need better friends."

"I agree," Rand said. "Though I'd hardly call Mr. Briggs a friend. We're only in town for a short while and... um... there are some important things I want to discuss with him."

Brannon gave a mirthless chuckle. "You mean to tell me he's capable of more than non-sensible grunts?"

"He has words of wisdom, but admittedly, they are few and far between."

The edges of Brannon's lip curled up. He seemed to appreciate the humor. Either that, or he was enjoying having all the power in the situation. Rand had always heard that people became police officers because they felt powerless all throughout their lives and the job finally allowed them to have the upper hand they'd lacked.

"Is there something we can figure out?" Rand asked. "Like I said, if I promise to keep an eye on him until he sobers up, and not let him drive?"

"Afraid it doesn't quite work that way. And to be honest with you, I'm being generous by only making him sleep it off in the cage." He nodded his head toward the far wall, indicating that the drunk tank was in the adjacent room. "By now, we should've hit him with all kinds of fines and a suspended license. But Arthur just isn't worth the paperwork these days. Better to teach him a lesson by locking him up for the night and hope he thinks about it the next time he drives home wasted from the Country Corner."

"What about some kind of bail?" Miller asked.

Brannon's attention shifted to Miller, then barked a laugh that was a little harder than before. "Bail? Nah. And consider your next words *very* carefully. I'd hate to think you were trying to bribe me."

Miller fidgeted beside Rand.

A Bible was open on Brannon's desk. Rand nodded toward it. "What're you reading?"

"The good book, clearly. Are you a man of God?"

"Yes, sir."

"Then you know a thing or two about punishment and redemption. Maybe in the morning you can bash some sense into your friend, because he sure won't listen to me. Look." Brannon leaned forward in his chair, which squeaked loudly again. "I don't take any kind of pleasure from arresting Arthur three times a week for the last..." He shrugged as he calculated. "... year or so. I'm not some heartless hardass. I've had my own issues too, so I recognize a man who's down when I see him. And Arthur's *really* down. We've tried reaching out, tried helping him, tried getting him to go and talk to somebody. He always refuses. There's a lot of pain in him that clearly runs deep. I don't know much about the guy, because he won't tell me. We've had many long nights in here to get to know each other, but he's a closed book. More like a vault, actually. The bottom line is, we lock him up in here because otherwise he'll hurt himself or someone else. My boss tells me it's only a matter of time before he does anyway, and the chief might be right, but... until then, I'll keep scooping him off the street when I catch him staggering home. Or worse, driving drunk." Brannon reclined in his chair. "Now, if you'll excuse me, I need to get back to my literature. Try to stay warm, fellas."

Rand sighed. Even if Brannon's speech had been half as long, it would've been enough to convince Rand that the officer was standing his ground. Had the situation not been so dire, Rand might have been touched by Brannon's sympathetic view of Arthur Briggs.

Rand glanced at Miller beside him. He looked like he was about to say something else, *wanted* to say something else, but then only hung his head and kept quiet.

"Right, okay," Rand said, his voice low. He turned and headed toward the door, and Miller followed. They walked back out into the cold.

"What do we do now?" Miller asked.

Rand didn't answer. He honestly didn't know.

Miller checked his watch. "It's not that much longer till morning. Maybe Arthur will be fine in there for a couple of hours?"

"We can't risk it," Rand thought.

The pentagram carved on Arthur's door had finally convinced Rand—he *had* inadvertently led the Bales straight to Arthur. And the Bagged Woman was one of their supernatural servants. He couldn't even begin to imagine the immense guilt he'd feel if their demon reached Arthur while he was trapped and helpless in a jail cell.

"But what are you planning to do?" Miller insisted. "Break him out of there like they do on TV shows?"

Out of the corner of his eye, Rand saw when Officer Brannon's shadow appeared in the door's frosted glass window. Rand grabbed Miller's arm and pulled him around to the side of the building.

Brannon went outside and down the steps that led to the sidewalk. He leaned heavily on the railing in the process, as if he didn't trust his legs on the way down. He was talking on the phone. "Yeah. Nah, it ain't just me tonight. Scottie's on, but he's doing a patrol right now, so I'm holding down the fort."

He used his shoulder to pin the device to his ear as he took a pack of cigarettes from his pocket. He put one in his mouth and cupped his hand to shield the tip of his lighter from the chilly wind as he lit it.

"Nothing crazy. Just me and Arthur, as usual." He paused as he listened to whoever he was on the phone with. "Yeah. Sad shame, these people with their liquor. I keep telling Dean down there at the Corner to cut him off and send him home whenever he shows, and the man keeps saying he'll do it, but here we are again. Must be one of those young bartenders who work for him who don't know any better. And God knows where Arthur gets all this money to afford all the whiskey he drinks."

The memory of Arthur straight up swiping the bottle from the bar ran through Rand's mind.

He and Miller stood together, crouched behind a nearby tree as they waited and listened.

Brannon started pacing farther down the sidewalk. "You ain't gotta wait up for me. Take one of those medatronins..."

"I'm going in," Rand whispered to Miller.

"What?"

The idea came to him instantly when he saw that Brannon was putting some distance between himself and the front of the police building.

"Stay here." He stepped out from behind the tree and crept around the corner of the building. He poked his head out and checked before making a move. Brannon was still facing away from the station's door as he continued to talk on the phone, though he was far enough that Rand couldn't make out what he was saying. The smoke from his cigarette rose into the air. Rand crouched as he went up the steps and inside the police building. The front area seemed eerie now that it was empty.

I won't have much time before he finishes his smoke break, Rand thought.

He spotted a doorway that led deeper into the building and opened into a room that was larger than the office. Black iron bars segmented off a majority of the space. When he walked in, he saw Arthur slumped in the rear corner of the cage, back against the wall, head hanging. He was lightly snoring.

Life's in danger and you can still take a nap? Rand thought. *Guess the whiskey finally hit you.*

Rand rushed to the far end of the cell to get as close as he could to the other man.

"Wake up," he hissed.

Arthur lifted his head and his saggy eyelids blinked several times, eyeballs shifting around as if guided by a tiny creature inside his brain, pulling levers.

"Arthur." Rand reached his arm through the bars and snapped his fingers.

Arthur jumped, reacting like the finger snapping was a firecracker. He turned and his unfocused eyes found Rand. Recognition slowly filled them.

"Wake up, buddy."

"You're very persistent," Arthur said, though the words were slurred from sleep and likely a rapidly approaching hangover.

"I'm getting you out of here."

Arthur chuckled. He then adjusted his weight, as if it were possible to get more comfortable on the cell's hard floor.

"Brannon said you're in here often. Surely you know where they keep the keys."

"This isn't some movie," Arthur muttered as he shifted around on the floor. "They don't hang the key on the wall so that people can piece together some sort of contraption to reach it."

"Yeah, I get that, Arthur, but come on, I'm trying to help you."

"I'm far beyond help, in more ways than one."

Now *is when he chooses to start regretting his drinking?* Rand clenched his teeth, sudden fury coursing through him. He was risking quite a lot for someone who wasn't interested in helping themselves at all. "I want to get you out of here before something bad happens."

Then Rand heard it. Shouting.

Miller.

Rand straightened, immediately wondering if Brannon had discovered his friend lingering outside.

But then Miller's voice was much clearer.

"Rando!"

31

I *wish he wouldn't do that,* Miller thought.

Rand had a bad habit of running off without saying much of anything. Or thinking things through.

But truthfully, that was why they made a good team. Miller, usually hesitant, lacked Rand's instinct to spot a limited opportunity and seize it.

So Miller was left alone in the cold, tense and waiting for his friend to get out of there before Brannon returned.

Brannon's voice steadily got louder as he neared. His pacing had brought him back in front of the police station.

"So, anyway. Scottie should be back soon." He put his phone between his cheek and shoulder as he checked his watch. "His wife's feeling better. He told me the physical therapist said she'll be at a full range of motion in a couple months." He took another cigarette from the pack in his pocket and tucked it between his lips. "Yeah, I'm laying off the smokes, no need to hound me. All right, love you. Try to sleep, okay?"

Brannon grunted in response to whatever his—most likely—wife said, and then hung up. He lit the cigarette and kicked at a loose stone on the sidewalk, smoking in silence.

Miller was too nervous to move. Now that Brannon was off the phone, the night was silent once again. Any sound Miller happened to make would easily cut through.

Crunch.

Miller went rigid. Held his breath. *Was that me? Did I step on something? I don't think I moved.*

He shifted his eyes to see if Brannon had noticed anything.

He had. But he hadn't turned toward Miller—he was peering in the other direction.

"Who's there?" Brannon dropped his cigarette onto the sidewalk to free up his hand. He seemed too distracted to stamp it out.

Miller couldn't see who Brannon was looking at. He gazed at a point somewhere farther down the sidewalk, perhaps even on the side of the road. The police station blocked the person from view.

"I said who are you?" Brannon barked, louder and more authoritatively. His hand went to his sidearm while his body stiffened. "Stop right there!" The pistol came out of its holster in a deft, practiced movement. Miller panicked, desperately hoping Rand didn't step outside in that moment.

"Don't—" Something changed in Brannon. His outstretched arm that supported his weapon seemed to lose its tension, and he blinked several times. "What the hell..."

The demon stepped into view. The same one Miller had spotted at Arthur's house. The woman with the bag tied over her head.

Brannon took a jumbled step backwards, but the woman's stride was too long. She reached him and— quicker than her lumbering form seemed capable of— she swiped wide and knocked the gun from Brannon's hand.

He yelped, turned, and ran down the sidewalk as fast as his chubby legs could carry him.

Miller tried to make himself small behind the tree. He peeked out with one eye.

The woman did not pursue Brannon. As the officer's footsteps faded into the distance, she craned her neck to face the police station.

She started up the steps.

Without thinking, Miller bolted from his hiding place. His whole being urged him to run in the other direction, just as Brannon had. But he couldn't let the demon walk into the building and corner Rand inside.

She was at the door by the time Miller reached the bottom of the steps. "Hey!"

She paused. Turned her entire body around. Looked down at him from the raised porch.

Then she came for him.

Miller took a couple of paces back. "Rando! She's here!" he shouted.

The demon was within range. She swiped at Miller just as she had to knock the gun out of Brannon's hand.

Miller attempted to dodge, but she made contact. A

blast of pain ripped through his chest and the force of her attack hurled him backwards and off his feet. He landed hard on the pavement in the middle of the street, his shoulder taking the brunt of his weight, and he cried out.

Get up!

He didn't have time to lie there moaning. Wincing, he twisted around and forced himself to sit up despite the pain in his torso. His softshell jacket had three jagged gashes in the material—a classic mark left behind by demonic entities. A sticky warmth had started gathering near the cuts.

Forget it. I need to get up before—

But the demon had turned her back on him and once again faced the entrance to the police station. The door opened on its own by some kind of unseen force.

Miller found his voice and called out, "Rando!" Shouting caused more pain, but he needed to warn his friend.

The woman walked inside and the door slammed shut behind her.

Miller mustered his resolve and shouted again. "Rando!"

32

Rand rushed away from the jail cell toward the station's front office. The way Miller had been shouting, he figured something had gone terribly wrong.

A door slammed.

Brannon's back.

When Rand rounded the corner, he nearly bumped right into the Bagged Woman.

"Oh, shit." He reversed and scrambled backward.

Worse than Brannon.

Rand couldn't get far enough away in time. She used both her hands to shove him aside. Her tremendous strength sent him spiraling across the room. He hit the hardwood floor and continued skidding even farther until his back rammed into the wall.

"Look who it is!" Arthur shouted, suddenly filled with energy, as if the sight of the demon had quickly sobered him up. He clasped the bars to pull himself to a standing position. "Did you like taking that bottle to the head? Ready for more?"

Rand twisted and used the wall to help himself sit up. The pain from his fall slowed him down.

The Bagged Woman stood right in front of the cage, her covered face inches away from Arthur's.

Arthur spat at her feet, then glared at where her eyes would be. "Fuck you! And fuck the Bales, too. Give them a message for me, will you? Tell them to kiss my ass!"

"Arthur," Rand said, forcing himself to stand.

The woman gripped the jail cell bars and pulled them apart, using her strength to bend them. In that moment, they didn't look like they were made of iron at all.

"That's right. Get in here. Just you and me, bitch!"

"Shit." Rand jumped to his feet, mind racing. Arthur had gotten lucky earlier when he'd hit her with the bottle, giving them time to escape. But now, in a cage, his back was literally against a wall.

The bars separated inch by slow inch. Soon there'd be enough space for the Bagged Woman to get through.

To Rand's right was another doorway—likely a rear entrance to the police station's main office area. An idea struck amidst his desperation. Rand rushed through the door, which brought him to where Rand had thought it would—Brannon's desk was nearby.

To his relief, the Bible that Brannon had been reading was still there.

"Fuck y—" Arthur's voice cut off with a wet gurgle.

She's through, Rand realized. He snatched up the Bible and ran back to the jail cell room.

The woman had her meaty hands pinned around

Arthur's throat. She held him flat against the wall at the rear of the cage, his feet lifted off the floor. His skinny ankles kicked, just visible beneath the hems of his dirty pants.

Then the Bagged Woman slung Arthur's body over her shoulders, like a firefighter's carry. She pivoted, then stopped short when she saw Rand in her path.

She's not here to kill him, Rand realized. *She's here to take* him.

Rand lifted the Bible, his arm outstretched, the book's leather cover facing the Bagged Woman. Her head twitched, as if suddenly bothered by something unpleasant.

The Bagged Woman shrugged Arthur off her shoulder. He landed hard on the ground behind her bloated ankles. Now that Rand had become a threat, the demon was giving him her full attention.

Rand knew he couldn't show fear in her presence. Demons like her fed off fear, and even though he was not immune to it, he had to remain steadfast.

"There's no place for you in this world. Leave here!"

The Bagged Woman's body tensed. She was eager to attack, but didn't approach. The Bible repelled her.

Rand took a step forward. Then another. "In the name of God, I command you to depart!"

She swiped her long arm at his hand that held the Bible, trying to knock it out of his grasp. Rand was quick, though. He pulled it back to his chest to dodge her strike, and then immediately extended the holy book toward her again.

"I told you to *return* to your shadows. You have no dominion here."

He took another bold step closer, and it seemed he'd

overwhelmed her enough. The Bagged Woman's body dissipated into an amorphous black shadow, which then faded away.

Rand lowered the Bible and looked around the room. The energy felt lighter. That was a telltale sign that the demon was truly gone.

For now, he thought.

Arthur had watched the whole thing with wide eyes. Sweat glistened on his face and he gasped for air. His spindly legs were bent at the knees as he laid on the floor. He'd fallen pretty hard, and Rand wondered if he'd been injured.

"Nice show," he said, his voice gravelly.

Rand heard something over his shoulder. He cocked his head and listened.

Brannon?

Rand moved quickly. He rushed back to Brannon's desk and dropped the Bible where it had been before.

The door to the police station suddenly opened.

"Get your ass over here right now!" Brannon shouted as he came in.

At first Rand thought those words had been for him, but when he looked, Brannon was on the phone, facing the door as he closed it. At the last second, Rand dipped into a small room behind Brannon's desk, which turned out to be a bathroom.

Rand was sure he hadn't been quick enough, but Brannon was so preoccupied with his phone call he apparently hadn't noticed Rand's scrambling. His boots thudded heavily on the wooden floor as he walked over to his desk. "I know what I saw, damn it. So get your ass over here!"

He hung up.

Brannon leaned over his desk, fists planted on the surface, head hanging. His body heaved with panted breaths, as if he'd been running. A dark circle of sweat had soaked through the back of his uniform.

Brannon straightened as he focused on the Bible for several drawn-out seconds. He ran his finger along the cover.

Shit, Rand thought as he peeked through the cracked bathroom door. The book had been open when Brannon had left, but Rand had closed it when he'd put it back.

"You been touching my things, Arthur?" Brannon called toward the next room. "Did you become a master lock-picker or something?"

Rand clenched his eyes and hoped Arthur wouldn't give Brannon a similar outburst as he'd given the demon.

But Arthur didn't respond.

"Must still be sleeping it off," Brannon muttered.

Rand silently let out the breath he'd been holding. If Brannon checked on Arthur and saw the bent cell bars, that would stir up some questions—and some trouble.

Although it sounds like we're in trouble anyway, Rand thought. *His partner's on the way...* He assumed that was who Brannon had been on the phone with. It'd be much harder to escape with two officers there instead of one.

Brannon's phone rang. Not his cell phone this time, but the one on his desk. The computerized ringing sounded abnormally loud in the quiet police station. A red light on the cradle flashed.

He lifted the receiver to his ear. "This is Brannon."

His expression immediately shifted as he listened. His jaw tightened before he spoke again.

"Yes, sir." His tone was humbled and low. Nothing like how he'd spoken to his partner.

Is it his boss? Rand wondered.

"I'm listening." Brannon snatched a pad of paper from the corner of his desk and slid a pen from his shirt pocket. He clicked the top and scribbled something.

"Right. Yes, sir."

Brannon returned the phone to its cradle and gave a deep sigh. He then took out his cell, tapped the screen, and brought it to his ear.

"Scottie. Never mind. Forget what I said." He listened for a bit. "Yeah, I was just a little spooked. No, no need to rush back. We can talk about it later. Pick me up a breakfast sandwich, will you? Thanks."

He hung up and stood by his desk for a long time, looking truly saddened and tormented. When he finally moved, it was to place his hand on the Bible. "God, please forgive me."

What's going on? Rand thought. *What's he about to do?*

Brannon ripped the paper he'd written on from the pad, folded it, and tucked it into his shirt pocket. He went around his desk and into the room with the jail cell. Rand waited to hear Brannon say something about the bent jail cell bars.

Instead, all Rand heard was, "On your feet. Get up."

"That's all you have to say?" Arthur's voice. "You're not going to ask about my super strength?"

"Hands."

Tense silence.

"Come on, Arthur." The tone wasn't unkind, but definitely authoritative. "Hands."

"Where are we—hey!"

Shuffling and jostling, followed by the metallic scrape of handcuffs sliding into place.

What's he doing? Rand thought. *You can't arrest someone who's already been arrested.* He considered jumping out and confronting Brannon, but had a strong feeling that would make the situation far worse. *Who was on the phone? What did they tell Brannon to do?*

The questions made Rand's heart thud.

Brannon and Arthur appeared again in Rand's line of sight. Arthur's wrists were cuffed behind his back, and Brannon held him by the shoulder as he forced the other man to walk forward. Together, they disappeared through the police station's door.

Once they were gone, Rand left the bathroom. The police station had taken on an unsettling energy. He knew he'd seen something he wasn't supposed to see.

What about your breakfast sandwich? Rand had a feeling that Brannon had never intended to stick around for it. He'd just needed to buy himself more time with his partner away from the office. Whoever had called had given him orders of some kind.

Rand went to the desk and picked up the pad of paper and angled it toward the light overhead. The paper was cheap and thin, and the pen had been pressed into it hard enough that Rand could make out the imprint of what he'd written on the page above.

A string of numbers. Coordinates.

Rand tore the paper from the pad.

33

Rand peeked through the window before leaving the police station. There was no sign of anyone outside.

Not even Miller.

Rand went out into the cold night and down the steps. He checked around the corner where he'd last seen his friend.

A few seconds later, Miller appeared from some unkempt bushes. "I had to hide when Brannon came back. Are you okay?" He stumbled toward Rand, arm held across his stomach at an awkward angle. "I wanted to follow you, but she—"

"Holy shit." When Miller was close enough, Rand saw blood staining his friend's forearm, which was crossed over his body and covering a wound. "What happened?"

"She got me," Miller said. "When I tried to stop her from going inside. I'm okay, though. It doesn't hurt too much."

"Let me see." Rand took Miller's wrist and urged his

arm away from his injury. There were three red gashes in his jacket. Blood stained the edges of the cuts. "Is it deep?"

"I don't think so. What happened in there, Rando?"

Rand hesitated before answering. Miller had never been injured before during one of their cases, and Rand felt his guilt growing. He also wasn't convinced that his friend was being totally honest about its severity.

And it seems like he's going to try to walk it off.

Rand tore his eyes from Miller's wound. "She attacked Arthur, but I sent her away by using that Bible Brannon was reading. What happened out here?"

"She appeared and spooked Brannon. He ran off, but doubled back around. He went inside and I thought you were busted. Then a few minutes later, he came out with Arthur in cuffs, put him in the police car, and drove off. Do you know where he's taking him?"

Rand held up the sheet from the notepad. "Here."

Miller took the paper and looked at it, flipped it over, and checked the other side.

"It isn't blank." Rand used his phone's flashlight to light up the indentions made from the pen.

"Ah, okay. I can barely see. Coordinates?" Miller took out his own phone and typed in the numbers. He stared at the screen for several long moments.

"What's wrong?"

"This is in Washington, D.C."

Rand deflated. He hadn't known what to expect from the coordinates, but it certainly hadn't been *that*.

"Where did you get this?" Miller asked.

"I was hiding in the bathroom. Brannon got a phone call, wrote those numbers down, then immediately took

Arthur away. Who obeys an order to illegally bring a drunk guy three states away in the middle of the night?"

Miller's forehead creased as his brain worked to come up with an explanation. "Well…"

"What?"

Miller hesitated. "We already know the Bales have some amount of control over the police."

It suddenly made sense to Rand. He couldn't believe he'd forgotten. Maybe he'd been too amped up over the confrontation with the Bagged Woman and the sudden need to hide from Brannon. Perhaps things had happened so fast that his brain wasn't connecting dots as it usually did. "Bernard, or someone else in the family, must've called and told Brannon to bring Arthur." Now that he thought about it, he didn't know how many of them there actually were in that family, besides Bernard and Miranda.

"How did they know he was here?" Miller asked.

"I have no idea. But it must have something to do with their demon. Maybe they can see what she sees, or know what she knows."

Rand couldn't begin to guess the intricacies of how it all worked. All he knew was that these twisted people had demons in their service.

"So after all that," Miller said, "Brannon is taking Arthur straight to them."

Rand hung his head and sighed. Things were rapidly spinning out of control.

"What do we do now?" Miller asked.

Rand paced, hands on his hips as he wracked his brain. There wasn't much to think about, though.

He already knew.

34

Once their decision to pursue had been made, Rand went back into the police station, where he rifled through Brannon's desk drawers. It didn't take him long to find an oversized plastic bag labeled "personal belongings." Arthur's name had been written by hand in black marker, and inside were the keys that Brannon had confiscated.

Rand and Miller returned to Arthur's truck and drove it back to his house, where Rand had left his Jeep. The ripped-off tailgate still lay in the yard, and the final embers of the fire near the cemetery hadn't yet stopped glowing.

"I'll drive," Miller said.

"You sure?"

"Yes."

"Do we need to go to the ER?" Rand eyed his friend's injury.

"We don't have time to sit in a waiting room for three hours. Brannon already has a head start."

Miller had a point, but he hadn't answered the question.

"Fine, but let's do this instead," Rand said as he opened the Jeep's trunk.

"Do what?"

He found the first-aid kit he'd driven with for years, but had never had a reason to use.

"Make it quick."

Miller sat on the lip of the trunk, unzipped his jacket, and gingerly unbuttoned his shirt while peeling the fabric away. His eyes were glued to the night sky as if he didn't want to see how badly he was actually hurt.

Rand used gauze to gently wipe the edges of the three jagged gashes in Miller's torso. The white material quickly became bloodied.

"The bleeding's stopped. I don't think they're that deep," Rand told his friend.

"Hurry up, I'm freezing." Sure enough, Miller had started to tremble.

Rand dressed the wounds with clean gauze and encircled Miller's stomach with medical wrap.

He felt like he'd learned something new about Miller that night. Generally speaking, when people suffered injuries, they either freaked out and let the pain overcome them or they pushed through it. It seemed his friend chose the latter.

"Done."

"Thanks." Miller buttoned his shirt and put his jacket back on. He then got behind the wheel and waited for Rand to pack up the first-aid kit, close the trunk, and get into the passenger seat.

Miller hesitated before driving away.

"What's wrong?" Rand asked.

"Give me a minute." Miller hopped out of the Jeep and hurried into Arthur's house. A moment later, he returned with the notebook Arthur had been referencing earlier.

"There's probably some good info in here," Miller explained as he got back in the car and dropped it into Rand's lap.

———

AN HOUR AND A HALF LATER, rays of sunlight emerged from the horizon. According to the road signs, they were passing through Athens, Georgia. The interstate was mostly clear, too early for rush-hour traffic.

Will there even be a rush hour today? Rand wondered. It might be the weekend. He'd lost track of the days. *Is Athens a big-enough town to have a rush hour? Why are so many American cities named after European ones?*

Notions like those rambled through Rand's exhausted mind as he slumped in the passenger seat. He pushed them away, but they were quickly replaced with thoughts of Arthur Briggs: what the Bales could want with him, and what they planned on doing to him.

Arthur was right about all of it, Rand thought. *They* were *following me and I led them straight to him.* They'd wasted no time in snatching him up. *It's my fault he was taken, so I have to do everything I can to get him back.*

Rand's eyelids were like lead. When they started to close, he slapped his own cheek a couple of times to wake himself up.

"Take a nap," Miller said.

Rand knew he needed to, but somehow it seemed wrong to sleep. It wouldn't be fair for him to rest while Miller drove, especially since Miller was the one who was wounded..

Rand's phone vibrated in his pocket. A darkness crept over him, assuming bad news.

It was a text from Dipika.

Rand's mind had gone to so many faraway places in the past couple of days that the last time he'd seen her felt like a distant memory.

Something about a test, he thought. *Didn't I give that back to her?*

"What's wrong?" Miller asked, concerned.

"Nothing."

"Who is it?" Miller insisted.

"Just a coworker."

"Oh." Miller relaxed. "The way you were looking at your phone was freaking me out."

I guess we're both on edge, Rand thought as he tapped the notification and opened his lock screen. The message included a selfie of her dressed in a black over-coat and scarf, standing in front of a building that Rand definitely recognized as iconic or historic—he'd probably seen it on TV a hundred times. He normally could've placed it, but his mind was too cloudy at the moment.

Her text read: *The tour guide says it's haunted. Maybe you'd like it.*

Then he remembered: Dipika told him she was heading to D.C. for the weekend for Arun Singh's event. He'd forgotten all about that. On any other day, the coincidence might have impressed him.

If it wasn't for me, there'd be no need for Miller and me to go there at all.

Rand quickly shut his thoughts down. He didn't want to spiral down the *if it wasn't for me* line of thinking. He'd noticed himself doing that far too often over the past couple of months.

He appreciated the friendly text and knew he should send a response. But there was just too much else occupying his attention at the moment.

Arthur's notebook at his feet caught Rand's eye. *I bet that would help keep me awake,* he thought as he slid his phone back into his pocket and grabbed the notebook. He flipped through some of the pages.

Arthur's handwriting was tight and messy, an urgent scrawl that at first Rand figured was some kind of code, since it was so hard to decipher. But if he squinted and held the notebook at an angle to catch the daylight, he was able to make out what was written. Barely.

April 22nd, 2015.

Made arrangements to visit the Tillett family in three days, but they called at midnight and urged me to come immediately. I did.

Marcy, 12 years old. Quiet, with only a handful of friends at school. Liked to read and watch people play computer games on the internet.

She lost interest in those hobbies. Then started talking back to her parents, which was apparently very out of character. Sometimes she lashed out violently. At first they thought common teenage nature, but when things escalated, they got in touch with me.

Normally I would have agreed that it was normal, yet

annoying behavior. But when I took out a series of religious objects, Marcy recoiled. That told me all I needed to know.

The exorcism lasted three days and three nights. Marcy had been possessed by Mezzalos. I'd encountered this same demon in 1997, when he'd possessed a seventy-eight-year-old woman.

Rand skimmed the rest of the case notes, then flipped the page.

June 9th, 2016.

Oliver Beckham, 9 years old.

Loved animals, always eager to help his father on the family farm. But then he became sullen, withdrawn. The Beckhams called their pastor when Oliver began harming the animals. The pastor then reached out to me.

Oliver turned aggressive as soon as I stepped in, started shouting at me in an unknown language. The pastor and I were able to exorcise him in about three hours.

Never learned the name of the demon that possessed the boy.

Rand skipped over a few more pages of case notes before coming to something different. Arthur apparently also drew things that seemingly had nothing to do with the rest of his paranormal research. He'd dedicated an entire page to the hand-drawn portrait of a woman. Although he'd used a single black-ink pen, there were enough details in her spirited eyes to bring her to life. Rand could tell that Arthur had put some love into the sketch.

He then remembered what Arthur had been about to say when they'd first met at the Country Corner.

"Maybe you'll lose her just like I lost—"

Rand frowned. From the little time he'd spent with

Arthur, it was hard to imagine the old man having had a woman in his life. Yet from the drawing, Rand sensed that Arthur cared about her very much. It seemed to be a tribute to her, whoever she was. Given the way Arthur currently lived, Rand had a feeling this woman was no longer in the picture and hadn't been for a while.

Rachel came to mind for the first time in a long while —Rand's most recent girlfriend, who'd ended things simply because she couldn't handle his lifestyle. He couldn't blame her. He'd sadly and reluctantly let her go. Tessa had broken up with him for the same reason. Their shared daughter was the only thing keeping her in his life, no matter how much she wanted to move on and forget him altogether.

There was a note beneath the drawing.

You taught me to look for the synchronicities, and to follow them.

Rand read and reread the sentence several times. He'd heard that word before, and it took him a minute to remember from where—Tessa. She'd talked a lot about synchronicities these days as part of the burgeoning spiritual phase she was currently going through. She mentioned them about as often as astrology. Rand hadn't put much stock into either concept.

But why is Arthur writing about synchronicities here? Rand wondered. The man didn't strike him as someone to entertain silly beliefs.

"Fuck what you believe," he'd said earlier. *"All that matters is what you know."*

Do Arthur and Tessa agree about this concept? Rand thought.

On another page, Rand found a drawing that was

strikingly familiar—a magic circle with jagged, demonic symbols written in the four cardinal directions. It was the same one he'd seen inside the Herron House. He'd stood in the center of it to communicate with Akhubel for the first time.

That same thing had been inscribed on the ceiling of his living room when his home had been desecrated.

So he's familiar with this, Rand thought, feeling just a little bit of hope. He wondered if Arthur knew how to remove the negative energy the circle had caused to infest his house.

But that seemed like such a small issue now with everything that had happened since then. It ultimately didn't matter *what* Arthur might know about cleansing his home if Rand and Miller couldn't save him from the Bales.

Rand paused on a page that was different from the others. It was not densely packed with writing, but rather was dedicated to a list of names and dates.

Joshua Ahmad — May 13th 2014
Manuel Roman — March 21st 2017
Rick Raine — April 20th 2019

Rand recognized Josh Ahmad. He was a college basketball player who'd been prominent a couple years before, a classic rags-to-riches story, leading his team to the National Championship game that season.

The night before the game, Josh had been stabbed in his hotel room. One of his teammates had discovered him a few hours later, still alive. He'd been rushed to the hospital, but had died on the way. The game was canceled, and both teams came together to honor his memory instead of playing.

It was a huge story at the time, made even bigger by the fact that the killer was never caught. Hotel staff claimed the security footage had been corrupted. That immediately sparked outcries of foreknowledge, or protecting the murderer, or a cover up. Eventually, as always happened with these things, it fell out of the news cycle, and the last Rand had heard of it, there were still no suspects or arrests.

"Do you remember Josh Ahmad?" Rand asked. "That basketball player?"

"Yeah. Whatever happened? Did they find the guy?" Miller looked at Rand. "Wait, why are you asking?"

"Arthur wrote his name right here." Rand took out his phone and searched for Joshua Ahmad. The results gave his dates of birth and death. The death date matched what Arthur had written. "He also has the day he died." Rand went to the next name on the list. This one he didn't know. "Who is Manuel Roman?"

Miller thought for a few seconds, then shrugged.

"He's got a date next to him as well. I'm assuming that's when he died," Rand said, looking up the name.

The results brought up Manuel Roman's stage name, which Rand recognized. It was Rex Haze, a recording artist who Rand's daughter used to listen to. She'd blare his music in her bedroom, which was distinct because of his falsetto voice.

Is he dead too?

Rand searched on his phone, and sure enough, Rex Haze had collapsed during a performance. No official cause was given, but the article mentioned that the family believed it to be drug related. That conclusion was contentious with some among the fan base who suspected foul play. Once again, Arthur was accurate about Rex Haze's date of death.

"It's the real name for Rex Haze," Rand told Miller. "You remember him?"

"Oh yeah. He had that one song I liked. Shame what happened. So Arthur's keeping a log of celebrities who died?"

"I guess so."

"But wait, is he *predicting* them dying?"

"I was wondering the same thing. I don't know." There was no way to tell when Arthur had written the list of names and death dates.

Rand turned the page, hoping that Arthur had expounded on his thought process. He had. The words were penned large at the top of the next page.

The Killing Ritual?

35

The words, "The Killing Ritual" had been underlined many times, the pen leaving several deep indentations in the paper.

Arthur's writing continued:

Demons feed off negative energy. They thrive off of it. More is always better.

I suspect "killing rituals" are designed for precisely that reason. I'm sure they have a more-accurate name used by those who conduct them, but killing rituals is essentially what they are.

When someone beloved, admired, or respected dies suddenly and publicly, it creates mass grief. The more famous and well known, the better the ritual works. Those responsible for the death are motivated by the demons in their service, who feed off this grief and grow more powerful in the process.

Killing rituals have been used throughout history to strengthen these entities.

Rand grunted.

"What?" Miller asked.

"Arthur's attributing these high-profile deaths to some kind of ritual that was done on purpose by people who are working with demons."

"I thought they said Rex Haze died of natural causes? Or was it drugs?"

"He may have, but Arthur seems to disagree."

"Is he talking about the Bales?"

"He doesn't specifically say, but they'd definitely be capable of something like this."

"I've never heard of such a thing," Miller said.

"Me either."

Rand already knew that demons thrived off negative energy. That was why they sought to create fear in their victims. But he'd never before considered that it could or would be done on such a grand scale.

Is that possible? Rand thought. *Did Arthur figure it out?*

"I don't remember anyone suggesting demonic killing rituals being related to either Josh Ahmad or Rex Haze at the time," Miller said. "We both know no one would've believed that."

Rand looked up from the notebook. "Maybe that's the point."

"Fuck what you believe. All that matters is what you know."

"Something like that wouldn't even come up in those investigations," Rand said, his mind now working in overtime. "People just don't have that in their paradigm. So in a way, it's a demonic ritual hidden in plain sight."

When it comes to Bales, I can't really discount anything, Rand thought.

Rand closed the notebook, feeling suddenly overwhelmed by the implications.

36

They did eventually hit traffic in Charlotte, North Carolina, which slowed their progress. Rand suspected it was a bad car wreck, but by the time the traffic broke up, the accident had been cleared, so he never saw what had caused their delay.

Miller—a lifelong devotee to the speed limit—tried to make up their time with some light speeding through the state of Virginia. Eventually, though, they were forced to stop at a rest area for a bathroom break and to stock up on snacks at the vending machines.

A wall-mounted television near the restrooms stopped Rand in his tracks. It was tuned to a news station, and the bottom caption said: *Arun Singh, supposed "psychic hero," to be honored tomorrow by the Bring Our Children Home organization.*

The screen was a montage of still photographs of Arun, who Rand only recognized from the handful of articles he'd read after meeting up with Dipika.

That must be the event Dipika told me about, Rand

thought. *The one she's going to.* He'd never heard of Bring Our Children Home, but he presumed their name was self-explanatory as to the kind of activism they did. They'd naturally want to show their appreciation for Arun Singh and how he'd recently helped rescue those kidnapped kids.

As they returned to the Jeep, arms filled with snacks, Rand asked, "Do you have another jacket?" Miller's ripped and bloodstained softshell had drawn quite a few stares.

"No. I pack light. And it's too cold to not wear it."

That was true. The overcast day was frigid and would only get colder when night came.

"How's your stomach wound?"

"Fine, thanks to your solid patch-up job."

Rand honestly didn't know if Miller was telling the truth or if he was gritting his teeth through the pain just so they could catch up with Brannon and Arthur.

"You want me to take over driving?" Rand asked.

"Nah. I can go a little longer."

As they pressed on, Rand found himself instinctively fixating on the passenger-side mirror, on the lookout for any cars acting suspiciously or aggressively. *We still don't know who rammed us off the road,* he thought. It was entirely possible that they might come for them again.

The delays, combined with the shorter winter days, meant the sun was rapidly setting as they neared the nation's capital.

"Decision time," Rand said as he peered at his phone's GPS. It wouldn't be long before they arrived at the coordinates Brannon had written down. "I know what I want to do, but I'd like to hear your thoughts."

"Okay," Miller said.

"We're getting close. Do we go straight there? Or do we find a hotel first and *then* go?"

Miller signed deeply. "I'm tired as hell, but we should see why we've come all this way."

"Yeah... I feel the same."

An uneasiness rose in Rand as the miles fell away. The checkered-flag icon, indicating their final destination, was fast approaching.

Will we come face to face with Bernard Bale? Or something worse? Rand thought. Well, if we do, I'll do exactly what I did last time.

That night in the Herron House, atop the mansion's tower, Bernard had attacked Miller, and Rand—desperate to save his friend—had just learned of the tesseract's destructive capabilities. He'd chucked the cube at Bernard, hitting him in the chest. He'd gone flying across the room and slammed into the wall. The force had seemed hard enough to kill a normal man, but Bernard had walked away as if nothing had happened. That was when Rand knew Bernard Bale was protected by some kind of dark magic.

In a way, that was a good thing—Rand wasn't prepared to kill someone. But he also had to do what was necessary to protect himself and his loved ones. And of course, that raised up the age-old moral quandary: was it okay to kill someone who had harmed so many others and planned to keep doing so?

The GPS brought them through an industrial part of the city. The streets were empty, all the workers having punched out hours ago. Ugly buildings loomed dark and lifeless, grey constructions of utility devoid of any architectural flourishes. For some reason, Rand felt as though they were being watched. He tried to tell himself that was only in his head.

"Left up here," Rand said, watching the highlighted path on his phone.

Miller turned onto a narrow road lined with dilapidated warehouses that had seen better days. The streetlights weren't strong enough to fully illuminate the area. Rand studied the soulless buildings and considered that maybe the workers would not return in the morning—the facilities looked abandoned.

This place is a perfect spot to bring Arthur if you're planning something dark, Rand thought with a frown. "This is it."

Miller pulled to a stop in front of one of the warehouses, which blended in with all the rest in the area. The only difference, Rand noted, was that the chain-link gate was open, leading to an empty parking lot.

"Someone's been here recently," Rand said.

Miller took that as his cue to turn into the lot. "What do you think we're looking for?"

"Just go up to that warehouse."

A square, nondescript building lay ahead with a sheet-metal door pulled down.

Miller did as he was told and parked the Jeep. Their surroundings were quiet, and the shadows of the buildings stretched toward them.

There was no sign of Brannon's police cruiser. Rand had wondered all day how much of a lead Brannon had. If he'd gotten through Charlotte before the car wreck that had held up traffic, then it could've been hours.

"I'm going to look around." Rand took off his seat belt

and stepped out of the Jeep. The cold air immediately assaulted him, as if urging him to get back inside where it was warm—and where it was safe. Miller followed Rand to the warehouse's sliding metal door.

"You hear that?" Rand asked, turning his ear. A soft rumbling sound came from within.

"Yeah," Miller said. "Sounds like... a car engine."

He's right, Rand thought. *But why here?*

Rand turned the latch, and it moved—the warehouse door wasn't locked. He hoisted it upward and it rattled on its tracks. The shrill, metallic noise cut through the empty parking lot. If anyone was within a mile radius, they'd definitely know someone was there poking around.

A noxious smell of exhaust and fuel immediately accosted Rand, causing both him and Miller to back away. Miller yanked his shirt collar over his mouth and nose. Rand did the same with his jacket as best he could over his face, resisting the urge to cough at the same time.

He held his breath and rushed toward the warehouse. He got underneath the halfway-raised door and shoved it open to let the fumes escape.

Brannon's police cruiser was inside, engine running.

"No way..." Miller said.

Still holding his breath, and his jacket still pulled over the bottom half of his face, Rand walked into the warehouse. He could almost feel the cloud of gasses surrounding him. There was no telling how long the car had been like that. It was dark in the warehouse, but there was just enough light coming from the floodlights in the parking lot that Rand could make out an unmistakable, large-framed body in the driver's seat—head lolled to the side as if taking a nap.

That was all he needed to see. Rand rushed back outside and away from the police cruiser, where the air was clean. He let out his breath and sucked in fresh, chilly oxygen. He bent over, hands on his knees as he raggedly gasped. Tears burned in the corners of his eyes.

"He's in there, isn't he?" Miller asked, and Rand nodded. "And Arthur?"

Rand shook his head.

"So..."

"They took Arthur and... left Brannon like that."

"Is there any chance he did that to himself? That's a... you know... common way people—"

"I don't think so. Remember what Bill told us—the story they were given at his office was that Jackson Herron had killed himself. And we both know it was a lie to cover up what actually happened."

Miller nodded sadly. "So someone set it up to make it seem like he did it to himself..."

We're starting to see their M.O., Rand thought. "I'm willing to bet on it."

Miller sighed. "What do we do?"

"We have to do the right thing."

Miller's face fell. "You can't call the police, Rando. The Bales control them. Brannon *was* the police."

Everything within Rand resisted the idea of walking away from a crime scene, but he knew Miller had a point. The police couldn't be trusted. Even Brannon, a small-town cop who lived over five hundred miles away, didn't —or couldn't—hesitate to do what the Bales had ordered him to.

Rand's phone suddenly vibrated in his pocket. His heart started beating faster. When he checked the screen, he saw that whoever was calling was using a hidden number.

"Who is it?" Miller asked.

Rand answered and activated speaker mode. He waited for the caller to talk first.

"Hello." A man's voice.

Rand looked all around, checking to see if they were being watched. As far as he could tell, there wasn't anyone.

But just because I can't see them doesn't mean they aren't there, he thought.

"We were taking bets." A slight mirth crept into the man's tone. "Would Randolph Casey follow Arthur all the way here, or decline to get involved? I put my money on you showing up, of course. You're *terribly* predictable."

Rand's mouth had gone dry. He licked his lips. "Who is this?" It didn't sound like Bernard Bale, but then again, Rand didn't quite remember the man's voice.

"Here's what's going to happen," the caller said, suddenly serious. Almost threatening. "Mr. Bale wants to welcome both of you to town, so listen very closely to my instructions. Leave everything you've found just as it was. I trust you know that any effort to tamper with it could implicate you. It won't be long before the local police show up, so you have to get out of there. Head downtown to a hotel called the Grand Sapphire. Go check in with a reservation that's under your name. Then wait for our next call."

Rand blinked several times as his mind tried to digest what he'd just heard. Miller's face fell into a puzzled frown. Of all the things the caller could've said, checking into a hotel had to have been among the last Rand would have guessed.

"Do you understand?" the man's voice cut in. He seemed irritated by Rand's silence.

Rand only managed a dry croak. "Uh…"

"Go now. You *chose* to get involved. It's too late to back out."

With that, the line went dead.

"A hotel?" Miller asked.

Rand suddenly snapped into awareness. The hotel part had thrown him for such a loop that he'd nearly forgotten the first thing the caller had told them. "He said the cops would be here soon. We need to leave right now."

37

They fled the crime scene, Rand now driving and taking the turns with a little too much speed. He wasn't heading anywhere specific. Not yet. First things first—they had to get away from that industrial section of town.

It wasn't long before police cruisers rushed past, heading in the opposite direction, sirens blaring.

"In a way, that guy on the phone saved us from being caught there," Miller said as he watched the flashing lights.

"I don't think he was trying to do us any favors." Surely whatever awaited them at the hotel was far more sinister than merely being arrested for suspected murder.

"So what now?" Miller asked. "Do we actually go to this hotel? It seems crazy to do that..." He chewed his lips as he thought it over. "Right?"

"I'm not sure we have a choice."

"Of course we have a choice."

"Technically, yeah. But they have Arthur."

"You think if we don't do what they say, they'll hurt Arthur?"

"I think they'll hurt Arthur even *if* we do what they say," Rand said. "We don't know where they took him after Brannon got here. So going where they want us to go could be our best chance of finding him. Maybe they'll have him nearby." Rand could hear the desperately hopeful tone in his own voice.

Miller sighed and nodded. "What did he say it was called again?"

"The Grand Sapphire."

Miller tapped on his phone and a few seconds later said, "Got it. Five stars. These new friends of ours have expensive taste."

———

RAND DIDN'T KNOW DC at all, but the Grand Sapphire appeared to be in a populated area near downtown.

"Central location and exorbitant room rates," Miller said. "I think this might be one of the nicest places in the city."

"That tracks." One thing Rand knew about the Bale family was that they had an extreme amount of wealth.

It's probably the first thing people ask for when they make a deal with demons.

"Up here and on the right," Miller said.

There were no clear parking lots, and anywhere that might've served as street parking had a sign that prohibited it. Rand turned onto the driveway at the front of the hotel, a crescent half circle that led to a porte-cochère near the main entrance. A man wearing a black uniform stepped away from his podium and toward the Jeep.

"I've never paid for valet service in my entire life," Rand said.

The man approached the driver's-side window, and Rand lowered it. Before he could ask how much the valet cost, the man said, "Orange Jeep Wrangler. You must be Mr. Casey."

"You... were expecting me?"

"Of course, sir." The valet—Richard, according to the name tag pinned to his shirt—flashed a bright, wide smile.

Rand and Miller exchanged a worried glance.

"Is something wrong, sir?" Richard asked.

"No, Richard. Sorry," Rand replied.

Richard stepped aside so that Rand could get out of the car. "We'll bring your things up. The front desk will let us know your room number. Please check in with them."

"Got it," Rand said, his tone flat. Normally this would be incredible service. That night, however, it just felt ominous.

The Grand Sapphire was everything the name promised it to be. The lobby had marble floors that were polished so well that every movement was reflected. Chandeliers hung from high ceilings and hotel guests occupied the plush furniture, attired in elegant dresses of black and red, avoiding the cold while they waited for their transportation to whatever event they were heading off to.

He and his friend were *very* much out of place—Rand

in his jeans, t-shirt, and jacket and Miller with his blood-stained softshell with three prominent tears.

As Rand approached the front desk, a woman wearing a white ascot around her slender neck beamed at him, and it seemed actually genuine. "Checking in?"

"I think so," Rand said.

The woman's smile didn't falter at his strange response. "Name, please?"

"Rand Casey."

She typed on her computer. "Randolph?"

"That's me."

"Okay. Your reservation is for you and a guest." Her eyes glanced up at Miller, lingered for a split second on the bloody marks on his jacket, then returned to her screen, pure professionalism. "Your room is ready now."

She produced a pair of key cards and handed them to Rand. He accepted them hesitantly, as if they were a cursed gift. As far as he knew, they were.

"Our valet team will bring your bags straight up. I've already sent a message informing them of the room number."

And who else knows our room number? Rand couldn't help but wonder.

38

Room 11-11 opened into the largest hotel suite Rand had ever seen.

Rand stepped forward into the den, the smooth, white ceramic clacking lightly beneath his shoes. Black leather couches faced a massive mounted television. Almost the entire far wall was floor-to-ceiling windows. Beyond them was a balcony that wrapped around the corner of the building. Though there were other buildings visible in the distance, the Washington Monument was the most eye-catching.

To the left, a large doorway opened into a bedroom. Rand saw a king-size bed, white sheets, and bedspread tight and neatly made.

Despite the luxury, everything felt off—dead and vacuous. The energy inside was thick and oppressive, similar to what Rand experienced whenever he walked into a home haunted by a demonic entity.

"I... have a feeling this room isn't available to the public," Miller said. He'd found a framed painting that

Rand hadn't noticed yet. The canvas dominated most of the wall, as if the entire suite had been built just to accommodate this one piece of art—if it could be called art. A creature with a twisted and distorted body stalked through a macabre landscape surrounded by fog. Its eyes glowed green and its mouth was open to the ashen sky, howling at the full moon. In its hand, it gripped a small, upside-down skeleton by the ankle—unmistakably the remains of what had once been an infant.

"... the hell is wrong with these people?" Rand whispered. He had a feeling Miller was right—Bernard probably stayed in this same room when he wasn't busy killing police officers or arranging a ritualistic sacrifice of his granddaughter to ancient demons.

A jingle sharply cut the silence. Rand's attention went to a polished desk in the far corner near the window that overlooked the city skyline. On top of it was an ornate rotary phone. It was incredibly gaudy, like something a niche collector might keep on a shelf but never actually use.

The phone trilled again.

Disgust slithered through Rand's body. Whoever was calling somehow had eyes on them. Feeling exposed, Rand surveyed the other buildings through the glass that wrapped all around them. A smattering of lights were on in various windows. He imagined one of Bernard Bale's grunt workers sitting there, binoculars in hand, downing energy drinks to stay awake, his only job being to let his bosses know when someone arrived in the suite.

Of course, there was no one clearly visible. If someone *were* watching them, then no doubt they'd be in a room with the lights off, hidden from view.

The phone kept ringing, this time seeming louder than before, as if urgently insisting Rand hurry and answer.

He walked to the phone and lifted it from its cradle. It was cold to the touch. A loose black wire rose with it as Rand put it to his ear. He said nothing at first, merely listened. There was silence.

Finally, he couldn't take it anymore. "Bernard."

The man on the other end chuckled. "No."

He immediately realized it *was* the same person that he'd spoken to at the warehouse.

"How's the suite?"

"We did what you wanted us to do." Rand was not in the mood for games.

"You're lucky. That room is a favorite of Bernard's—you mentioned him, so I assume you two have met. He never books it for his friends or colleagues—only people he has a *special* interest in."

Smug smiles had a certain sound to them, and although Rand couldn't see the person he was speaking to, he could hear the man's smile.

"Right," the man said, sighing. "No small talk with you. Bernard always takes a liking to the boring ones." He paused for a second, waiting for Rand to respond to that. He didn't. "Here's the deal. My boss wants you to join him for some fun. Both of you."

Rand wasn't sure what that was supposed to mean. *Your boss?* he wondered.

"Take the same elevator you just used," the man clarified. "He's at the rooftop restaurant. Go now."

39

D *ing.*

The elevator doors slid open. It was empty.

"This seems insane, Rando," Miller said.

Rand stepped inside and scanned the collection of buttons. There were fifteen floors. The top-most option merely read "R." A sign bolted beside the button panel indicated the amenities on each floor: pool, fitness center, meeting rooms. Next to "R" it was labeled, "Sapphire Skies Restaurant."

Only after Rand pressed the button did he notice that Miller hadn't entered the elevator. Rand used his arm to block the door from closing.

"Would it be better if we split up?" Miller asked. Rand gave his friend an incredulous look.

"I'm not trying to flake out on you," Miller quickly explained. "We came here for Arthur, not to play games with this guy who keeps calling. Maybe you could distract him and I could... you know, have a look around. Then if he says something that tips you off, text me."

"I have a feeling he'll figure out what we're up to," Rand said. "Not that I don't think it's a good idea. But he specifically told us *both* to go to the roof."

Miller considered that for a few seconds before he finally relented and got into the elevator. Rand removed his arm and allowed the doors to close.

They glided past the twelfth floor, then the thirteenth.

Miller's eyes were glued to the number-shaped bulbs over the door, each one lighting up in succession as they rose. "It's just that at some point... we need to stop doing what we're told and do what *has* to be done. You know? And I have a feeling that if we wait too long, we'll miss our chance."

Rand nodded slowly. Miller was right. The last thing Bernard Bale wanted to do was let them take Arthur back after he'd been searching for him for so long. Whoever was calling them had to be aware that they were only there because they were trying to save the man.

And only a few nights before, Rand had proven himself to be capable of disrupting Bernard's carefully laid plans. The Herron House debacle was likely to still be fresh in the man's mind.

As the elevator rose, Rand caught a glimpse of himself in the mirrored walls. He was struck by his pallid skin and how there seemed to be new lines in his face he hadn't noticed before. He saw a man slowly succumbing to total exhaustion—it went beyond mere physical fatigue.

Just press on, Rand thought to his unfamiliar reflection. *For Libby. For Arthur.*

The elevator dinged one last time, and the doors slid open to reveal a narrow hallway. At the end was a single door that presumably led to the rooftop restaurant. Two men in matching suits flanked each side of the door.

At first Rand assumed they were hotel staff, but as he approached and the two men silently glared at him and Miller, he realized they were security. They said nothing and kept the door blocked with their broad bodies.

"I'm staying in room eleven-eleven. I've been told to come up here by someone who's probably your boss," Rand said begrudgingly.

One hefty guard looked at the other. They held each other's gazes for a while, neither betraying a hint of emotion, nor any indication of what they were thinking.

Finally, the bigger of the two spoke. "Let's go." He pushed the door open with his long arm and stood aside to allow Rand and Miller to enter first. He accompanied them while his partner remained at his post.

Blood red was the predominate color of the decor. The open-air restaurant gave expansive views of the city skyline, sparkles of white against a blanket of pure black. The night's chill was warded off by the metal gas torches that rose like columns in a Roman temple, punctuated by yellow and blue flame at the top. Cocktail tables were dotted around the area, draped with navy tablecloths. Rand saw how servers didn't let an empty glass linger long before swooping in to take it away. Sofas were along the periphery of the restaurant, in more intimate areas near the edges of the roof. Lights on wire strings hung loosely from the ceiling, giving off a dim glow. People mingled about, drinks in hand, wearing suits and elegant evening gowns. Rand knew he and Miller *definitely* stood out in their grimy attire.

Them being escorted by security like prisoners also

drew attention. Rand noticed the finely dressed people's conversations trailing off when they caught sight of him, craning their heads to watch as he passed.

The guard brought them to a VIP section. One of the restaurant's corners had been cordoned off, the border delineated half by red velvet rope, and the other half by a fifteen-story fall off the hotel's roof. Plush black sofas formed a horseshoe pattern within. Two men sat side by side on the middle sofa with their backs to the skyline, speaking to each other. A handful of others were in the area, talking low amongst themselves and sipping at their cocktails.

Rand's eyes rapidly bounced around at all the people, searching. Miller did the same. But Rand didn't recognize anyone.

Bernard isn't here?

The escorting security guard handed Rand and Miller off to a pair of guards who were supervising the VIP section. One unlinked a part of the velvet rope and gestured for the two to enter.

One of the men on the couch noticed them, and by the way his eyes lingered, Rand could tell that he was the "boss" they were there to meet.

But where's Bernard? Rand thought.

The man wrapped up his conversation with the tuxedo-clad gentleman, who then took his leave. As he went out, he cast the slightest of puzzled glances at Rand and Miller.

The man reclined, crossed his left ankle over his right knee, and spread his arms onto the back of the couch. "Glad you could join us." His smile was wide and white. "Please." He gestured to a smaller couch that faced his own. A circular table was the only thing between them, leaving enough space to still have an intimate conversation. A cocktail rested beside an orb-shaped lamp that gave off a soft blue glow. Torches in each of the four corners of the VIP area kept them warm; they were more than necessary in the open-air restaurant.

This must be the boss we're supposed to meet, Rand thought. He and Miller didn't move.

"Sit," the man said, his smile lingering on his face. "I know you both must be tired. You've had one *hell* of a day."

Rand sat first, then Miller. The couch was about half the length of the other—they were so close that their thighs brushed together.

Rand shot a quick glance over his shoulder. He couldn't help but feel exposed now that his back was to most of the restaurant.

"No need to be nervous, Randolph. We're just here for a chat."

He was very handsome, with a chiseled jaw and a very symmetrical face. His smile was flawless, and you could tell it came easily and often. His thick black hair was slicked back, but not so much as to suppress the natural waviness. Now that the other man had left and he was alone on the couch, there was an excess of space on either side of him.

"I need a picture. I'll want to remember this." He leaned forward and took his cell phone from his coat pocket. He aimed the camera and Rand and Miller as he pecked at the screen with his index finger. "Smile or something." The man waited, studying his subjects with anticipation through the screen. "Ah, whatever. Doesn't matter." He tapped the screen with one decisive motion. "Good enough." He lowered the phone and started typing with both thumbs. "I'm sending this to Dad. He'll get a kick out of it."

Dad?

Only when Rand looked closer could he see it. The structure of the man's brow, maybe even the shape of his mouth. Rand hadn't been in Bernard Bale's imposing presence for long—that misfortune belonged to his daughter—but could indeed make out the resemblance.

This is Bernard's son.

Miller's eyes found Rand's, the same flicker of realization passing silently between them.

"Anyway, I know you two met my father. My name's Nathan." Nathan Bale returned his phone to his pocket and resumed his relaxed posture, one leg crossed over the other. His eyes lingered on Rand. "You are *exactly* as I imagined you." Nathan let several moments pass before continuing, "I'm jealous of you, Randolph. You were there."

Rand didn't know where "there" was, so he waited for Nathan to elaborate. The seconds dragged on, and Rand realized that Nathan Bale was completely comfortable with staying silent until he got a response.

Rand cleared his throat. "Where?"

"At the old Herron House. You know..." the smile finally faltered from Nathan's lips, "...to tell you the truth, I didn't have much faith in Jackson. Didn't think he had the stones to do what he needed to do. But from what Dad told me, he was about to go through with it. The only problem, of course" — Nathan nodded toward Rand, almost as if in admiration — "was that you were there, and you stopped it. It's a shame, really." Rand couldn't read Nathan's face well enough to see if the man *actually* felt it was a shame or not. "Jackson could have been good for the family. If he could find it in himself to do what was being asked of him that night, then he would've done *anything* for us. But he failed at the last second, and that can't be tolerated when you're trying to earn your place."

A fiery anger swirled in Rand's chest as he listened to the casual way Nathan spoke about ritualistic child sacrifice. He wanted to throw the man's own glass at his forehead and give him a bloody gash to mar his near-perfect face.

How many others...

"Dad's already looking for my sister's next husband. Didn't even wait for Jackson's body to get cold." Nathan shook his head. "He's always been like that—in a rush. Anyway, he has his eye on some businessman from Hong Kong. Poor bastard—my sister can be a real pain in the ass sometimes. Well, you know. And your daughter knows too, from what I've heard recently."

Rand's hands clenched into fists at Nathan mentioning Libby.

Nathan took a long sip of his drink. His eyes fell to the ground, lost in thought, before snapping back to Rand as if suddenly remembering something. "Do you have it?"

"Do I have what?"

Nathan nodded his head almost imperceptibly at Rand's chest. His jacket. In the pocket.

Rand hesitated. He felt Miller stiffen beside him.

"I know how it works, Randolph," Nathan said. "You can try to get rid of it as many times as you want, but it *always* comes back. It has to be in one of your pockets." He smirked.

Rand sensed he had no choice. He pulled out the black cube, which felt cold to the touch, as if it had absorbed the winter air.

Nathan's eyes glimmered, as if the cube was an ancient artifact that he'd convinced himself couldn't possibly exist. He casually lifted his hand like he was asking to be tossed a baseball or a hacky sack.

Rand had gone to great lengths to keep people from touching it. Even before Arthur had filled him in, he sensed it was cursed. Surely Nathan knew that as well, along with *all* the intricacies of how it worked.

It probably doesn't curse him like it does everyone else, Rand thought. *Another benefit from having already sold your soul.*

He tossed the cube over the lamp-lit table and Nathan snatched it out of the air with a practiced catch. The man leaned forward and set his drink down so he could dedicate both his hands to turning the tesseract over and over, staring at it like it was the world's most perplexing Rubik's Cube.

"I haven't seen one of these in a while." He glanced up at Rand without lifting his head, his strong eyebrows folding his forehead into wrinkles. "You didn't let anyone else touch this, did you?"

Rand shook his head.

"Good man. This was meant for you and only you."

Nathan started tossing the cube a foot into the air before letting it fall easily back into his palm. With a flick of his wrist, he put a slight spin on it. His eyes followed it up and down as it twirled.

Rand winced with each toss. He didn't know a lot about the tesseract, but he knew what would happen if Nathan threw it at him—or someone else. He remembered how the little cube had destroyed stone and incapacitated Bernard Bale.

"Yeah, I haven't had much use for one of these in a while," Nathan said, "but it's always interesting to see who Dad's going to give one to next. He loves a good old-fashioned tes—" He paused, catching his words before he said something he apparently hadn't intended to say.

But Rand already knew, thanks to Arthur.

"Tesseract," Miller spat the word—the first he'd contributed to the conversation.

Nathan's eyes flew to Miller, finally acknowledging him. The cube came down on his knuckles while he was distracted and rolled into his lap.

Rand shot Miller a look. For some reason, it seemed like it would've been better to *not* let on about how much they knew. But it *was* nice to wipe the smile off Nathan Bale's face.

"Someone's done his homework," Nathan said slowly. He retrieved the tesseract from where it had fallen and tossed it back to Rand.

In the split second that it flew through the air, Rand's heart seemed to freeze. As if by instinct, his hands rose defensively in front of his chest. His body tensed up, waiting to be blasted backward, but he wasn't. He then became aware of the weighty chill in his palms. He'd caught the tesseract, and nothing had happened. Rand released a slow exhale. Beside him, Miller had recoiled as well.

Nathan shook his head and chuckled, enjoying

Rand's reaction, as if what he'd done was a mere hazing prank.

Nathan turned his attention back to Miller. "You're Miller, aren't you? You were there at the Herron House, as well. You said something to my father that night. Do you remember what it was?"

Rand's eyes bounced between Miller and Nathan. *What's he talking about?*

Miller's face fell into a mixture of confusion and fear. He glanced at Rand, as if seeking the right response. But Rand didn't know.

"You might not remember," Nathan said. "Dad told me he was about to kill you, but then you said something that made him change his mind."

Rand saw in Miller's eyes that his friend was slowly starting to recall what Nathan was talking about.

"You mentioned the Lords of Hell," Nathan went on. "And *that* was the moment Dad decided to spare your life, Miller. Because *that* was when he realized you knew Arthur Briggs."

Miller's gaze dropped to the floor. He shifted in his seat and looked like he'd collapsed inwards.

Rand surmised that the exchange Nathan was talking about had happened just before Rand had saved Miller by throwing the tesseract at Bernard.

That's how the Bales knew to follow us, Rand realized. *Miller accidentally tipped them off.*

"A unique Arthur-ism, the Lords of Hell," Nathan said. "Clever term… but a little dramatic, if you ask me."

Even without knowing what Nathan was talking about, Rand could see how easily Nathan had wormed his way into Miller's head, crushing his spirit.

Enough of this, he thought.

"Where's Arthur?" Rand demanded.

Nathan shifted his attention from Miller back to Rand. Studied him, as if considering whether to tell Rand the truth or avoid the question entirely. "He's around."

Rand clenched his jaw, glaring at Nathan. "Where?"

Nathan flashed a knowing smile and shook his head. "Come on, Randolph. I shouldn't need to explain to you that I can't divulge that information."

"You killed that police officer," Rand said.

The accusation didn't faze Nathan at all. "Well actually, that was more *your* fault than mine. My lady friend tried to grab Arthur for me. But as usual, you were there to screw everything up. The cop was an improvised contingency plan. So really... who's more responsible? Me or you?"

Rand's fury flared.

"And speaking of Arthur... I have a long night ahead of me, plus a busy day tomorrow. I shouldn't even be talking to you right now, but I couldn't help myself. I *had* to meet the great Randolph Casey." Nathan checked his watch, frowned, then looked back up to Rand and Miller. "Look, I'll level with you. Dad's pissed at what you both did at the Herron House, but the truth is that there are other priorities tonight. In fact, there's no reason for you to be here. Why couldn't you have just let Arthur go? It would've saved you a massive headache."

It was true. After Brannon had taken Arthur from the police station, Rand and Miller could've returned home, but they'd chosen to follow.

"I guess you can blame your hero complex," Nathan continued. "Fine. As long as you insist on being here, I might as well be a generous host. That's Dad's favorite room you're staying in, by the way."

"If we weren't supposed to be here, then why are we being watched and followed?" Rand asked. Nathan's eyes narrowed at the question.

"That's Dad for you," Nathan said, sounding almost exasperated. "Always trying to do everything at once. You don't need to worry about the man you've been speaking with on the phone. He's just one of my assistants. But..." Nathan looked to the side as he thought about something. "I do believe you know the man who ran you off the road a few nights ago."

Rand straightened. "Who?"

Nathan scoffed. "All these questions and no answers to give you. You might as well ask me where Arthur is again. Anyway, like I said, there's lots to do, and I've distracted myself enough already." Nathan lifted his hand and signaled for one of the security guards, who promptly left this post outside the roped off area and came over to him. "Enjoy the room and be sure to stick around. After this business with Arthur is done, my father will want to have a word with you both."

The guard positioned himself between Nathan Bale and Rand, as if he'd suddenly become a threat to the man's boss. He extended his thick arm, gesturing toward the exit of the VIP area.

40

The elevator chimed as they descended in silence.

On the eleventh floor, the doors opened and they stepped out. While they walked toward their room, Rand asked the question that had been nagging at him since they'd been escorted away from the hotel rooftop. "What was Nathan talking about? The thing you said to Bernard."

Miller paused as his shoulders sagged and a heavy sigh escaped his chest. Rand stopped alongside his friend. "That night, at the Herron House... before you saved me from Bernard. I mentioned the Lords of Hell." He shook his head, eyes fixed on some spot on the carpeted hallway floor. "I'd been reading Arthur's posts on that forum, and I had *no idea* Bernard would know who Arthur was, and that he was the only one who used that term."

"You couldn't possibly have known," Rand said, his tone sympathetic.

"So I guess, technically it's *my* fault that we were followed to Rose Grove. And *my* fault that Arthur got taken."

Rand could recognize a spiral when he saw one. For once, it wasn't him falling down the path of negative thoughts. Still, it pained him to see Miller like that. He wished he could take it from him. "I don't think—"

"Honestly, Rando, I completely forgot I said that. I swear. I was so scared when Bernard was there, I just—"

Rand clasped both of Miller's shoulders. "It's okay. You didn't do anything wrong."

"Obviously I did. Because—"

"Nathan said Bernard spared you *because* of what you said."

"Only because he wanted to use us to get to Arthur."

Rand gave Miller a single, firm shake. "You did what you had to do to survive, and it worked. That's all that matters."

Miller fell silent.

"You did the right thing," Rand said.

"But what are we going to do now?" Miller asked.

Rand released Miller's shoulders. "The way Nathan was talking about Arthur, it seems he's still alive. So we have time to figure something out."

How much time they had, though, Rand didn't know for sure.

"There are other priorities tonight," Nathan had said. Had he meant Arthur?

Rand checked his watch. It was approaching midnight. If Nathan had been referring to Arthur, then it could be they only had a few hours.

THEIR BAGS WERE WAITING for them in the hotel room; Arthur's notebook rested on a table by the door. The valet worker must have seen it in the front seat of the Jeep and decided on his own to bring it up as well. Perhaps he thought it looked important.

Miller snatched up the notebook and headed for the couch. "Maybe there's some kind of clue in here." He sat down and started flipping through pages.

Rand unzipped his bag and retrieved two small vials of holy water from their wooden case, then slipped them into his jacket pocket. Having them on his person would make him feel better. *Especially after I showed up at Arthur's house empty-handed.* A whiskey bottle had helped them, but it would never have been his weapon of choice against a demonic entity.

Rand remembered what he'd read in the notebook earlier. "There was that stuff about killing rituals. You don't think..."

"It sounded like those were for famous people. I'm not sure Arthur's a candidate."

Rand sat down on the couch opposite Miller. "There still might be some kind of ritual happening. Everything's a ritual, remember? If they wanted to just murder Arthur, they wouldn't have bothered to bring him all the way here."

Miller nodded slowly as he considered that. "I see what you're saying."

He laid the notebook on the coffee table in front of him and squinted through his glasses to read Arthur's overly small writing.

Rand remembered Miller's earlier suggestion of splitting up. "While you're reading through that, maybe I could look around for Arthur."

"You think he's in this hotel somewhere?" Miller asked without looking up from the page.

"It seems too simple and obvious, but still, it's *something* I could do."

Miller paused his flipping when a passage seemed to catch his eye. His eyes danced along the lines as he read.

Despite his desperation, Rand felt fatigue creeping up on him now that he was sitting. They'd spent most of the night before at Arthur's house and the Rose Grove police station, and he hadn't dozed much on the car ride to D.C.

I need to start moving, otherwise I'll fall asleep, Rand thought.

"Look, Rando, this right here might relate to what you just said about bringing Arthur here." Miller started reading out loud, using his index finger to trace along the page: " 'There are many energy vortexes around the earth. These are areas where energy is more easily harvested. Cities that control the world in the modern day were purposely settled upon these vortexes because the ancients knew they existed, despite what historians say. London, Vatican City, and—' " Miller looked up. "Washington, D.C."

"Those cities pretty much *do* run the world," Rand said.

Miller read on. "'Within these cities, certain structures are built for harvesting this energy, like giant antennas. These include homes, government buildings, monuments, and memorials. This knowledge is only for the benefit of a select few. The general public only knows a location's or building's *ostensible* purpose, never its *true* purpose.'"

Rand didn't like the implication of that at all. He glanced out the hotel window and eyed the Washington Monument in the distance, a massive obelisk reaching to the sky as if trying to pierce the heavens.

A thought came to him. "Bernard Bale likes to stay in this very room. Do you think maybe this hotel is one of those buildings?"

"I hope not... but I guess we have no choice but to consider that possibility," Miller said, frowning.

Miller turned the page. Rand waited for him to read something else out loud, but Miller only scanned the text silently. The quietness in the room once again encouraged Rand's sleepiness. He leaned his head back and realized this was the most comfortable he'd been in days. He tried to force himself to sit up, but his tiredness fought against him.

Miller started saying something else, but his words seemed distant. Rand's entire body relaxed, and he closed his eyes.

41

R and woke suddenly. He straightened his head, which had bent backwards at an extreme angle while he slept, resting on the back of the couch. He rubbed his neck and looked around, unsure at first where he was.

Bernard's hotel room.

He sat on the hotel's plush, comfortable sofa. He remembered sitting there while Miller read Arthur's notebook, but Miller was no longer in the room. It was dark, and the only sounds were of distant traffic coming from the streets far below.

Did Miller go somewhere? Rand thought.

His eyes still burned and were heavy with sleepiness. He found himself frustrated that Miller had let him sleep. No matter how exhausted he was, there simply wasn't time.

Rand stood and stretched. His body had stiffened despite only having a quick power nap. *How long was I out?*

He turned toward the floor-to-ceiling windows to check if there was a hint of daylight. There wasn't. The sky was still black, the lit-up Washington Monument the most prominent thing in the distance.

Rand had only ever been to the capital city once in his life—on a field trip in the seventh grade. At the time, he'd been too preoccupied with getting a seat on the tour bus beside to Tiffany Mooney whenever they loaded up to head to the next site. He vaguely remembered visiting the Washington Monument, but the nation's history had not been at the forefront of his mind.

Life had been so simple then.

Hell, life was simpler two weeks ago, before I knew about the Bale family, he thought.

His eyes drifted to the building across the street. When they'd first arrived at the hotel, he'd imagined someone watching him from those windows, shrouded in darkness. He wondered if they were still there, tasked with staying up all night and keeping tabs on him and Miller. Rand waved, curious to see if there'd be some kind of response.

One of the dark windows lit up. The light flickered three or four times before filling the pane—revealing a figure.

Rand took a step away from the window, a sharp gasp catching in his chest. The Bagged Woman.

Just like when Rand had seen her outside of the hotel in Rose Grove, the demon held another body by the throat.

She finished the job, Rand thought. *Arthur...*

She effortlessly lifted the corpse by the back of the neck to display the face to the Rand, as she'd done before.

It wasn't Arthur.

Rand blinked several times, trying to process what he was seeing.

Dipika.

Eyes half closed, mouth hanging open, blood streaming from her lips.

The very next moment, Rand was staring at the darkened ceiling.

Did I faint?

He lifted his head, the same pain shooting through the back of his neck. Then he realized he was waking up again.

"Couch must be pretty comfortable." Miller still sat where he'd been before, his face lit by the glow of his laptop screen. Arthur's notebook was open beside the computer.

Another damn dream.

His chest felt pinched at the sight of his dead colleague. Heart pounding, Rand whipped around on the sofa to check the office building across the street. The Bagged Woman wasn't there, and the window she'd appeared in was dark once again.

Except it isn't just *a dream.* The Bagged Woman had actually gone after Arthur.

"No," Rand whispered to himself. "Not her."

"What'd you say?" Miller asked.

Rand was tempted to not disturb Dipika, but the haunting memory of the Bagged Woman showing up at Arthur's home shortly after Rand had had a similar dream propelled him forward.

Rand shot up from the couch and took his cell phone from his pocket.

42

Rand returned to the hotel window and stood in the same spot as he had in the dream, facing the office building. It had seemed so *real*. He dreamed often, but rarely did they reflect reality so accurately. Everything he saw—the dark sky, the Washington Monument—even the handful of windows that were lit up across the street had been the exact same in the nightmare.

More a vision than a dream, Rand thought.

He had a feeling that the dreams were being placed there somehow. Injected into his head like poison.

"Rando, are you all right?" Miller asked.

"I think we have a new problem." Rand checked the time on his phone screen; it was now just after one o'clock.

She'll be so pissed, he thought, deflating. But if he hadn't already seen what had happened to Arthur, he would have let it wait until morning.

He opened his text messages. The most recent was from Dipika.

The tour guide says it's haunted. Maybe you'd like it.

From the message, he tapped her name and then the call icon. He gripped the phone as it rang, his stomach feeling hollow with each new unanswered ring.

"Who are you calling?" Miller's tone held a fearful edge.

Her not answering doesn't mean something has happened, Rand told himself. *It means she has her phone on silent at one A.M. like a normal—*

"Hello?" she answered, voice thick with sleep and perhaps a touch of concern.

Rand stiffened. "Dipika?"

"Rand?" She definitely sounded worried.

"Hey. Sorry to call you so late. I know this is going to seem weird, but... are you okay?"

Only after the words were out did he realize how truly ridiculous they came across. If she was in danger, then she wouldn't have been sound asleep, nor answering strange phone calls in the middle of the night.

"Yeah... I'm fine. Why? Are... you okay?" She seemed hesitant to ask.

It had taken the Bagged Woman roughly an hour or so to show up at Arthur's house after Rand and Miller had rushed there. Dipika wouldn't be in danger now— the demon was telling Rand that she'd be in danger *later.*

He suddenly wished he'd organized his thoughts before calling her. "I'm... well, it's complicated."

There was rustling on the other line. It sounded like she was shifting around and then sitting up in bed. "What's going on?"

"I don't know how to explain it, but I believe you're in danger."

"Excuse me?"

"Look... I'm in D.C. Are you still in town?"

She hesitated for a few seconds. "I am."

"Can we meet? So I can explain everything?"

"Um... I guess. I should I have some time tomorrow."

"I mean now." Rand had no idea where in the city Dipika was staying. It could be far. And *even* if *she agrees, the Bagged Woman might get to her first,* he thought.

"Now? Rand, it's—"

"I know. I wouldn't ask if I didn't think it was important."

Silence hung on the line. She was probably deciding if she would entertain the whims of a colleague who was quickly proving himself to be crazy. "Rand, are you okay?" Although she'd already asked him that, those same words felt like an entirely different question, like she meant *mentally* okay. "You looked very upset the other day when we shared the classroom. Then when we met that night, you still seemed... off. Kind of strange to say, because I don't know you that well, but... I sensed something."

Rand wondered if she was asking from a place of concern, or if she was now a little afraid of him. Maybe a bit of both.

"You're right. There's a lot going on, and I think you might be involved."

"How?"

"Can we meet?" he asked again. "Please. I promise I'll explain everything."

Silence for several moments. Finally, she said, "Where are you?"

"The Grand Sapphire Hotel."

"Are you serious?"

"Yeah."

That was another can of worms to explain. *She knows I couldn't afford this place on a college instructor's salary.*

"In that case, *you* get to send the Uber, since you clearly like to splurge. I'll text you my hotel's location. It isn't far from you."

"Great. Thank you."

Dipika hung up and Rand lowered his phone. He peered out at the black sky, the empty streets, and the glowing Washington Monument. The window that had lit up to reveal the Bagged Woman. He glared at it, waiting for the demon to show herself—daring her to. It remained dark.

"Rando, what's happening?" Miller asked.

"I had another vision. She's going to attack again." He turned around to face his friend. As he did, the large, wall-mounted mural clawed at his attention from his periphery. Rand refused to look at the green-eyed creature carrying a baby's corpse.

Miller straightened, his focus fully taken away from Arthur's notebook. "Arthur?"

"No. Dipika."

Miller blinked. "Who?"

Rand realized he hadn't mentioned her to Miller before. "She works with me at the college."

"Oh. But why her?"

It was Rand's turn to pause. Now that he had a moment to think about it, he... wasn't completely sure.

"If Nathan Bale controls the demon, then how does he know to send her after your colleague?" Miller continued.

Rand thought it over for a few more seconds, but could only come up with one likely reason. "Because she's here. And because he can."

Rand now wondered if he'd been followed even before he and Miller had departed on their trip. Had someone working for the Bales seen him meet with Dipika at O'Conner's? If that was the case, then that meant they'd also started keeping tabs on Dipika on this trip to D.C.

And who else? Rand wondered. *Libby? Tessa? Maybe Bill?*

"Nathan knows it'll distract us from searching for Arthur," Miller said.

"And it worked." Rand tucked his phone into his pocket and headed for the door. "But she agreed to come here, so that's a good start. She'll be safer here rather than alone. I'll go meet her in the lobby."

"How are you going to explain all of this to her?" Miller's eyes followed Rand as he crossed the room.

"To be honest, I haven't figured that out yet. She'd probably never believe the truth, but if I lie, she'll pick up on it and not trust anything else I say."

"You want me to come with you?"

"I think it's better if you stay here for now. She might be overwhelmed if there's two of us."

Miller nodded. "Well. Good luck, I guess. Call me if something goes wrong."

43

The lobby of the Grand Sapphire was quiet at that hour. A single clerk manned the desk, though he suddenly stirred into action when Rand came into view. He almost looked alarmed, as if Rand had walked in on him doing something he wasn't supposed to be doing.

Or maybe he's working for the Bales. Keeping an eye on me.

The lobby seemed so much larger when it was empty. He chose one of the many cushioned chairs and sat down. He checked his phone, the ride-sharing app on the screen. It tracked the car he'd sent for Dipika, which was now only a few minutes away.

He drummed his fingers on his thighs. A fresh wave of nervousness coursed through him. He got this way every time he had to explain his double life to someone who had no clue what he did outside of his day job.

Well, after our conversation the other night, at least she knows a little, Rand thought. *But she definitely doesn't under-*

stand the extent of it, nor would she like hearing that she might be involved. If only these demonic bastards left everyone else alone.

The hotel's rotating door spun a few minutes later, announcing her arrival. Dipika spotted him instantly since he was the only one there besides the employee at the desk. She had an inscrutable expression on her face as she approached. She wore jeans and a t-shirt with a leather coat cinched around her torso. Her thick black hair was pulled into a tight ponytail.

Rand stood as she neared. Dipika's eyes quickly scanned him from head to toe, then glanced around the lobby, as if checking if there was any sign she might've walked into an ambush.

She tucked her hands into the pockets of her jacket, her elbows at right angles at her sides. "I've always heard we were underpaid when compared to the national average. Now I see it's just me."

That's a decent start, Rand thought. Since she was cracking jokes, perhaps it'd be easier than he expected to get through to her.

He cleared his throat. "I'm so sorry to do this to you."

"I told myself I'd never let a man call me to his hotel room in the middle of the night," Dipika said. "So this needs to be good."

Rand glanced over at the desk clerk. His back was to them, head bent over his phone. Rand wondered if the high ceilings of the lobby would cause their conversation to echo, but they would have to talk there. Getting Dipika to come at all had been pushing his luck. He didn't want to ask more of her by suggesting they go to a more private place.

They sat. Of the four chairs that were arranged around a small, circular table, Dipika chose the one farthest from him. She waited patiently as he searched for the words that would best convey the situation.

"I'm not really sure where to begin," Rand said. "You... already know a little bit about my work outside of the classroom."

"You're Mr. Exorcist."

"I know it's hard to believe, but in this world, there is true evil. I've come face to face with it many times. I'm well aware that I'm the laughingstock around campus, but every single thing I teach my class is very real. I can promise you that."

Dipika let that sink in for a minute. "What does that have to do with me? Especially in the middle of the night?"

"It isn't unusual for me to be followed by these... demons." He was nervous about using the word, afraid that it might lose her. Dipika didn't react. "The one following me now is showing up when I sleep. *Harming* people in my dreams. Earlier tonight, I dreamed that she hurt you."

"Me?"

"You were dead, actually."

Her eyes fell to the ground and she shifted in her chair.

"It's a pattern that I've unfortunately gotten used to. These demons will attack me, but they also threaten and target people I know. It's a common method of causing fear and chaos. I talk about it in my class."

"So you're saying they go after your coworkers?"

"Not usually. You're actually the first."

266

Dipika looked around the lobby again, including over her shoulder. "It doesn't seem like I'm in danger."

"It could happen at any time," Rand explained. "Which is why I called you. You're safer as long as you're with me."

The skepticism written on her face was clear. "Be honest, Rand. What do you *expect* me to make of all this?"

"I don't know. But all I can ask for is a little faith."

"Faith." Dipika gave a mirthless chuckle. "I teach about all the major religions of the world, most of which emphasize faith... yet I haven't felt or believed in faith for a long time."

"Do you have faith in your friend Arun?" Rand asked.

Dipika blinked at the mention. "What about him?"

"If you can believe him, then maybe you can believe me."

Dipika took in a deep breath as she thought that one over. It was only logical—if what Arun said was true, then other supernatural claims could also be.

"I forgot I told you that story."

"There's a good reason I remember what you shared. The girl he sees... Tara. I've seen her too."

She leveled her eyes at him. "Really."

"Yes."

"Why didn't you tell me that the other night?"

"I figured you wouldn't believe me."

She shrugged, as if saying Rand had a point.

Rand caught the man at the desk watching them—he quickly glanced away.

Dipika followed Rand's gaze. "He can probably hear us," she whispered.

"Yeah."

She exhaled sharply and looked like she was considering her next words carefully. "Is there somewhere else for us to go? So you can tell me more about this."

Rand felt some of the tension leave his body. *She's willing to listen.*

"We can head up to the room and talk more there."

44

Ulvareth's head poked up at the foot of Libby's bed as he peered at her. It might've been comical, had he not looked like an exhumed corpse.

Libby sighed. "Don't you have anything else to do?"

The demon did not respond. She knew he never would.

Libby silently chastised herself. She shouldn't be talking to him. That was probably exactly what he wanted. If she got into that habit and slipped up in a public place, then people would think she was seeing things. Technically, she was. Before long, she might not be any different from the unfortunate folks who had full-length conversations with themselves while others were not around.

Libby's phone chimed. She checked the notification, and her heart pounded harder.

Arun Singh had responded.

Her hand trembled as she unlocked her phone and

tapped on the screen to open the social-media app she'd used to message him.

'Are you related to Randolph Casey?'

She inhaled sharply. How did he know who her father was?

Her thumbs hovered over the keyboard as she considered how to respond. Something in her gut told her to go with the truth.

'Yes.'

The message delivered. A few seconds later, the app indicated Arun had seen her response. She felt like the man was near, like they were connected.

'The person you are looking for can be found close to where you met her.'

Libby blinked several times as she read and reread the message from Arun. *He's actually helping me.* Though her brief rush of excitement was replaced by hesitation. *But why?* Of all the messages he likely received, why had he picked hers specifically to reply to?

Does it have something to do with Dad? she wondered. Arun had only answered her question after confirming that she was Rand's daughter.

Regardless of Arun Singh's motive, Libby knew she had to go with it. His message had given her the only potential clue she now had about Carmen Herron.

Close to where I met her... It took Libby a couple of seconds to remember where that had been.

At that crappy motel. She'd stayed there with Carmen while Miranda Herron had mysteriously left. Libby now knew that she'd stepped out because she was coordinating the rest of the ritual meant to happen that night.

But he says close to there, she thought. *Not specifically there.*

That most likely meant the creepy mansion itself. The Herron House. The motel had been about a ten-minute drive away.

Another message suddenly appeared.

'I also have a strong feeling that you shouldn't go there. I don't think there's anything you can do to help her.'

Libby didn't know what to make of that. After what Arun Singh had done to save those kidnapped children, wouldn't he want every possible child to be found?

She also wasn't sure if it was a mere suggestion or a full-blown warning. Either way, she felt her body pulled forward, as if by some kind of determined energy. She already knew that she had to check to see if what Arun said was true.

She had to return to the Herron House.

It was late at night, so Bill and her mother would be asleep. Bill's house was so huge that they wouldn't hear her slip out and drive away.

A few seconds later, she grabbed her car keys and jacket and headed downstairs.

ONCE, in elementary school, Libby had a crush on a boy named Michael Belen. After class had let out, she'd spotted him sitting on a bench by himself, reading a novel while he waited for his ride to pick him up. She'd resolved to walk over and ask him to be her boyfriend.

Her friend at the time, Amber, had tried to tell her that she shouldn't. She'd said it was the boy's job to ask the girl to be his girlfriend. Libby didn't like that idea—what if Michael wanted to ask her, but was too afraid? It might never happen.

But as she walked over to Michael that day, resistance pushed against her. Each step closer seemed to bring with it a new image that arose in her mind and tried to talk her out of her decision.

What if he said no?

What if he laughed at her?

What if everyone found out, and they laughed at her too?

What if he thought it was weird because he *also* believed that boys were supposed to ask out the girls?

All of those thoughts had crashed through Libby's head like waves, each one building into an invisible force field of energy that tried to pull her away, to convince her to abandon her plan.

Libby felt a similar aversion as she drew closer to the Herron House. Back then, she'd ultimately given in to the resistance—she'd chickened out and never asked Michael Belen to be her boyfriend. This night, though, she was barreling forward. The stakes were much higher.

The winding road ahead had no streetlights—her car's headlights were the only thing that cut through the darkness. She felt like the only soul within a twenty-mile radius. Because of her speeding, she'd shaved the drive down to just over an hour.

Going back seemed wrong in so many ways. It felt like returning to the scene of a crime, or like she was turning her back on whatever good fortune had allowed her to walk out of there alive the first time. Only fools would return to a place that had almost killed them.

Dad died there. The mental image returned, unbidden and unwanted—his lifeless body sprawled in the upper room of the mansion's tower, the floor covered with his dark-red blood. There had been so much blood...

She reached out and touched the cross that rested in the passenger seat of her car—not for the first time. She needed the assurance that it was still there, that it hadn't suddenly vanished, abandoning her.

Now and then, her eyes went to the rearview mirror. She caught the faint outline of Ulvareth in the backseat, watching her in the reflection with his usual detached expression. He sat stoically, like a silent, well-behaved passenger, his hands resting on his thighs.

Libby turned onto the dirt path that brought her through the main entrance gate. She passed the caretaker's cottage on the right, which now stood vacant. That was where she'd met up with Miller, and together they'd proceeded to the mansion.

She drove on farther until she came to the front of the mansion. Once there, she parked her car and took the cross from the passenger seat before getting out. The large structure was a shadowy silhouette against the moonlit night. Her eyes were drawn to the tower that reached toward the stars—the place where her father had died.

Libby zipped up her jacket against the cold and looked around. From what she could tell, she was alone. Even Ulvareth had disappeared from the backseat. She glanced left, then right, but for the first time since she'd spoken with Miranda Herron, the demon wasn't in sight. Libby would've thought she'd enjoy the break, but found the demon's sudden absence unsettling.

Is he afraid of the mansion too? Libby thought.

Libby ascended the stone steps toward the mansion's front door, using her phone as a flashlight. In her other hand, she clutched the cross to her chest like it was some kind of shield against evil.

God, please protect me, Libby prayed. *Tara, if you're still inside the cross... please protect me.*

She felt silly imploring the angelic being for protection when she'd never actually encountered her before. Yet she trusted her father's judgement and experience.

She reached the porch and shone her light at the massive front door. Her dad and Miller hadn't bothered to close it when they'd left the other morning, and it was still cracked open.

Libby gripped the handle and pulled. The hinges creaked.

What if it closes behind me and traps me in, like what happened to Dad? Libby thought. *No. Don't be paranoid. Akhubel was the one who did that, and he's dead.*

She used her light to scan the mansion's entrance hall before going inside. She saw the familiar grand staircase and the pillars that lined the edges of the room, supporting the domed ceiling.

Her phone's light caught something lying atop the black-and-white checkered floor.

Libby gasped and abruptly lowered it. Still, she knew what she'd seen. An invisible, intrusive hand clenched her heart and gave it a tight squeeze.

Arun Singh had been right.

Libby forced herself to step through the cavernous entrance, which looked like a gaping maw. She raised her phone light, once again illuminating the truth.

Carmen Herron's small frame, diminutive against the expansive room around her.

A heavy lump formed in Libby's throat as she neared. She fell to her knees, the coldness of the tiles seeping through her jeans.

The girl was on her back, chin lifted, blonde hair spread out on the floor. She almost looked asleep. Her flesh seemed pale in the darkness.

"No." Even though it was a whisper, Libby's voice echoed off the high walls.

Tears came, then sobs. She reached out with a trembling hand and placed it on the girl's chest, feeling for a gentle rise and fall. There was none. She had a feeling there hadn't been any breath for several days.

Eyes blurry with tears, Libby held out the cross in the air over Carmen's body. It had worked for her father. Could it work for Carmen?

"Come on, Tara," Libby begged. "Please."

She waved the cross around the girl's still form. After a few seconds, she felt foolish, like she was a child playing with a pretend magic wand. Carmen didn't move.

Libby pressed her face into Carmen's stomach and cried.

I'm sorry. I let you down.

Would things be different if she'd only searched harder? Or messaged Arun sooner? Maybe this could have been avoided. Maybe she could have saved the girl from her vile family.

A part of her told her it wasn't possible. Libby was no expert, but she got the impression that Carmen had been dead for a while. That meant that her family had disposed of her soon after the ritual had failed. If

Akhubel wasn't able to feed, then the girl was useless to them—there'd been no need to keep her around.

The darkness of the realization crushed her. She felt her limbs go limp as all her emotions rose into her chest and escaped through her cries, which echoed off the walls.

Libby had barely known the girl, but it didn't matter. No one deserved what had happened to her. When Libby had first met Carmen, she'd been coloring, fully absorbed in her artwork—oblivious to the fact that her parents were planning to sacrifice her to a demon that night.

Maybe Carmen knew a boy like Michael Belen and had a crush on him, Libby thought. *He might be wondering why Carmen vanished from school.*

Another emotion exploded inside of Libby. Anger. It tried to displace the grief, but then the grief pushed back, and the two made an uneasy truce in her heart. She felt angry that she'd taken on this mission of saving Carmen while her father was away. She'd wanted a more active role in his cases, and had forced herself in, despite him trying to stop her. Her first true attempt at fighting the evil in the world had ended in a complete and tragic failure tonight. Her dad always seemed to emerge victorious. He'd literally *died* the other night, yet had *still* managed to disrupt the dark ritual in the mansion's tower.

And there she was. Unable to help anyone. The only thing she was good for was finding the body after it was too late.

Humiliation came knocking next. She'd told Miranda

Herron to her face that she would save Carmen... and the woman had already known her daughter was gone.

Libby wiped her eyes. Her sobs caught in her throat when she noticed her forearm—it was *glowing.* She blinked away the tears, wondering if the wetness distorted her vision.

But that wasn't the case. A shimmering purple aura outlined her hand, wrist, and forearm. She checked her other arm and found the same. It encapsulated her entire body.

"What..."

Narrow tendrils of the purple light rose from her body and into the air. She followed their slow drift upward, craning her neck.

Ulvareth had apparently decided to reappear, ending Libby's brief reprieve from his constant presence. He now hovered above her, and his mouth gaped open while the rising purple light was sucked down the black hole of his throat. His feeding looked strikingly similar to what Akhubel had been doing to Carmen before her father had interrupted the ritual.

Libby had a distant thought that whatever was happening wasn't good, but she was too mesmerized by what she was seeing to do something about it.

She was startled by the sound of footsteps.

Libby jerked her phone's flashlight toward the mansion's entrance—Miranda Herron had followed her inside.

Libby knew she should've felt cornered, knew she should've been looking for a way to bolt out of there, because what if she was next? What if Miranda planned to kill her and lay her body beside Carmen's in the dark tomb of the Herron House?

But instead, Libby's insides roiled at being in the presence of true evil.

"You're a monster." It was all Libby could think to say.

"I don't expect you to understand," Miranda said. She almost sounded sympathetic to the roller coaster of grief Libby was going through.

Ulvareth still floated above Libby as he consumed the aura released from her body, and suddenly she understood what was happening. Her father had explained it a hundred times: dark entities were drawn to negative energy. That negative energy made them stronger and anchored their presence in the material world. She was witnessing that process. Her sadness, anger, grief, and feelings of failure—emotions that all humans experienced, but rarely at the same time—had to have been a strong cocktail for the demon to indulge in.

Another realization struck Libby. "You *wanted* me to find her."

"I could tell you felt strongly about my daughter. So it seemed like a good opportunity."

Opportunity.

Libby clenched her jaw at the implication. Carmen's true purpose had been foiled, so this was a consolation prize.

Fatigue washed over Libby. Her limbs were limp and exhausted. It had to be a side effect of Ulvareth feeding off of her as if she was some kind of supernatural battery.

She understood now. It was one of the most common questions her father received from his clients: if demons hated humans so much, then why not just kill them?

Because death was rarely ever the ultimate goal. What they cared about was the *energy* they could harvest from their victims. That was why demons endeavored to incite fear, anger, and paranoia. All of that negativity was expressed as energy the creatures could feed from and use to grow stronger.

Libby fought through the sudden tiredness and rose to her feet. *Enough.* The only way she could think to fight back against the demonic parasite was to lift the cross above her head, displaying it to Ulvareth. When she did, the demon fled immediately, zipping into the air and vanishing into the darkness that gathered at the domed ceiling of the entrance hall. To her relief, the purple aura around her body faded.

Libby hadn't expected the cross to deter him. The last time she'd confronted him with it, he'd sent her flying across the room.

"There'll be plenty more for him later," Miranda said.

Maybe that's why he didn't attack me again when I showed him the cross just now, Libby thought. *I'm more valuable to him now.* What she'd experienced that night would not be a one-off thing. This was why trauma was so desirable to demonic entities. For the rest of her life, Libby would *never* forget the sight of Carmen's lifeless body. She'd relive those emotions each and every time the memory sprung back into her thoughts. And as long as Ulvareth was there, attached to her, he'd feed. Again and again.

"You've had a rough night," Miranda said. "I think you should go." The woman stepped aside, clearing the path to the mansion's exit.

She's letting me go? But then Libby understood...

Miranda's goal had been achieved. Libby would now be a perpetual energy source for her demonic attachment.

Tearing away from Carmen's side and walking past Miranda Herron felt like a walk of shame. The woman's smug smirk of triumph made it so much worse.

45

ing. Six.

Ding. Seven.

The backlit numbers in the panel above the elevator door lit up one by one. Rand's stomach lurched whenever the elevator rose. He felt like it was taking its time, somehow purposely going as slow as possible.

Dipika stood as far away from him that the little square compartment would allow. She folded her arms across her chest and fixed her eyes on a point on the tiled floor.

"I'm not here alone," Rand said, and Dipika's eyes flicked up to him, snapping out of her trance. "You'll meet my friend, Miller, in the room. He helps me with these... supernatural situations."

She eyed him for a long moment. "So you have, like, a whole team?"

"No, just—"

The overhead lights flickered. Both Dipika and Rand looked up.

Oh no, he thought.

It was then that he realized he should've taken the stairs.

Whenever the demonic were present, there was always a chance of interference with electronic equipment. In the past, Rand had experienced otherworldly voices breaking through radio signals, cell phones suddenly dying despite having a full battery, and even medical equipment randomly malfunctioning. As they'd seen a few nights ago, something demonic had even intercepted Miller's phone call when he'd tried to book the hotel in Rose Grove. Elevators were no different.

I should have known, Rand mentally chastised himself. Maybe he'd have insisted on the stairs if he hadn't been awake for nearly two days straight, running on fumes.

It almost didn't surprise him when the elevator slowed, despite them only passing the ninth floor. Then, it lurched to a stop that felt *wrong*. Premature and sudden.

"What's going on?" Dipika asked. It came out more like a statement than a question. She knew, but didn't want to face the fact just yet.

Rand went to the panel and repeatedly pressed his thumb into the button for the eleventh floor, as if pressing it harder and deeper would register his request as urgent.

"Shit."

"How is this happening?" Dipika left her self-appointed zone in the corner and joined Rand at the panel. "Nicest hotel in town, and the elevator breaks down."

Fear crawled up Rand's spine. He knew this wasn't just some mundane malfunction.

It's her. The Bagged Woman.

Dipika pressed a red-rimmed button that was separate from the others. It lit up a bright orange and chimed loudly. The nearby speaker clicked and came alive, presumably opening a direct line to security. Static crackled on the other end.

"Dipika," Rand began, "I think—"

Dipika brought her mouth close to the speaker. "Hello? Is someone there?"

The static grew louder. Rand already knew what was going on. There wasn't anyone on the other side of there. At least, not anyone they'd want to speak to.

"The elevator stopped. We're stuck in here. Can you send someone?"

More garbled static. Just beyond it was a voice, barely audible.

A woman laughing.

Dipika shot Rand a wide-eyed look. Confusion with the beginnings of fear. Rand jabbed the orange emergency button, which shut off the speaker.

"Why—why was she laughing?" Dipika asked.

"We aren't broken down. We've been stopped."

"Stopped? What for?"

Rand wished he could explain to Dipika how demons tampered with electric equipment, but there wasn't time for that. Rand dug his fingertips into the tight slit between where the two elevator doors met and forced them apart just enough to get the rest of his hands between them. He adjusted his grip and pulled. The heavy doors slid open to reveal a shaft of ugly dark metal, bolts, and beams. It was a look completely at odds with the rest of the hotel—clearly a section that was never meant to be seen.

They were stuck between floors. The bottom half of the sliding doors that would lead them out of the elevator shaft were higher than Rand's head.

"Can you reach?" Dipika asked.

Rand was just tall enough to touch the space where the two doors met. He gritted his teeth as he worked his fingers to get them in between the doors. Sweat broke out on his forehead; the air ventilation must have shut down at the same time as the elevator. Finally, he felt the doors shift. He figured they were equipped with mechanisms that allowed them to give way when forced open— precisely for situations such as this one.

"I... don't think I want to crawl through there," Dipika said. "I've seen enough movies of people getting cut in half."

Although the elevator seemed solidly stuck in place, Rand realized perhaps Dipika had a point. If they *were* being held there by some kind of demonic force, then it could be released. What if someone was watching them and waiting for them to crawl out?

Despite these thoughts, Rand continued to pull on the outer doors. Once he got them started, it was easier to spread them apart.

The doors opened to reveal a pair of legs—milky skin, bare feet, and thighs covered by the hem of a dirty, torn dress.

Rand opened his mouth to shout a warning, but he

wasn't quick enough. The knees bent into a crouch, then the Bagged Woman's long arm snaked into the elevator from above. Her large land gripped the collar of Dipika's jacket and yanked, lifting the woman off her feet as if she weighed nothing. She shrieked. Rand tried to grab her legs to pull her away, but they slid through his grasp. In a mere second, the Bagged Woman had snatched Dipika from Rand's side, pulled her through the elevator doors, and hefted her into the hallway.

"Dipika!"

The pasty legs of the Bagged Woman turned and stalked away from the elevator shaft, vanishing from Rand's view within a few steps. All the while, Dipika screamed his name over and over.

Rand backed up as far as he could, and with a running start, leapt toward the ledge above. He gripped the edge and pulled himself up, scrambling fast in case whoever was holding the elevator let it drop in the hopes of taking a bleeding half of his body with it. He hoisted himself into the carpeted hallway and got back on his feet.

The Bagged Woman's long strides carried her down the narrow hallway. She held Dipika in front of her, one arm encircling her waist while her other was clamped over her mouth, smothering her desperate screams. Dipika's feet shot out every which way, trying to kick herself free as she struggled hopelessly against the demon's strength.

Rand broke into a sprint and bolted down the hall. As he gained on the Bagged Woman, he suddenly realized he didn't *know* what he was going to do when he caught her.

I have holy water in my pocket, he remembered. He'd have to use that.

The demon pivoted, shifting Dipika so that her left arm encircled her captive's body. She then lashed out at Rand with her right arm and cracked him against his face with a solid backhand that left his head reeling from the blow.

"Rand!" Dipika managed cry out before the entity's massive hand clamped down over her mouth again.

With Rand disoriented, the Bagged Woman had no trouble seizing the front of his shirt and lifting him off his feet. She drew back and threw him with tremendous force. His body crashed into the wall before crumpling to the floor—pain lanced through his right knee and upper back.

Dipika continued to screech Rand's name, giving him no time to sit there and wonder if he'd broken something. The Bagged Woman had resumed her unhurried walk away from him, carrying Dipika away.

Something on the floor caught Rand's eye. The tesseract. *It must've fallen out of my pocket when she threw me,* Rand thought. It caught the light from the fluorescent bulb in the ceiling, seeming to absorb it. He remembered what it had done to Bernard Bale.

Rand set his jaw and pushed himself up, trying his best to ignore the pain. He darted forward, scooping up the tesseract like a baseball player fielding a ground ball. He closed some of the distance between himself and the Bagged Woman, then wound back and pitched the black cube forward.

It struck her in the back and propelled her forward, causing the Bagged Woman to lose her grip on Dipika with a dark, guttural growl of pain. Dipika dropped to the hallway floor. The power from the cube hurled the Bagged Woman forward through the air several feet before she landed and rolled, her thick arms and legs thrashing every which way.

Rand rushed to Dipika and crouched down to where she'd landed. "Are you all right?"

Dipika sat up and scooted away from where the Bagged Woman lay to put as much distance between herself and the demon as she could. "What the hell *is* that thing?" Her voice shook.

The Bagged Woman writhed on her back, seeming like she was struggling to stand up.

She's weakened, Rand realized. *This is my chance. Might not have another opportunity where she's vulnerable.*

He left Dipika's side and rushed toward the demon. He stood over her as she squirmed. Her groans lessened, as if the pain was subsiding, and Rand knew it wouldn't be long before she was on her feet again.

He reached into his jacket pocket and grasped the two vials of holy water he'd taken earlier. He bent down and slapped them onto the Bagged Woman's chest, right where her dirty dress's neckline ended and her flesh began.

"God, send this creature back to hell." Rand stomped his foot onto the two glass vials, crushing them. The Bagged Woman howled so terribly that Rand wanted to cover his ears. Her gaping mouth was imprinted beneath the sack that covered her head. He twisted the heel of his shoe, grinding the glass shards and pressing the holy water deeper into the woman's chest. Black smoke rose from beneath his shoe. Her legs and arms trembled less and less until they became still, and her otherworldly voice faded. Rand's foot sank concavely into the woman's thoracic cavity as the holy water melted a hole in her body.

The Bagged Woman dissipated into a burst of smoke, then was gone. She left behind a wide puddle black smudge that ruined the carpet underneath where she'd laid.

Dipika still sat on the ground, watching Rand with wide eyes, wearing an expression he'd seen many times before.

She finally believed him.

46

They took the stairs the rest of the way to Rand's hotel room.

As they ascended, Dipika kept her body pressed against Rand, as if she refused to get too far away from him. She quietly sobbed. Rand limped on his knee —the pain had come back in full force now that the adrenaline had worn off. He was sure he'd be able to walk it off. At least he hoped he could.

With a calming hand on her back, Rand led Dipika to his room. He used his keycard on the lock and they went inside.

"Rando, I—" Miller called out.

Dipika cried out, startled, and jumped behind Rand's shoulder, which she gripped tightly.

"It's okay," Rand whispered. "It's only my friend Miller, who I was telling you about."

Miller rounded the corner, looking visibly confused.

"Come on, let's sit down." Rand guided Dipika past

Miller and into the living room. She lowered herself onto the couch and tried to get her sobbing under control.

Rand hung his head. He'd seen people go through this before. The skepticism that defined their worldview had been shattered all at once, like an antique lamp knocked over by a rowdy child. Not only had Dipika witnessed the horror that existed in the world, she'd been attacked by it.

"I'm so sorry you had to go through that," Rand offered. It hardly seemed worth saying. In that moment, there were no words that could make Dipika feel better.

The room was silent except for her quiet crying. She sniffed and wiped at the edges of her eyes, took some breaths, and looked up at Rand. "What... what was that thing?"

"Like I said downstairs... there's true evil in this world."

She peered at him, giving him a look that suggested *he* was some foreign, supernatural creature. "So that's why you called me?"

"Yes."

"What happened, Rando?" Miller whispered beside him.

"Our little friend stopped the elevator and tried to take her."

Miller frowned. "Then what?"

"I got her. I don't think she'll be bothering us anymore."

Miller blew out his breath through puffed cheeks, looking relieved.

"This is Professor Sharma, my colleague who I was telling you about. Dipika, this is Miller."

Dipika continued to wipe at her eyes. She'd gotten her tears mostly under control. She drew her legs up onto the couch and pressed her back against the armrest. "What are you doing here, Rand? In D.C. You never said."

"That's a... long story."

"I'd probably believe anything you told me after..." She let a resigned sigh.

"You might. But I don't think we have time to get into—"

Rand's phone vibrated in his pocket, and his heart thudded a bit harder. There were only a handful of people in his life who would call him that late at night, and only if something was wrong.

It was Libby.

47

He answered and his daughter appeared on the screen. Her face was red and streaked with tears.

"Libby, what's wrong?"

Miller's forehead creased with worry. Dipika furrowed her brow.

"I'm fine," Libby said quickly. She was in her car, the phone's front-facing camera pointed up at her from her lap. She sniffled and wiped at her nose. "But I... I found Carmen."

Rand swallowed. "Where are you?"

"Leaving the Herron House."

"You went *back* there?" He shot up from the chair, his worry suddenly replaced with panicked anger.

"Dad, there's some stuff that's been happening since you left, but I didn't want to bother you while you and Miller were off doing your thing."

"You *need* to tell me when things happen," Rand said. He began pacing.

"And that's what I'm doing now. Miranda Herron showed up at my school the other day. After that, this demon started following me around wherever I went. I... I still see him."

Rand's stomach sank. While he'd been out of town, his daughter was being attacked at home. He suddenly wanted to rush there to be with her, but felt himself pulled in two directions.

"Send him away," Rand said. "Use the cross. You know what to do."

"I tried, and he—he fought back. It didn't work. It's like he knew what I was about to do."

Rand seethed at the thought of Libby being harmed by one of the Bale family's demonic servants.

"He only hurt me when I tried to send him away," Libby explained. "If I don't do anything, he just kind of... stands around and watches me."

"That doesn't make it okay."

"I know. But that was why I was going to wait for you to come home before I told you about it."

Rand remembered what Libby had started with. "What about Carmen Herron?"

"I shouldn't have done it, but I messaged that guy Arun Singh on social media." From his peripheral vision, Rand noticed Dipika's hand go to her chest. "I didn't expect him to answer. I'm sure people message him all the time about their missing kids, since he's so famous. But he replied to me, and he asked if I was your daughter. He knows you somehow."

Now Rand and Dipika held each other's gazes for a long while. Rand tried to read her expression, but thoughts must've been crashing through her head just as fast as his. He could see it in her eyes that she was trying to make some semblance of sense of what she was hearing.

Tara, Rand realized. The white-eyed girl must've told Arun about him. *But why?*

"He said I could find Carmen near where I met her. But he also told me not to go there, and that there was nothing I could do to help her."

Rand knew where this was going.

"I... I couldn't help myself. I assumed he meant the old mansion where you and Miller went. I went back and... she was just lying there. Like a discarded piece of *trash.*" She spat the word and began to cry harder. "I think she's been dead for days. I wanted to save her so bad, but I never even had the chance." Her words were almost lost between her sobs.

Rand hung his head as his daughter started bawling all over again. It was one of the worst sounds in the world. Miller removed his glasses and wiped at his eyes.

"I'm sorry, Libby," Rand said. The weight of the news settled on his shoulders and in his heart.

It wasn't only Libby. He'd worked hard to save Carmen from Akhubel's ritual—and he'd *succeeded.* Every part of him had wanted to pull the girl away from her murderous parents and grandfather, but when she'd woken up, she'd run straight to them with no recollection of what had happened to her. They'd taken her, and Rand had strongly suspected it was best to let them go. He'd barely scraped by that night, and he couldn't expect to claim all the victories. He'd foolishly assumed that even though their plan had failed, they wouldn't just murder Carmen. But the Bales were constantly proving that he had no idea of the lengths they would go to in order to please their demonic allies. The girl truly *had* been born for a single purpose: to eventually sacrifice. If that didn't happen, then in their eyes, there was literally no reason for her to exist in their family.

"I think... I think they wanted me to find her," Libby said, sniffling.

Rand snapped out of his spiraling thoughts. "Why?"

"Something weird happened when I saw her. The demon following me. He started... I don't know... *feeding* off my sadness. You always say demons feed off negativity, right? I'm pretty sure that's why Miranda let me leave earlier," Libby continued. "They didn't want to hurt me. At least, not tonight. They wanted to use me for energy."

Rand's mind whirred as he felt the pieces coming together, prompted by what his daughter had just said.

"Dad, what are you thinking?" Libby asked. He must have been quiet for too long.

"Where are you now?" Rand put his thoughts on hold.

"Driving back to Bill's. I pulled over to call you."

"You should've told me all of this sooner," Rand said.

"I know. I'm sorry for waiting so long. I only wanted to help."

In a way, Libby *had* been a help. She'd just connected some dots for him. "Go to Bill's, stay put, and don't leave until I come back. And that cross I gave you? Keep it close." His words came out a bit sterner than he'd intended, but Libby didn't react. "I took the rest of my supplies with me, so that's all you have. Remember what you did to Akhubel. Do the same to this demon following you, if you can."

Libby nodded. "Okay. When are you coming home?"

"I don't know yet." He cast a quick glance at Miller and Dipika. "There are some things I need to handle first."

"Please be careful, Dad."

"I always am."

Libby hung up, which left a heavy silence lingering in the room.

"I feel terrible for her," Miller finally said.

Rand was only half listening. His mind had wandered to a possible alternate reality where Libby *hadn't* gotten to walk away from the Herron House. He remembered how, when he'd been there, the door had suddenly shut behind him, sealing him inside for most of the night. He recalled the ordeals he'd come across as he'd traversed the decrepit mansion. He couldn't bear to think of Libby having to do the same.

Something else swirled in Rand's gut, an emotion that he hadn't expected to be there. He was kind of pissed at Arun Singh.

If he knew the location was dangerous, he shouldn't have even told Libby where to go.

Surely Arun understood that. There *had* to be a reason.

"Rando?" Miller asked.

Rand turned to Dipika. "Can you get Arun on the phone? I want to talk to him."

48

Dipika hesitated, seemingly put off by Rand's curt request. She eventually took her phone from her jacket pocket, tapped the screen, and then handed it to Rand. Arun's contact page was there.

Rand pressed the camera icon to video call Arun.

He answered quickly. "Dipika?" His phone laid on a surface, pointing up at a ceiling. It shook as it was picked up. Then a man appeared. "Are you—" He cut off when he saw it was not Dipika on the other end. He blinked a few times and this his face softened, as if his worry had been assuaged. "Randolph Casey. This is *quite* the synchronicity."

Rand paused. *There's that word again,* he thought. *The same one Arthur wrote in his notebook.*

"Friends call me Rand."

Arun nodded once. "It's nice to finally speak with you, Rand."

"Dipika's right here," Rand said. Dipika went to stand

over Rand's shoulder, and he pointed the phone's front camera so that Arun could see her.

Arun smiled when he caught sight of Dipika. "I must admit, I didn't expect this to come together like this."

I'm sure it is, Rand thought, but he had other concerns. "I just got off the phone with my daughter. I learned that Dipika isn't the only mutual friend we have."

"It seems that way, yes." Arun's words were gentle, yet firm.

"Quick question." He heard the edge in his own tone. "My daughter was looking for someone. If you knew it was dangerous, *why* did you tell her where to go?"

"Rand." Dipika's voice was barely a whisper. He felt her hand lightly touch his shoulder, and then pull away. Rand figured she'd sensed the coming confrontation between her two friends.

Arun held Rand's gaze through the video call. "You're upset."

"Put yourself in my shoes as a father."

"Sadly, I cannot. But when our mutual friend gives us answers to our questions, I know we must seize them, or else they will be gone forever."

"You're saying that was Libby's only chance to hear the truth of what happened to Carmen Herron?"

"Was that her name?" For the first time, Arun's calm tone dipped into sadness. "If your daughter didn't learn tonight, then I'm afraid she never would. She'd wonder for the rest of her life. Would you want that for her?"

Rand couldn't answer in that moment—it would require some serious debate. Would he prefer Libby to never know what befell Carmen Herron if it meant she avoided what had happened tonight?

"These are very negative entities and evil people you've entangled yourself with, Rand," Arun went on. "It's foolish to expect complete safety at all times."

Am I being scolded? Rand thought. It was hard to tell from Arun Singh's soft-spoken nature.

"I also got the strong feeling that your daughter takes after you. And you, it would seem, don't always heed sound advice either."

Definitely being scolded.

But Rand wasn't quite sure what Arun was talking about. "What do you mean?"

"I sense from Tara that she tried to guide you away from the situation in which you currently find yourself. And you didn't listen."

Rand remembered the last time he'd seen the white-eyed girl. It felt like so long ago, even though it really hadn't been. She'd appeared to him in the depths of the Herron House.

'You are not ready for this fight,' she'd told him. *'Your actions have pleased all who watch over you, but there is still much that you do not yet understand.'*

That night, Rand figured the girl had been talking about Akhubel. At the time, Rand had thought he was there to help Jackson and Miranda Herron. He hadn't yet learned that Jackson had lured him there as part of the ritual.

'You cannot fight him,' she'd also said. *'You will not win.'*

Fight who? Rand wondered now. *Bernard? Nathan?* Maybe she *had* meant Akhubel after all. As it turned out, fighting the demon was a lose-lose situation. Even though Libby had killed him, his death had earned them the ire of the Bale family.

"In fact, it cost you your life."

At the mention of Rand's recent, albeit temporary demise, Miller's gaze shifted downward, a cloud of sorrow settling over him. Rand had been spared the grief-invoking sight of his own corpse—after all, he'd been dead—but he couldn't escape the emotional toll it had taken on his loved ones. Over his shoulder in the video feed, Dipika looked perplexed.

"Yeah, well..." Rand found himself short of words. In hindsight, it was easy to see that maybe he should've stopped while he was ahead. "I wish Tara would speak a little more clearly."

Arun reminded Rand of the psychic mediums he'd worked with in his past cases. When they connected with the spiritual world, the messages came across as cryptic and vague, requiring sharp intuition to decipher. This often frustrated Rand, whose mind preferred being literal. But hazy communication was a reality of dealing with the other side.

Arun chuckled. "You and me both, my friend. I must confess, I'm also guilty of not always following her guidance."

"But you helped rescue all those kids," Rand said.

"I mean for myself."

"Yourself?"

"Let's just say that I have a strong feeling traveling to D.C. for this little charity event wasn't in my best interest."

"Are you okay, Arun?" Dipika cut in, leaning forward.

"Yes, I'm fine."

"So then why did you come?" Rand asked.

"For many reasons," Arun said.

Rand waited for the other man to elaborate, but he only fell silent and looked to the side, as if someone had entered the room. Rand glanced up at Dipika, who only shrugged.

"Rand..." Arun's voice was suddenly heavy and serious. "You are also searching for a lost person, just as your daughter was."

Rand's eyes flicked up to Miller. His body stiffened and his face shifted into a hopeful expression.

Arthur.

"I am."

"He's near."

Dipika glanced between Miller, Rand, and Arun, once again seeming like she was trying to play catch-up.

Rand looked around. There was no indication that anyone was there save for the three of them.

"Do you feel the energy?" Arun asked.

"Yes." Rand had sensed the negativity as soon as he'd walked in. Even hours later, it hadn't abated at all, and it definitely wasn't something he could just become accustomed to.

"That room is connected to a very evil place," Arun said. "And the man you're looking for... he's there."

"Where?"

Arun was silent for several long moments, as if trying to divine the answer. "Perhaps I shouldn't say," he finally said. "It's very dangerous. You'd be ill-advised to go."

Rand saw his jaw muscles clench in the video. "Not gonna play that game, Arun." Although frustrated, Rand now understood Arun's decision to tell Libby where to find Carmen.

"He's below," Arun said.

Below? Rand thought.

"Underneath you, somehow," Arun went on. "And... there's something happening. Something dark. If you hurry, maybe you can stop it before it's too late."

49

R and shot up from the couch, handing Dipika's phone back to her.

"Arun, what's going on?" Rand heard Dipika whisper.

If Arun responded, Rand didn't hear it. His mind was too busy racing.

"Below," Rand said to Miller. "Downstairs?"

"Elevator?" Miller offered.

The last thing Rand wanted to do was use the hotel's elevator again. "But that would mean leaving the room. There's something in here..."

"*That.*" Miller's attention snapping to the grotesque mural on the wall.

Rand walked over and inspected it, running his hands along the side of the gilded frame. Almost immediately, he felt that it wasn't well-attached. He pulled, and the top of the painting folded down, controlled by squeaky metal hinges as it lowered like an attic door.

Behind it was a rectangle hole in the wall. It led to a hollowed-out room.

"What in the world?" Miller muttered.

Rand stepped through the hole. He had to crouch to keep from bumping his head against the roof of the small area. It only continued for a few paces before coming to the end of the passage, where a narrow, spiral staircase descended into darkness.

"What's in there?" Miller asked.

"There's a way down," Rand called over his shoulder. Miller and Dipika watched him from just outside the secret passage.

"And you're going," Miller said. It wasn't a question.

"I have to. Arun said Arthur's down here somewhere." Although he felt compelled to see where the stairs led, he hesitated.

What if Nathan wanted *us to find this?* he wondered. *Why would he put us in this room if some part of him didn't intend for this?*

Despite the possibility, Rand knew what he had to do.

He started down. The steps were steep, and there was no railing. He ran his palms along the walls to support himself and keep his balance. The stairwell was completely shrouded in darkness, built within a very narrow section of the hotel's walls.

He heard footsteps above and behind him. Miller had followed.

"You can wait for me," Rand called up, though inwardly he was relieved.

"No way. You can't go down there alone."

Miller appeared around the curve in the stairs. Dipika

was on his heels as well. They both held their cell phones, flashlights activated.

"What did you find?" came Arun's voice from Dipika's phone.

Rand *really* didn't want Dipika to come with them, but decided not to protest. Arun had strongly suggested they hurry.

Down and down they went, the tight spiral of steps making Rand feel like he was being flushed down a drain.

There were no other doors or exits along the way. Nothing led out or connected to other rooms in the hotel. This whole stairwell and passage had been built specifically for the room Bernard Bale liked to occupy.

Which means there's an entire section of this hotel that was made just for him, Rand thought. If that was the case, Rand wondered if Bernard actually owned the building. It was entirely possible.

Rand couldn't track what floor he was on, but he did get the feeling they were going all the way to the bottom. Maybe even *further*, to a basement.

The spiral staircase ended in a dark passageway that only led one direction. Dirt crunched under Rand's foot.

"Unbelievable," Miller whispered.

The passageway brought them through an arched doorway. The way forward became less narrow, widening before passing through a second large arch. The walls grew farther apart as Rand continued, and then he walked beneath a third, even larger arch. It reminded him of the bizarre architecture inside the Herron House.

"What's Arun got to say?" Rand asked over his shoulder to Dipika. "Are we hot or cold?"

"The call dropped," Dipika said. "There's no signal here."

That came as no surprise to Rand. He sensed they were currently *underneath* the building. He didn't remember an option to go to the basement on the elevator button panel. Where they were was off limits to the public. Rand wondered how many of the hotel workers actually knew this area was down there.

Probably none.

Rand pushed forward, intent on seeing where it all led. His gut twisted itself into knots, a strong, overpowering fear taking him over, urging him to go back.

Tara might also tell me to turn back if she appeared, he thought.

The final arched doorway opened to a massive chamber—something that *definitely* wasn't a simple basement. They'd emerged into a room so large Rand would never have expected to see anything like it beneath the hotel. It was dark except for several burning torches.

Rand froze in his tracks when he realized they weren't the only ones inside the chamber. He extended his arm to block Miller's path, silently indicating to him not to go any farther.

There was a raised platform in the center of the chamber, built upon concentric, circular slabs of concrete that got smaller as they rose, serving as steps. A pair of semi-circular, waist-high walls wrapped around the center platform. The gaps in the wall appeared to serve as entrances—one to the north and the other to the south—to access the main platform. A dozen people stood behind the walls, leaving about an arm's length of space between each other. They wore matching brown smocks and identical masks made of metal; all of them faced the central platform.

Atop the platform was a single, simple chair.

In the chair sat Arthur Briggs, wrists and ankles bound.

50

Arthur pulled against his restraints, but with nowhere near enough force to break free. His movements seemed hopeless, as if he'd been trying for a long time. He wore the same jeans and t-shirt as when Officer Brannon had taken him away, except now they were stained dark with blood.

I was right, Rand realized. *They kept Arthur alive and brought him here for a reason.*

The masked onlookers chanted, but not in unison. From what Rand could tell, each person vocalized something different, producing a twisted harmony—if it could be called that. He was immediately reminded of his experience in the Herron House, where he'd been surrounded by record players, each playing a unique demonic track that grated on his ears.

The chanting was unintelligible, a hellish language that Rand didn't understand. Despite that, the energy was palpable. A dark, heavy force weighing him down. His chest was tight. He suddenly felt unable to take in an adequate breath, as if the oxygen was being sucked from the room.

There's a demon here, Rand thought. *These people are summoning him.*

And Arthur was right in the middle of it all.

But why? A sacrifice?

Rand's entire body was numb with a level of fear he had never quite experienced. In his past cases, he'd mostly dealt with simple things—teenagers who'd messed around with a Ouija board, or a small group of spiritualists who had gotten carried away and inadvertently invited a demon into their home. Never before had he seen a ritual like this, large and organized with this many participants.

The masked chanters suddenly lifted their arms in unison, as if receiving a cue from a director. They raised their palms toward Arthur and began to sway. Their chanting escalated.

Arthur's body jerked as if he'd been slapped in the face by an invisible hand. His eyes rolled back into his head, and his chest heaved like he'd started suffocating.

I need to do something, Rand thought. *But what?* He was hopelessly outnumbered.

The chamber's high roof was supported by thick columns, similar to an ancient temple. Rand peeked out from behind one of them as he watched the proceedings. Miller and Dipika were just over his shoulder. Miller's jaw hung open in astonishment and he adjusted his glasses, as if he didn't trust them about what he was seeing. Dipika's hands covered her mouth, seeming like she was holding in a scream. No one involved in the ritual gave any indication that they knew intruders had wandered in.

There was movement in the shadows in the room's periphery. Whoever it was walked slowly, their attention on what was happening at the core. He or she did not chant along, but rather supervised, making sure everyone was contributing, playing their part. They were dressed the same as the others—brown smock and metal mask.

Rand's focus was on this person now. They carried something that resembled a spear. They left the shadows and made their way to the southern opening of the central altar, holding the spear in both hands.

Rand gritted his teeth as he wondered what this person was going to do with it. He briefly imagined them winding back and hurling it through Arthur's chest, like a hunter killing a deer.

But the masked leader turned the blade toward the floor and started to etch. The leader's movements were deft as the sharp edges glided along the stone, scraping symbols and glyphs similar to what Rand had seen written on the walls of his desecrated home. The sound of steel on stone should've been grating, yet it seemed to blend in with the dark chanting that filled the room, masking it and harmonizing with it at the same time. The symbol was comprised of criss-crossing lines, straight and precise, as if the leader was a machine rather than human. It almost looked as if they had no control over their own body. Maybe they didn't.

The masked leader went to the north side of the altar. There, they turned the spear against the floor again and continued. The symbols matched, except for being inverse to each other. With each new complete symbol,

Rand sensed the energy in the room further constricting, like a large snake was slowly squeezing the life out of him, content to wait before finally consuming him.

Once done, the masked leader stepped away. The symbols carved into the floor began to glow, radiating with what resembled a black flame. The dark substance swelled into the air above them. The chanters did not react to the anomaly creeping up around them; they were either unfazed or too far gone in their trance to notice.

Or maybe they've seen it before, Rand thought.

"Rise up!"

They were the first words Rand had understood since he'd entered the chamber. They came from the leader who'd gouged the symbols into the floor. Rand also recognized the voice: Nathan Bale's.

"We summon you, Vyraxus!"

Rand's breath caught. *That... that's the name from Arthur's story. They're handing him over.*

He and Miller exchanged a fearful glance.

"You stated your desire, and I have fulfilled it. Accept this offering. May it please you. May this atone for our recent failures."

The blackness that rose from the two sets of symbols floated high, arched, and came together about six feet over where Arthur sat, forming a shadowy orb.

Rand had seen balls of dark energy like that before. They represented a demon's amorphous form when not appearing as an apparition.

The collection of shadow unraveled itself like a ball of yarn, tendrils of black twisting around each other in a double-helix spiral toward the crown of Arthur's head.

As soon as it touched him, Arthur's entire body went

rigid and vibrated as if struck by electricity. His shriek echoed off the chamber's high walls.

Rand wanted to rush forward and interrupt this ritual, just like he'd done to the one with Akhubel, but he felt Miller's hand gripping his shoulder, urging him to stay put. His friend must've sensed what he was thinking.

"They won't let us walk out of here," Miller whispered into his ear.

When Rand looked back, the black energy was gone, all of it having been absorbed inside Arthur. He went limp and his head sagged.

The chanting ceased all at once.

All the masked people watched Arthur in silence. Rand could hear his own heart thudding in his ears. Dipika had pressed her body against him, and he felt her trembling.

Nathan removed his mask, then let it fall to the floor with a loud clatter, all the while keeping his rapt attention focused on Arthur.

Arthur lifted his chin and peered at Nathan. His eyes had turned into pools of black.

Nathan held the demon's gaze, seemingly unafraid. "Vyraxus. You've been reunited with your old friend." His tone contained a slight mirth.

Arthur effortlessly broke out of the restraints that bound him to the chair with a Herculean strength Rand had seen many times before in those possessed. Now free, he rose.

"Everything is in place for the morning," Nathan said. "Bringing you here tonight was the final thing we had to do to prepare."

What's in place? Rand thought. He remembered Nathan mentioning earlier that he had a busy day ahead.

Arthur inspected his palm, then the back of his hand. He looked down at his legs and feet as if studying his new, temporary body.

"We meet again, Arthur Briggs." It sounded as if two voices came simultaneously from his throat—Arthur's natural voice was buried beneath an unnaturally deep, otherworldly one.

"I assumed you'd appreciate involving the old man," Nathan said. "He's a last-minute addition to the plan, but a good one, I think."

Rand was struck by how casually Nathan Bale spoke to the demon.

Arthur descended the steps from the raised platform. Vyraxus carried Arthur's body differently—his shoulders were no longer hunched and his limp was gone. He went to stand a few paces from Nathan. Given Arthur's short stature, the demon had to crane his head upward to meet Nathan's eyes.

"You are right," Arthur said. "But it is only a small detail. What about the most important thing? Have you determined a suitable sacrifice?"

Nathan grinned. "Of course."

Sacrifice? Rand thought. *If it isn't Arthur, who else could it be?* Then it struck him. *Me?*

Before, Jackson Herron had been instructed to sacrifice him. Were they coming after Rand again?

But those explanations weren't right. Something didn't quite add up.

Nathan told me I shouldn't have followed Arthur here,

Rand remembered. *That means I was never meant to be a part of whatever this is.*

Then, like a flash, it all came together in his mind. Rand now had a strong suspicion that he knew what was going on.

A killing ritual.

Rand retreated behind the column that hid him and planted his back against it. Sweat prickled on his forehead. Dipika looked sick. Miller's face was pulled into a fearful frown. Rand figured his friend had just put the pieces together as well.

He silently gestured that they needed to leave. Every moment they lingered increased the risk of them getting caught. Besides, Rand had seen and heard enough.

There needs to be a target for a killing ritual, he thought as he and the others quietly retreated from the underground chamber. *A suitable sacrifice, as Vyraxus said.*

Rand was pretty sure he knew who the "suitable sacrifice" was meant to be.

51

They scrambled up the spiral staircase. None of them spoke until they'd emerged into the hotel room.

"Rand, what..." Dipika wiped away the tears on her cheeks.

"It's Arun," Rand said. "They're going to fucking kill him."

"A killing ritual," Miller said as he shoved the mural back into place, seeming like he was trying to barricade in the evil he'd just witnessed.

"And they're using Arthur to do it," Rand said. "He'll take the fall for it."

"Rand, what—what are you talking about?" Dipika managed to ask, despite her shaky voice.

There was simply too much to explain. It would have to wait. "Arun said he knew he shouldn't have come to D.C. Now I know why. Can you call him again?"

Dipika immediately took out her phone, tapped the screen a couple of times, and handed it back to Rand.

Arun answered quickly. This time, he appeared nervous.

"Arun, you were right about not coming here," Rand said. "That event in the morning that Dipika told me about? You *can't* go. You'll be in danger if you do."

"Why?" Arun seemed almost ambivalent, as if he'd been warned of something similar a hundred times before and nothing bad had ever happened.

Rand sighed as he searched for the right words to explain himself and his dire warning. "Do you know a man named Nathan Bale?"

Arun looked away as shame slowly filled his eyes. Dipika's posture was rigid, clearly waiting for Arun's response.

"Yes." Arun breathed the word, as if admitting some kind of wrongdoing.

It shouldn't have been a surprise. Arun Singh, before his sudden rise to fame, had accomplished a lot in the tech world—surely earning him plenty of money. Wealthy people had a way of knowing each other. Rand had suspected Bill had known Jackson Herron, and he'd turned out to be correct.

"He's sponsoring the event," Arun said.

Rand exchanged a look with Miller.

"It's a setup, Arun," Rand said. "They're... going to do something to you. Trust me, Nathan Bale's *definitely* not your friend."

Dipika's face pinched, as if she might start crying again. Rand felt for her. Things were moving so fast, jerking her around like an old roller coaster on a rusted track, and he knew it just left her confused and afraid.

"I admit that I get a bad feeling from the man, but why would he want to hurt me?" Arun asked.

Because it's a killing ritual, Rand wanted to say, but he held back. Arun had said Nathan was sponsoring the event. That meant Nathan had chosen Arun as the sacrifice well in advance. It wasn't like Nathan was merely seizing the opportunity to kill a beloved celebrity who happened to visit the city. Nathan had planned and paid for the whole thing to lure Arun there.

But why Arun specifically?

A possible answer dawned on Rand. He cleared his throat. "Those kids you helped locate... what exactly did Tara show you? How did you know where to tell the police to look?"

Miller and Dipika both eyed Rand, waiting to see where he was going with this.

"I kept seeing visions of the church where they were discovered in my dreams," Arun said. "And hearing the cries of the children as if they were actually all around me." His voice was choked, as if the memory pained him. "I searched online and found photos that matched what I was dreaming."

As miraculous as it sounded, Rand knew it wasn't enough. "I read that the kids were in a secret basement underneath a church. How did you know it was there?"

Arun gently set his phone down, propping it upright on something atop the table at which he sat. With his hands free, he took a nearby pad of paper and a pen from his shirt pocket and started drawing.

"Besides the church, I saw something else. I told the police to look for this symbol." Arun tore the paper from the pad and held it up to his phone's camera.

The broken, uneven pentagram. The Bale symbol. It perfectly matched what had appeared on Arthur Briggs's front door.

Rand swallowed hard and turned the phone screen toward Miller, whose lips pressed into a thin, anxious line when he saw what Arun had drawn.

"Arun..." Rand began, although he had no idea how he was going to articulate this. He turned the camera back around to himself. "This will sound crazy... but Nathan Bale and his family had those children kidnapped."

Arun lowered the pentagram, revealing his face in the frame. His expression in that moment was unreadable. "Why?"

At least he isn't outright denying the possibility, Rand thought.

"I'm not sure," Rand said, "but I have a theory." He remembered Carmen Herron sprawled on the floor as Akhubel fed off her. "And I *do* know that Nathan and his family are involved in some very dark and evil things. Supernatural things."

"It's true, Arun," Dipika interjected. Rand turned the camera toward her so Arun could see the earnestness in her face. "I've seen a lot tonight." She sniffed in an attempt to bury the new tears. "More than I ever could've imagined. Rand's telling the truth."

Arun was quiet for a long time before he spoke, but eventually said, "Do you work often with these dark and evil things, Rand?"

At hearing his name, Rand once again turned the phone camera back onto himself. "Yes."

"Tell me. Do you feel fear?"

Rand wasn't sure where this was headed. "Of course."

"And what do you do when that happens?"

"I press on."

"Exactly. So you know that I have to do the same."

"But—"

"There are a lot of people who want to see me go away," Arun continued. "They didn't suddenly appear today, right before the ceremony. They've been there ever since those children were rescued. Many assume I'm trying to take credit for what the police did on their own. Others think I only knew the location because I was somehow involved in the abduction."

Rand remembered reading about those opinions of Arun in the media.

"Some of these people lurk in the shadows, while some shake my hand and smile to my face," Arun continued. "I know that, but I can't let them intimidate me. I can't let them win. For those who believe in me, for the kids we've made a difference for, I have to stand my ground. And even if I'm afraid sometimes, I break through that fear and do what's necessary to push back against the evil in our world."

Rand took a steadying breath. He understood where Arun was coming from, but the other man was missing the point. It seemed like he was going to need to hear all the details in order to be convinced.

"I'm not talking about social-media trolls," Rand said. "I'm talking about a very large and well-connected network of people who have sold their souls to demons in exchange for power. Nathan Bale is one of them, which is why you get a bad feeling from him. That symbol you just drew? That's some sort of crest or emblem for his family.

Those children *belonged* to them. They were probably going to sacrifice them to their demons."

Despite the supposed insanity of what Rand was saying, Arun didn't react.

"You messed that up for them," Rand pressed on. "Now they're mad. Trust me. I know, because I've pissed them off too. I interrupted one of their rituals recently and that's how I learned all of this. Nathan offered to sponsor this event for you because they're planning what they call a killing ritual. That means they're going to assassinate you in a high-profile way. Demons feed off of negative emotions, so it's in their interest to generate as much negativity as they can. The very public murder of someone as positive and benevolent as you is *precisely* what they want."

There it was. Everything was laid out. Arun, to his credit, had patiently listened to every word. There weren't many people who would have done the same.

"I believe you, Rand, I do," Arun said. "But I have to say this. It seems like you and I have the same philosophy: the evil in this world must be confronted with as much strength and fearlessness as we can muster, otherwise it will run rampant. Evil thrives on the inaction of the masses."

"You can still confront evil, but can you just... *not* do it tomorrow?" Rand asked—he could hear his own desperation.

"There'll be a lot of people there who need to hear what I'm going to say." Arun almost muttered the words derisively under his breath.

"What's *that* supposed to mean?" Dipika asked, taking a step closer to Rand.

"Let's say I skip the ceremony," Arun said, ignoring Dipika. "What then? Won't these people just come after me later?"

"Maybe, but—"

"I appreciate that you are afraid for me, Rand," Arun said. "But remember how we're meant to handle fear."

Rand faltered, forced to reflect on his self-doubt. Never before had he approached any supernatural situation with failure as an option, yet this time he was. Entertaining the possibility of failure almost always manifested that very outcome.

Fear. He was afraid. After all he'd witnessed and experienced recently, Rand realized he felt smaller than he'd ever felt in his life. Usually, his cases were one-on-one confrontations with a single demon. Now, he was up against a potent network of corrupt elites and their powerful demons. For the first time, it seemed that the work he had to do was too great for one man. The past couple of days and nights had proven to him that he was far out of his league.

And my immediate instinct is to run, Rand thought. He hung his head.

Adding insult to injury, he realized that he wasn't going to convince Arun.

"In light of all these new developments, Dipika, I think it's best if you don't come in the morning," Arun said. "I'm sorry you traveled all this way for me. I'll make it up to you soon. I promise."

"Arun, please listen to Rand," Dipika pleaded.

"I'll tell you what, Rand," Arun said. "I meant what I said about facing evil, but at the same time, that doesn't mean I won't take some precautions." He glanced at his watch. "There's still time for me to make arrangements. I'll hire a private security team. Also, I'll only be present long enough to give my speech. I'll fly in by helicopter, go on stage to say what I need to, and then immediately fly away."

Rand slowly shook his head. "I... don't think that'll be good enough, Arun." Arthur came to mind, possessed by a powerful demonic entity. Regardless, he knew there wasn't much else he could say. Arun had made his decision.

"I have to make some phone calls. It was nice to finally speak with you, Rand."

With that, Arun Singh hung up.

52

Silence lingered between the three of them.

Dipika broke it first. "Did I mention that Arun can be stubborn? He's been that way since we were kids."

"This is more than stubborn." Rand handed the phone back to her. "This is *stupidity*. Sorry to be blunt."

"I agree with you," Dipika said.

"So what do we do?" Miller asked.

Dipika looked at Rand expectantly, also interested in the answer.

"We have to go to the event tomorrow and stop the killing ritual from happening," Rand said.

"I knew that much," Miller said. "I meant more specifically. We don't know *how* Nathan is planning to... do it." He glanced at Dipika as he carefully chose his words.

Rand didn't have the energy to be as delicate. "You're right. He could have Arthur use a gun, a bomb, poison..."

Dipika shook her head with an anguished expression.

Rand wondered if he could've learned more details if

he'd stayed behind in the underground chamber longer, but he'd also known he had to get out of there while he still had a chance.

"What can I do?" Dipika asked. Her fear seemed to have been replaced by some semblance of resolve.

Rand hesitated. It was only natural that Dipika wanted to help save her friend when he was in danger, but Rand couldn't shake the feeling that involving her further was wrong.

If I'm in over my head, then she's definitely way *in over hers,* he thought.

"Maybe it's... best if you don't come," Rand said.

Dipika's defiance rose even before all the words had left his mouth. "No. I'm going to help."

"Dipika, these people—"

"I know. I've seen what they do." She gestured toward the painting, seeming to indicate the ritual they'd witnessed in the chamber beyond it. "I don't care. I want to protect Arun."

Rand sighed. Arguing with her wasn't worth the energy. It seemed none of them—Miller, Dipika, Arun, or himself—were willing to stand by and let evil succeed.

"What time's the event?" Miller asked Dipika.

"Admission starts at ten-thirty," Dipika said. "Arun was scheduled to give his speech at noon." Something occurred to her. "What if they try to attack Arun before then?" Dipika asked. "It seems strange for us to just wait around."

"We have to wait because they're going to wait too," Rand explained. "This ritual needs to happen in front of a lot of people. All eyes need to be on Arun."

Dipika seemed to accept that, albeit reluctantly.

"If it doesn't open till ten-thirty, then that means we have a few hours," Miller said. "Maybe we should all try to get some rest. If that's even possible."

Rand already knew it wouldn't be.

———

DESPITE IT BEING AGREED upon that they'd take a break, no one seemed interested—or able.

Miller climbed into the king-size bed, his back against the cushioned headboard, open laptop resting on his thighs. The glow of the screen lit up his face and reflected in his glasses.

Dipika sat at the desk in the far corner of the room. Nearby was the old rotary phone Rand had answered earlier. She leaned forward, chin propped on her palm as she peered out of the floor-to-ceiling window.

Rand wondered what was running through her mind. The quiet moments were always when his own negative thoughts came crashing in like waves.

He went and stood just over her shoulder. "You okay?"

"Ask me again tomorrow," she said without turning around.

He strived to come up with something to tell her that would put her at ease. "The demon who tried to take you is gone," Rand said, though he already knew it was a weak attempt. "It should be safe for you to go back to your own hotel. You might be more comfortable—"

Dipika swirled in the chair and gave him an incredulous look. "You *really* think I want to be alone after all this?"

"Fair enough." Something else occurred to him. "I'm

sorry I scared you earlier. By calling you in the middle of the night and freaking you out."

"Are you serious? I *wish* the only thing I had to worry about right now was an insane, creepy colleague. *That* I could deal with."

Rand had to chuckle. "Yeah, I guess. One quick call to the Dean, tell him I was harassing you, and I'd be out on my ass."

Pretty sure most of the other teachers in the Religious Studies department would be happy to see me go, he thought. Before, he would've put Dipika in that category, but he wondered if that was still the case.

"How's the Dean going to help me from sixteen hours away?" Dipika asked. "I was ready to handle you myself." She reached into her jacket pocket and withdrew a palm-sized canister of pepper spray. She placed it upright on the desk, as if presenting it to Rand.

Rand could only chuckle and shake his head. "You came prepared, I see."

She then reached into the other pocket and pulled out a handheld Taser and set it next to the pepper spray.

Rand stared at the metallic, menacing prongs. "Very prepared, actually."

"I trusted you, but not *that* much."

"What about now?"

Dipika softened as she thought it over. "Completely." She shook her head. "This is what you do regularly? When you're not teaching?"

"Not quite," Rand said. "Things being this intense is new to me."

Dipika dropped her gaze as she considered that. Rand could tell she hadn't been comforted by those words.

Unfortunately, it's the truth, he thought.

"Do you think we can actually save him?" she asked.

Rand's decision to go to the event had been made so quickly that he hadn't taken the time to consider his odds of success. Sometimes, that wasn't beneficial because it ultimately didn't matter. He still had to try, even if the odds were low.

"I do," he finally said.

"I do, too." Dipika tore her eyes from Rand and looked back out the window. The first rays of daylight were chasing away the night as the sun began to rise over the city.

53

The next morning dawned clear and with a blue sky. Rand felt like it had been forever since he'd last seen the sun. He wished he could take that as a good omen, but he couldn't. The darkest of deeds could be committed on the brightest of days.

The traffic thickened as they neared Willow Creek Park, the large outdoor area where the Bring Our Children Home event was being held. Rand drove while Dipika rode in the passenger seat, Miller in the back.

Many finely dressed people were on foot, clearly having parked far away.

"We're going to have to get out and walk," Rand said. "Arun draws a crowd."

"I didn't know it would be like this," Dipika said.

The more eyes, the better for Nathan, Rand thought grimly.

"You two go, and I'll find a place to park," Miller said. "Then I'll meet you."

"Good idea." Rand and Dipika got out of the Jeep

while Miller quickly transitioned from the backseat to the driver's seat. He drove off, and Rand and Dipika fell in with the rest of the crowd walking toward the park.

Rand watched her out of the corner of his eye. She'd traveled to D.C. thinking this would be a joyous occasion to celebrate her lifelong friend and his accomplishments. Now she looked around suspiciously, unsure of everyone. Worry marred her face.

She'd been through a lot the last several hours, having both seen and heard things she probably would've preferred to remain ignorant of. Dipika had every right to flee from him and the situation, yet she was still there, believing him and ready to support him.

Rand placed his hand on her arm, interrupting her thoughts. "Don't worry. We're going to help him." As he said the words, he tried hard to believe them himself. Dipika didn't seem reassured.

A line of people had formed in front of a booth at the park's entrance. Attendees showed their invitations on their phones to a well-dressed lady, who scanned them with a barcode reader. A burly security guard stood nearby, looking over the woman's shoulder. Rand wondered if he was part of the team Arun promised he was going to hire.

Rand and Dipika fell in line with other men and women wearing crisp suits and colorful dresses. The pair's casual clothes made them stand out. Rand had finally had time to change into the second pair of jeans he'd packed and a clean t-shirt, but he hadn't brought anything formal. Dipika had a dress for the event, but she'd left it at her hotel.

Dipika pulled up her invitation on her phone. "We're

lucky that Arun gave me a plus one," she said as the line progressed. The barcode reader chirped loudly with each ticket scanned. "I told him I wasn't bringing a date and that he should give that spot to someone else, but he insisted I keep it, just in case."

When it was their turn, Dipika turned her screen to face the woman, who aimed the red laser light over the barcode. It blurted an obtrusive noise that was unlike the ones it had made before.

"Oops." The woman pointed her machine away for a second, and then tried scanning the code again. It gave the same sound. She set the scanner down on a nearby table and picked up a tablet. She squinted through her glasses as she read the barcode number of Dipika's invitation and manually typed it into the device. The security guard beside her seemed displeased by the interruption.

"Uh oh," the woman said, sounding disappointed. "It seems your invitation was recently rescinded."

"*Rescinded?*" Dipika said. "That's a mistake."

The woman checked her tablet's screen again and regretfully shook her head. "I'm afraid it's not."

"No." Dipika's voice rose slightly. The guard unfolded his arms. "Arun Singh is a personal friend of mine, he wouldn't do that."

"Damn it," Rand said as it occurred to him what happened. He whispered into Dipika's ear. "Arun probably *did* cancel your ticket. He told us not to come, remember?"

Dipika paused when she realized that was likely the case, but was no less displeased—or ready to give up. To the woman, she said, "I have the invitation right here, for me and a guest."

The security guard put himself in front of the woman. "Ma'am," he said, a warning edge in his tone.

Rand also took a half step forward, mind racing for something to say. They *needed* to get into the park, regardless of whether Arun wanted them there or not.

A second guard swiftly joined the first, seemingly coming out of nowhere. His suit matched his colleague's, and he was much larger. He towered over Rand.

Rand was appalled at how fast backup had arrived without having to be called. The two of them hadn't even been causing a scene.

I suppose if Arun's paying top dollar for these guys, then this is how he expects them to operate, he thought.

Rand looked up at the second guard and had to shield his eyes from the sun. His insides froze when he recognized the man's face.

Him?

The same man who'd served as a bodyguard for Deckard Arcan, the unscrupulous pastor who'd allowed himself to be possessed by a demon.

Hoby. That was his name.

He'd kidnapped Libby so she could be married off the Deckard's weasel of an assistant. That had been months ago, but Rand would never forget what Hoby had done.

Rand felt his face twist into a fierce glare. Any desire to reason with the ticket-scanning woman was suddenly gone. His fists clenched as his anger blazed.

Dipika glanced between Rand and Hoby, likely detecting the sudden, intense energy.

Hoby broke his gaze. He leaned down and whispered something into his colleague's ear.

"You sure, boss?"

Hoby gave a terse nod, then turned and walked away. Rand watched his broad back as the man fell in with a crowd of people, his head towering above them all.

"Move on through," the first guard said, standing aside so both Rand and Dipika could enter.

Rand barely heard him. He was too busy glaring at Hoby.

"Rand," Dipika prodded, taking his arm and lightly pulling him past the entrance booth.

He got us in, Rand thought. *But... why?*

"Friend of yours?" Dipika asked.

"Something like that." Rand scanned the grounds, looking for where Hoby had gone, but he'd lost sight of the guard.

Rand hadn't satisfactorily settled the score with Hoby. They'd briefly fought that night in Deckard's mansion, but when the demon Hazul had revealed himself, Hoby had fled in fear. Perhaps it was for the best he'd walked off—the man was almost twice Rand's size. Still, that was irrelevant to Rand. He felt an irrational surge of confidence at the incendiary memory of Hoby and Libby.

Focus, Rand told himself. *He's not the reason I'm here.*

But a hollow feeling formed in his chest when a realization dawned on him. Knowing Hoby's past client, it wouldn't surprise Rand if Hoby had somehow gotten involved with Nathan Bale.

Which means this security team that Arun hired might not be loyal to him, Rand thought grimly. He sighed. Dipika was already worried enough, and he hated to give her more bad news.

"You need to text Arun," Rand said.

Her eyes snapped to him. "What for?"

"Tell him the security is very likely working for Nathan."

Dipika set her jaw and searched his face for any sign that he might be mistaken. "Does this have something to do with that guy back there?"

"Yes."

"But if he's with Nathan, then why did he let us in?"

"I don't know." *And that scares me,* he wanted to add, but refrained.

Dipika took out her phone and started tapping out the message. "He also said he was going to fly in by helicopter. You think that'll be compromised too?"

Rand sensed that it was a rhetorical question, but nonetheless couldn't dismiss the possibility.

All around, the philanthropists and their friends, guests, and colleagues were smiling and laughing— enjoying the day while anticipating hearing from the country's newest sensation. White tents had been erected on the grounds, like a medieval army encampment. Balloons and ribbons attached to the tents swayed in the light breeze. Tables draped in silver linen sported pans of catered food.

Children played nearby, the boys wearing clip-on bow ties and the girls in floral, frilly dresses. They laughed and called out to each other as they ran around the area. A band performed on a small stage to the left.

Toward the rear of the grounds, a raised platform had been set up. There was a podium and a single row of chairs behind it. More chairs arranged in rows, like soldiers, faced the main stage. All of them were empty, but he knew they'd be filled once the man of the hour arrived. Above was a massive banner that read BRING OUR CHILDREN HOME. On either side of the words was the organization's logo: an emblem of Earth flanked by two sets of open palms—one large and the other small —to symbolize adults and children, respectively.

Several video cameras were positioned in strategic spots, aimed at the stage. The film crew that would likely operate them later were currently milling about.

Of course it's going to be televised, Rand thought. Now that he knew the plan, Rand could see the makings of television history unfolding—Arun Singh's murder would be seen live by *thousands* of people.

Dotted amongst the guests were the suited guards. They surveyed the event with stoic faces, occasionally speaking into their earpieces.

"I can't believe Arun would cancel my invitation," Dipika said.

"He's only doing what he thinks is best for you," Rand said, trying to reassure her.

"I know. But I wish he would do what was best for *him.*" Dipika let out a scornful breath. "Anyway. We're here. What's the plan?"

"Still formulating it," Rand said. That wasn't quite the truth—it would've been more accurate to say he was making things up as he went.

He once again scanned the crowds. Everything and everyone seemed so benign. It was hard to imagine a demon-possessed Arthur lurking among the guests.

"Arthur will show up at some point, if I'm right about what they're planning to do," Rand said. "We need to keep an eye out for—"

"Nice day, isn't it?" came a familiar voice from behind Rand. His body went rigid. He felt Dipika also freeze beside him.

I should've known it wouldn't take long.

54

Rand pivoted. Behind him, Nathan Bale flashed his easy smile. He wore an impeccable black suit, which helped him blend in with the rest of the attendees. Just over his shoulder, perhaps ten strides away, was a stoic-looking security guard. His uniform matched the others on his team. His gaze casually scanned his surroundings, but Rand wasn't fooled; the man's attention was diligently focused on his boss.

What unsettled Rand the most was that Nathan shouldn't have been expecting him there at all, but nonetheless almost seemed happy to see him.

Maybe he had a way of listening in on our conversation in the hotel room last night, Rand thought. That wouldn't be too far outside the realm of possibility.

"Walk with me, Randolph." Without waiting for a response, Nathan strode past Rand and Dipika, and the bodyguard started to follow.

Dipika gave Rand a questioning look.

"Give me a minute," Rand told her. He felt like he

didn't have the option to refuse. He fell in beside Nathan, who strolled forward at a casual pace.

It *was* nice out, as Nathan had said. Yet despite the sunlight warming the clear winter day, tension prickled beneath Rand's skin. The foreboding energy was thick around him, and he wondered if anyone else was picking up on it.

"You couldn't bother to put on a suit?" Nathan said. "Yesterday evening you had an excuse because you'd just arrived in town. But you've had plenty of time to clean yourself up since then. I should be embarrassed to be seen with you."

Rand said nothing. He was quickly realizing that Nathan Bale enjoyed a little fluff talk before getting to the point.

"So who's the girl?" Nathan asked.

Rand felt his hackles rise. The question sounded innocently inquisitive, but Rand detected something sadistic buried deep underneath Nathan's honeyed tone.

"She's no one."

"You might as well be honest with me, because I already know." Nathan drew his phone from his tuxedo coat pocket, tapped the screen, and put it to his ear. "My five o'clock. Woman wearing jeans and a leather jacket. Looks to me to be of South Indian descent. Keep an eye on her as well."

Rand halted and turned to face Nathan fully. "She doesn't have anything to do with this. Leave her out of it."

Nathan mirrored Rand, staring back at him without fear. "She *didn't* have anything to do with this until you decided to follow Arthur here. So I sent Janet after your little girlfriend to teach you a lesson about minding your own business."

Janet? Rand tried to place the name, but came up empty—until a second later. "The Bagged Woman," the words escaped his mouth.

Nathan gave a nod, as if impressed. "We just called her Janet. You *really* need to work on your nicknames, Randolph. They're too literal, don't you think?"

Rand's anger flared at remembering Dipika's shrieks from the night before as the Bagged Woman had tried to carry her off. He glanced back at her. She still stood where they'd left her, alone. Her hands worked together worriedly in front of her stomach.

"You're thinking too much," Nathan said. "You don't need to worry about it now. But did you have to hurt Janet like that? She was only doing her job."

With a gentle prod on Rand's arm, Nathan urged him to keep walking.

"You saw things last night that you weren't supposed to see, Randolph," Nathan said—an icy wave coursed through Rand's insides. "Though I have to commend you. Most people would've had a breakdown after witnessing something like that. I'm surprised your girlfriend is still hanging around with you."

He knew I was there the whole time, Rand thought as he swallowed the lump in his throat. *I should've known.*

"Because of what you saw, and since you aren't stupid by any stretch of the imagination, I have a pretty good idea as to why you're here."

Nathan waved at a man standing amidst a group of people, who returned the gesture with a smile. Rand thought he recognized him from television.

"That's Senator William Collinsworth," Nathan said. "He once confessed to my father that he was willing to leave his wife to marry my sister, but Dad declined his offer."

Rand had to wonder how tight of a grip Bernard held over his family. Nathan had mentioned before that his father had picked out a businessman from Hong Kong for Miranda, now that Jackson was dead. Everything they did was pre-planned and executed for their maximum benefit.

Rand quickly checked Nathan's ring finger; he wore a simple gold band.

He's married too. How many kids is he raising to carry on the interests of his family?

Their stroll was interrupted by a group of people headed the opposite way. A tall woman, made even taller by her heels, smiled and waved at Nathan.

"Good morning, Vee," Nathan said, his tone switching instantly to something friendlier..

"Hey Nate." The woman had to bend her knees slightly to give Nathan a quick hug and a kiss on the cheek. She held a flute of sparkling champagne. "Wasn't sure I'd see you here. You never got back to me."

"I wasn't aware you called," Nathan said with a smirk and a nonchalant shrug. "I'll have to fire my assistant."

Vee rolled her eyes playfully. "Whatever. Is your sister here?"

"Unfortunately not. She's been busy with some other things lately."

Rand's jaw grew tight. Those "other things" were tormenting Libby.

"That's too bad," the woman said. "Tell her I said hello."

"Will do."

She caught up with her friends and continued on.

"Veronica Donovan," Nathan explained. "CEO of WorldLife Pharmaceuticals. I know you've heard of it."

The name did ring a bell.

"Dad's on the board of directors. He's the reason why her company went from her garage to international so quickly. Journalists and TV hosts salivate over her—a determined woman from a humble upbringing who built her empire from scratch. Well, between you and me, what's fed to the public isn't... quite true. My dad had a significant role, but as I'm sure you've noticed, he doesn't like to stand in front and take all the credit. People around the world are inspired by her story, and she helms a massive corporation Dad can easily influence. Everyone wins."

Rand could only wonder how extensive the Bale family's reach was. *I almost don't want to know,* he thought.

"What were we talking about?" Nathan continued. "Ah, yes. So about what you saw last night..."

Nathan paused as his gaze dropped to the ground, searching for the precise words he wanted. He then looked Rand straight in the eyes. "I'd like to encourage you to not do anything stupid. This is just some friendly advice. I know you think that after everything that happened with my sister and her husband that you're somehow in the middle of some grand scheme. But Randolph... I mentioned this last night, but it bears repeating: you're not as important as you think you are.

No offense, but we have other, more significant things to worry about right now."

"Like Arthur," Rand said, his glare unyielding.

"Exactly." Nathan sighed. "As far as *I'm* concerned, he's a washed-up old man. He would've eventually drank himself to death in that shit town where you dug him up. But we have certain *partners* who very much want to see him punished for the things he's done in the past."

"Partners like that demon you allowed to possess him," Rand said.

"Yes. Vyraxus."

"And you'll use Arthur to kill Arun. And as far as the world is concerned, Arun Singh was murdered by a random, unhinged lunatic."

"That *is* the narrative that'll be crafted, yes," Nathan said. "You'll learn that the narrative is more relevant than the truth."

"This isn't just about the narrative, or even about Arun," Rand said, voice rising. "You want the collective *energy* from all the people who will witness this. Because this isn't just a murder. It's a killing ritual."

Something fleeting crossed Nathan's face, but Rand had been looking for it, so he caught it—the same surprise that Nathan had revealed the night before when Miller mentioned the tesseract.

"I hope you learned a lot from Arthur when you had the chance," Nathan said. "I have a feeling you won't be hearing much from him again."

"You're a psychopath," Rand snarled.

Nathan smirked. "I've been called worse. But I see all this as a very pragmatic way to live."

A distant thrum grew increasingly louder until it

drew Rand's attention upward. A silver helicopter cut across the sky, flying low.

Nathan shielded his eyes from the sun. "And that'll be our friend. He's chosen to travel in style for his final moments."

The chopper leveled out and slowly descended into a clear, flat area about fifty feet away from the stage. Nearly everyone at the event also watched the helicopter land, many of them filming it with their phones.

I didn't think about cell phones, Rand thought. Surely tons of people in the crowd were planning to record Arun's entire speech. Even if mainstream television networks decided Arun's murder was too gruesome to air after it was first caught live, the cell-phone videos would be circulated around endlessly.

Nathan shifted his attention back to Rand. "Enjoy the show, my friend. I'll see you soon."

With that, Nathan turned and walked away. He fell into a crowd of people he knew, shaking their hands and saying something that made the group laugh as if it was the funniest thing they'd heard all week.

55

Once Nathan was gone, Dipika returned to Rand's side. "That was the guy from the underground room last night, right?"

"Yeah." Rand nodded toward where the helicopter had landed.

"What did he want?"

"Basically, he knows we saw everything and also knows why we're here today."

That seemed to make Dipika sick. "Who are these people, Rand?"

"To be honest, I'm... still figuring that out myself." He looked back at the rear area of the park. The helicopter was no longer visible, blocked from view by the crowds. "Let's see if we can get Arun's attention. One last-ditch effort to talk him out of this."

They maneuvered through the throng of spectators that had gathered around the helicopter's landing site, shouldering their way past and pushing toward the front.

Security had set up a perimeter to prevent the crowd from getting too close.

The helicopter door slid and open and a burly man dressed in the security team's same suit was the first to disembark. The morning sunlight reflected off his thick sunglasses. Next came Arun Singh. People clapped and cheered, and he acknowledged them with a warm smile.

Dipika waved in his direction, though Arun didn't spot her among the crowd. He disappeared into a nearby private tent behind the stage.

"He didn't see me," Dipika said.

A woman emerged from the tent that Arun had just entered. White hair framed her face, and she wore a tailored, deep-burgundy tailored blazer with a silver brooch pinned at her left shoulder. She tread over the grass carefully in her dark heels before walking up the small set of steps on the side of the stage.

"Something's happening," Rand said.

The woman went to stand behind the microphone and, as if on cue, the band on the far end of the park stopped playing mid-song.

She gently tapped the microphone to make sure it was on. The muffled *thump* confirmed it, so she leaned in close. "Ladies and gentlemen." Despite her confident demeanor, she seemed a bit unsure, as if she were about to deliver some bad news. "There has been a *slight* change in schedule." She forced a smile, as if trying to force it to not be a big deal. "It seems Mr. Singh has suddenly been needed elsewhere this morning. However, he didn't want to cancel last minute. So, you will hear from him now instead of at the previously scheduled time."

There were murmurs among the crowd. Rand

couldn't tell if people were disappointed at the change, or happy to get what they came for sooner. The camera operators sprung into action, caught off guard now that their job was starting earlier than anticipated.

"I'll only be present long enough to give my speech." Rand remembered Arun's promise, his attempt at compromise.

"I know not everyone who was invited has arrived yet," the woman went on, "but these are the circumstances. I think we're all grateful Mr. Singh was able to make it here at all. So if you could all take your seats and gather round, then we can hear from the man of the hour."

"In and out, just like he planned," Rand said as the crowd around him shifted all at once, moving toward the stage and rushing to claim the spots closest to the front.

"Do you think maybe the early start will throw off the plan?" Dipika asked, a hopeful edge in her voice.

Despite the hundreds of people in the vicinity, Rand caught sight of Nathan Bale, as if his attention were instinctively drawn to the man. He stood just behind the final row of seats that had been set up to face the stage and was focused on his phone, tapping out a message. He seemed calm and unperturbed by the change.

"I don't think so," Rand said.

"Then what do we do?"

Rand's phone vibrated in his pocket. It was a text from Miller.

'Arthur's here.'

56

Miller drove Rand's Jeep through bumper-to-bumper congestion on the narrow roads surrounding Willow Creek Park. It had been at least half an hour since he'd split up from Rand and Dipika, maybe even longer.

I'll miss everything before I even find a place to park, Miller thought.

He'd almost decided to abandon Rand's Jeep in a no-parking zone and risk having it towed when he spotted a patch of grass a few other cars had used for overflow parking. To his relief, there was just enough space for him to fit.

He killed the engine and looked around, not quite sure where exactly he was in relation to the event. He'd made so many turns while searching for a place to park that he'd lost his bearings.

I can just follow the crowd, he decided. *They'll lead me there.*

A familiar figure sauntered past the windshield.

Arthur Briggs.

Miller only caught a brief glimpse of him before the old man blended in with the crowd.

The sighting stunned Miller, sending a chill through him. He snatched up his phone from the center console and shot off a quick text to Rand.

'Arthur's here.'

Taking a deep breath, Miller exited the Jeep and hurried in the direction he'd seen Arthur go, hustling to catch up. He only had to push through a few groups of people before spotting the leather jacket again. Because of the entity within him, Arthur seemed to glide with an uncharacteristic, uncanny grace through the crowds.

'I don't like being followed,' a voice suddenly resonated inside Miller's mind, a direct telepathic communication. A prickle crawled up his arms, and he halted. Miller knew in theory that demons often communicated telepathically, but he'd never experienced it himself. It was a stark reminder that he'd given up operating completely behind the scenes when it came to Rand's work.

Miller composed himself and kept following.

'Let what you witness today be a lesson to you,' the voice continued. *'This is what happens when you interfere.'*

Interfere? Miller thought, but then realized Vyraxus was not talking about him—the demon was talking about *Arthur*, and what Arthur had done in the past.

Arthur veered to the left, moving against the human tide. Miller twisted and turned as he dodged the clusters of people walking the other direction, his shoulder lightly glancing off several of the well-dressed guests.

"I just got a text from Paul," a woman said to her companion as she passed Miller. "Apparently Arun's speaking *now* instead of at noon. Some sort of last-minute change. We need to walk faster."

'Arthur Briggs has had this coming for a while,' the voice kept going in Miller's head. *'He has involved himself in our affairs for far too long.'*

Unlike Miller, Arthur made no effort to sidestep the people. He thrust his shoulder into anyone who got in his way like a bully walking down a high school corridor. Those shoved cast bewildered and incredulous glares at Arthur's back.

The man strode forth into a large group, who parted around Arthur and reassembled once he'd passed, causing Miller to lose sight of him. Miller frantically scanned the crowd, standing on his toes as he tried to spot Arthur again.

Miller picked up the pace. A few minutes later, the crowd thinned when Miller came to an area a ways off from the park's entrance. Several vans and trucks were parked nearby, branded by logos that suggested to Miller they belonged to the day's service providers: catering, music, and other logistics. Despite being away from the masses, Miller still couldn't see where Arthur had gone.

He disappeared, he thought, his heart sinking.

'Not quite.'

The voice jolted Miller and he whirled around. Arthur had reappeared behind him, now glaring at him with pure-black eyes.

Miller's face flushed and his temples pulsed. Despite having followed Arthur for the last couple of minutes, he instinctively wanted to put as much distance between himself and the demon-possessed old man as he could.

Arthur lashed out before Miller could react, pressing

his hand hard into the center of Miller's gut—right where the Bagged Woman had clawed gashes into his flesh. Burning pain surged from the wounds.

Arthur pushed Miller back and sent him stumbling, taking quick steps so as not to topple over. The man then forced Miller up against the side of one of the trucks, where he *clanged* loudly against the vehicle. Arthur continued to drive his hand into Miller's stomach as if trying to impale him with his forearm. Miller gripped Arthur's wrist with both of his hands, tried to pry him away, but the possessed man was too strong.

'I must thank you for revealing Arthur's location to us.'

Arthur twisted his palm against Miller's wound, making the pain flare once again.

Why did I follow him? The thought banged around in his head like an alarm, as if his survival instinct was scolding him. Pinned down, he couldn't hope to overcome the demon. There wasn't even anyone close by to see what was happening. *He lured me here.*

Then Arthur pulled his hand away from Miller's stomach.

'Go and watch. You're a part of this ritual too.'

With that, Arthur launched himself onto the roof of a nearby van with superhuman strength. He leapfrogged from one vehicle to the next, displaying an agility incongruous with Arthur's frail external appearance. He eventually disappeared from Miller's sight atop a large, big-rig truck.

Miller's chest heaved as the fear dissipated from his body. *He wants me to witness Arun's death,* he thought. *To feed off my negative emotions along with everyone else's.*

In a way, Miller figured his grief would be far more

potent than most who saw the killing ritual. Since he knew about the plan and wanted to prevent it, failure would cause even deeper despair.

He took out his phone and sent Rand another message.

'He's coming inside and so am I.'

57

"Miller says Arthur's here," Rand said.

"He'll be hard to spot with all these people," Dipika said, looking around.

"But we know exactly where he's going." Rand turned toward the stage. Three of Nathan Bale's muscular brutes had planted themselves in front of it like security at a concert. With that impenetrable barrier in place, Rand wouldn't be able to get close.

After being prompted by the announcement, the seats facing the stage had filled up fast. There weren't enough to accommodate all those in attendance, so those who hadn't claimed a chair were forced to stand behind the last row of seats. The video camera operators were in position, checking their frames one final time. The silver-haired woman patiently waited at the podium as the attendees got situated. Behind her, four other people now occupied the chairs on the stage, likely other executives of the Bring Our Children Home organization.

Rand and Dipika had positioned themselves on the

outskirts of the crowd, affording them a better vantage of the entire scene. Rand internally debated with himself if he should move closer, but being trapped in the dense mass of people would limit his ability to react quickly.

The clamor started to die down.

"Thank you all for your cooperation," the woman began, "and once more, I apologize for the unexpected change." She cleared her throat and smiled. "Good morning. I'm Lesley Reisser, executive director of Bring Our Children Home." A smattering of applause broke out. "Today we're here to honor a man who needs no introduction. Arun Singh."

The crowd applauded again, this time far more powerful.

"I'll never forget waking up to the news of twenty-seven children having been successfully rescued from their captors. These children were given a second chance at life." Lesley Reisser intermittently referred to her notes as she spoke. "Over my decades of work, I've seen first-hand the devastation that child abduction inflicts on a family, a community, and even our nation. Sadly, many of these cases go unresolved. But today, we're here to honor a man who has single-handedly shifted that balance. So without further ado, I'd like to introduce one of our country's newest heroes, Arun Singh."

Arun received a standing ovation as he walked onto the stage. He had to wait at the podium for a long while, just to give the thunderous clapping time to die down. Rand could see the anxiety behind Arun's eyes, even from afar.

Dipika stood beside Rand with her arms crossed, watching Arun with a mixture of nervousness and sadness. Rand knew this was supposed to have been a happy occasion for her. She'd traveled there to celebrate her lifelong friend, and instead, things had taken an abrupt and terrifying turn.

Arun adjusted the microphone nearer to his mouth. "I'm honored and moved by that welcome. Thank you." He paused before continuing, "The horrific plight that faces the world's children is unseen to most as we go about our everyday lives. Evil people who seek to exploit these vulnerable members of our society know this very well, and they operate almost out in the open with impunity. Unfortunately, many of us do not have the eyes to see it all for what it truly is." Arun let a heavy and poignant silence ripple through the crowd as they anticipated where he was going next. "There are plenty of you who are ostensibly here today because you support the rescue of these endangered children. But to those same people, you need to take a hard look in the mirror and be honest with yourself. Is what you're doing *really* for the benefit of humanity? Or are you contributing to the problems that we have gathered here to address?"

The silence shifted to one of awkwardness. Rand felt the heavy tension grow. Some in the crowd kept their eyes on Arun, while others looked down at their laps. A few glanced around, as if wondering who exactly Arun was referring to.

Is he calling them out? Rand wondered. He remembered what Arun had said the night before. *"There'll be a lot of people there tomorrow who need to hear what I'm going to say."*

Nathan Bale had definitely been responsible for the kidnapped children Arun had helped locate. Rand found himself wondering, how many others who were there at this event also had their hands in similar activities?

His phone suddenly buzzed again with a message from Miller. Dipika kept her eyes glued on him as he read it.

'He's coming inside and so am I.'

"Looks like it's go time." Rand tucked his phone back into his pocket. "I'm going to see if I can get past those guards and make it closer to the stage."

"But there's three of them," Dipika said.

"I know, but—"

Rand became aware of an imposing presence just over his shoulder—Hoby. Dipika gasped, startled by the sudden appearance of the large man. Rand took Dipika by the elbow and shifted her behind him.

Nathan must have told him to keep me from doing anything, Rand thought. He clenched his jaw as he felt what little hope he had crash through the floor.

Arun continued his speech, but Rand was too focused on this new threat to hear what he was saying.

"Come," Hoby said in his baritone voice.

"Fuck off," Rand spat. Dipika widened her eyes, clearly unsure of his decision to be so aggressive. However, Hoby didn't seem put off by Rand's defiance. "Don't think I've forgotten about what you—"

"You'll need my help to save him."

58

Rand blinked as his mind raced to process what the man had just said. "What?"

Hoby held Rand's gaze, his expression stony and neutral. "You're here to save him, aren't you?" He nodded toward Arun.

A few seconds passed before Rand managed a response. "Yes." The word was hesitant, as if he were admitting a secret.

"Then come with me. I can get you close."

Rand and Dipika exchanged a glance. She gave a near imperceptible yet desperate nod. She didn't understand his and Hoby's history; she only saw an opportunity.

Rand sensed he had mere seconds to decide if he was going to trust this man who'd once kidnapped his daughter.

Is it a trick? It has to be...

"Alright," Rand finally said, the decision mostly urged by Dipika's sudden flash of hope. Hoby went around them and started walking toward the stage. "Wait here," Rand told Dipika.

He caught up to Hoby, who easily parted the standing crowd that formed a semicircle at the backs of the chairs. They approached the right side of the stage about fifteen feet away from where the chairs had been set up.

"Why are you doing this?" Rand knew there were other urgent matters at the moment, but he couldn't help but ask.

"Because enough is enough," Hoby said. Rand didn't know what that meant. *What has he gotten involved in since he worked for Deckard?*

Hoby broke through to the front of the crowd. The nearest guard who protected the stage snapped out of his stoic trance when his boss came into view. He cast Hoby a skeptical glance as Rand was escorted beyond the perimeter, yet he didn't question what was happening. Although now only a few paces past the guards, Rand felt as if he'd traversed something insurmountable. Perhaps he had—nearby were the steps that led up to where Arun was giving his speech. He and Hoby were the only ones in the area.

"Arun Singh thought he was the one hiring your team, but y'all work for Nathan, don't you?" Rand said.

Hoby didn't answer him, but Rand could read the man's face—he couldn't deny the accusation.

"But you're turning on them," Rand prodded. "Nathan and his family."

"Nathan wanted someone to keep an eye on you," Hoby said. "Someone *human.* I volunteered so I could try to stop you from getting any closer. Nathan was using you to find the old man."

Rand was confused at first, but then understanding struck him like lightning. "Wait... it was you. *You* were driving the car that ran us off the road."

"Once Nathan figured out where the old man was, he let his demon handle the rest. After that, I realized it was too late to stop you from getting involved, and that the best chance any of us had was to let you come here."

Any of us. Rand wondered who Hoby was referring to. It wasn't like they had ever been on the same team. *Or is he trying to join me?* As much as Rand wanted to puzzle out Hoby's true motivations and loyalties, he knew it would have to wait.

"I don't know the details, but it's supposed to happen any minute now," Hoby said. "I've gotten you close. The rest is up to you."

"Thanks," Rand said. "But this doesn't make up for what you did to my daughter. I'm not done with you."

Hoby gave a single, understanding nod before returning to the crowd in front of the stage.

This is a huge risk for you, Hoby, Rand thought as he watched the big man go. Hoby might be strong, but at the end of the day, Nathan Bale held far more power than what simple strength could overcome.

Rand's thoughts were interrupted by applause. People were once again reacting to something Arun had said.

'I was hoping you'd be here.'

The demonic voice filled Rand's head telepathically.

He gasped and stiffened. His eyes darted around, searching.

'Behind you.'

59

Rand took a deep breath and turned. Arthur Briggs stood about fifteen paces away. He still wore the same clothes as the night before. Now, though, his eyes were as dark as midnight.

He isn't afraid that I'm here, Rand thought.

'You're right. It's actually much better this way.'

Rand realized that Arthur had read his mind. The possessed man began closing the distance between them, and Rand's heartbeat raced. Arthur drew from his belt a knife that appeared to be made of black glass.

He held it up for Rand to see. *'Look familiar?'*

It did. Jackson Herron had wielded a similar blade when he'd attempted to sacrifice Rand that night in the Herron House.

And this one's meant for Arun.

Rand stood his ground as Arthur walked toward him. Rand's attention bounced back and forth between the pitch-black eyes and the knife.

Arthur made no move to lift the knife or otherwise

threaten Rand. When he was near, he paused and let his gaze bore into Rand's. *'Everything is a ritual.'*

He then bent low and yanked Rand's leg from under him, sending him sprawling onto his back and slamming to the grass with a jolt.

'And you are just as much a part of it as Arthur is.'

With that, Arthur surged forward, lithe and swift.

Rand shoved himself up and tore after Arthur.

Arthur leapt over the steps and landed on the stage, then bounded toward Arun without breaking stride. A collective gasp rose from the crowd.

"Arun!" Rand shouted.

Arun had already spotted Arthur. Arthur raised his knife and lunged.

Arun tossed the podium onto the stage, right at Arthur's feet, which made shrill feedback from the microphone burst from the speakers. Arthur was moving so fast that he tripped over the downed podium and stumbled to the ground.

Rand clambered up the steps.

Cries and shouts rose from the crowd. Lesley Reisser and the others who'd been sitting behind Arun abandoned their seats and fled.

Arthur's trip had bought Rand enough to time to catch up. He clasped Arun on the shoulder—the other man hardly seemed surprised to see Rand.

"Get out of here," Rand said to Arun.

Arun didn't seem disturbed at the attempt that had just been made on his life. He also ignored Rand's order.

The cries of the crowd grew louder, filling the air. Some people started running.

Arthur rose to his feet again, facing away from Rand and Arun.

Rand darted from Arun's side and tackled Arthur back to the ground, wanting to give Arun more time to flee. They both went down hard. The black knife spiraled from Arthur's grasp.

Rand tried to stay on top of Arthur and subdue him, but the demon-possessed man was simply too strong. He shoved Rand off with ease.

Arthur straightened, picked up the knife, and glared at Arun, who still had not fled.

"Go!" Rand shouted at him.

Arthur snarled and lunged at Arun again. Arun leapt back and dodged the swift strike that turned the black knife into a shadowy blur.

Rand guessed that Arun must've had some kind of combat training. Maybe that was the reason he hadn't been afraid to show up. But Rand knew it wouldn't be good enough. He wasn't facing a human opponent.

Arthur attacked again, a horizontal slash, and Arun ducked. In the same movement, he seized one of the chairs that had been knocked over when the people on the stage had fled.

Arun put the chair between himself and Arthur just in time—Arthur's next attack sent the blade stabbing through the fabric. Arun deftly twisted the chair, prying the knife from Arthur's hands, then threw the chair far off the stage.

Arthur was still and didn't attack again. Instead, his black eyes followed the blade to where it landed in the grass, still embedded in the chair. Although Arun was right in front of him, Arthur leapt away to retrieve his weapon.

He needs to kill him with the knife, Rand realized. *There's some kind of significance to it.*

"Come on, Rand!" Arun called.

With Arthur distracted, Rand got back to his feet. He and Arun ran off the side of the stage toward the helicopter. Its rotors had begun to spin, as if the pilots had been ready for the possibility of an evacuation.

Who's rescuing who? Rand couldn't help but think.

Halfway between the stage and the chopper, someone leapt in front of them and blocked the way—the security guard who'd first been accompanying Arun.

Rand and Arun halted.

"I'm afraid I can't let you go any further," the guard said to Arun.

60

"So you were right," Arun said to Rand out of the corner of his mouth. "When Dipika messaged me about my security team possibly betraying me, I assumed she was just being paranoid."

The guard started toward them.

Even though it was two against one, Rand knew this wasn't about winning a fight—this was about wasting precious seconds. Arun had to get back on the chopper before Arthur caught up to them.

From their right, someone suddenly appeared and barreled into the guard, tackling him off his feet. Hoby, despite being large, was apparently also fast. The two started wrestling on the ground, each trying to force the other into some kind of submission hold.

Arun took the chance to rush toward the chopper, pulling Rand along with him. Once there, he unlatched the door and slid it open.

"Get in," Arun called over the rotors' deafening wind.

It rushed against Rand, tugging at his clothes and tousling his hair.

Arun leapt inside, and Rand followed. As he did, Rand cast a glance back to where they'd come from. Arthur wasn't in view.

Rand's line of sight was cut off when Arun threw the sliding door closed. A moment later, Rand felt the helicopter start to lift off.

———

ARUN HAD APPARENTLY SPLURGED on the helicopter. The cabin was large enough for both him and Rand to stand up. Along the rear part of the cabin were cushioned seats that allowed for maybe five or six passengers.

Rand peered out the window as the helicopter straightened out. The ground drew farther and farther away as they rose higher. The people who'd once been Arun's audience were tiny specks now, and Rand watched them scatter around the park.

Arun took a wall-mounted headset and placed it over his ears; Rand did the same with the one that was nearest to him. Once the cushioned speakers were in place, he could hear the conversation that was already happening.

"—flight path confirmed." Rand guessed the tinny voice belonged to one of the pilots.

"Sir, are you okay?" came the voice of likely a second pilot or co-pilot.

"You shouldn't have come," Arun said as he peered at Rand from across the cabin.

"Neither should you," Rand shot back. "I told you this was going to happen."

"And thanks to you, I was ready."

Rand had indeed been surprised by Arun's quick and competent self-defense. Still, he knew it was a fight that Arun would never win on his own.

"Where to, sir?" the pilot asked.

Arun didn't respond. He and Rand held each other's gazes. Rand figured they were wondering the same thing —had they truly gotten away?

Rand turned to the door's wide window just in time to see something shoot up from the ground like a missile— as if a single person among the crowd had suddenly discovered their ability to fly.

It's him.

Resembling a comic-book superhero, Arthur arched through the air toward the helicopter. His leap reached its apex, and he started to fall. Rand estimated—hoped— they were just out of his each. Arthur dropped out of sight, his arm outstretched.

He missed.

The chopper suddenly lurched sideways, throwing Rand off balance.

"What was that?" Arun asked as he braced himself.

"Shit," Rand said. Arthur hadn't missed—he'd grabbed onto the landing skids below.

The sound of rending and crunching metal filled the cabin a second before the sliding door was ripped from its latch and forced open. Arthur clutched the outside of the helicopter as it flew, the wind whipping at his clothes. He climbed the rest of the way inside, once again holding the black knife. His eyes were affixed to Arun on the opposite side of the cabin.

Rand positioned his body to block Arthur's path, but

Arthur only shoved him away again with the same frightening strength. Rand slammed against the wall that separated the cabin from the cockpit. His headset—attached to the roof by a cable—was yanked off, which made the roar of the chopper fill his ears yet again.

With one wide stride, Arthur crossed the cabin and raised the knife over his head.

Arun kicked out, buckling Arthur's knee.

Rand took that chance to pounce. He wrapped his arms around Arthur's chest and peeled him away from Arun.

The full extent of the dire situation crystallized in Rand's mind. He had no supplies with which to exorcise the demon. There was nowhere else to flee in the cabin.

I have to throw him out, Rand realized. It was the only way to save Arun—and himself.

And no matter how much strength and resilience Vyraxus leant to Arthur's body, there was no chance Arthur would survive a fall from a few hundred feet up.

The real Arthur's still in there somewhere, Rand thought. *I can't just—*

Rand's hesitation was enough for Arthur. He gripped Rand's arms and, with a single swift motion, yanked Rand around him and thrust him backward through the chopper's door—out into the open air.

61

The uproar began before Miller even reached the entrance to the park.

Shrieks and disjointed cries.

It's happening, he thought. The air around him seemed to thicken.

Miller picked up his pace and arrived at the park's entrance less than a minute later. Since the event had begun, it was manned only by a single security guard. The guard's attention had been captured by the panicked voices. To Miller, he looked to be debating with himself about what to do. Ultimately, he decided to leave his post.

So Miller scrambled over the turnstile.

The stage loomed in the distance. The surrounding crowd had become a hive of turmoil. Some people dashed past Miller as they fled, rushing toward the exit.

Miller pressed forward, fighting against both the retreating attendees and his own instincts. On any other occasion, he would've joined those who were running away. But today, that simply wasn't an option. There was a chance that after today, it wouldn't be an option for him ever again.

His eyes flitted across the stage, looking for any sign of Rand, Arun, or Arthur, but saw no one.

Am I too late?

"Miller!"

Dipika had spotted him in the frenzy. She rushed over to him, weaving through the running crowds.

"What's—"

"It happened," she cut in, her finger stabbing toward the stage. "That guy attacked Arun, and Rand tackled him."

A mechanical roar split the air, and a helicopter near the stage lifted off.

"That has to be them," Dipika said when she saw it.

"Did Rand go with him?"

"I—I don't know. I couldn't see everything that happened."

And where's Arthur? Miller thought. That was probably the most important question.

"What do we do?" Dipika asked.

Miller wasn't sure. For some reason, it felt wrong to assume Rand and Arun had actually escaped in the helicopter and that everything would be fine.

"Enjoying the show?"

The familiar voice came from Miller's left.

Nathan Bale. He was accompanied by one of his security guards. "In case you were wondering—yes, your friends are on that chopper."

So they did *get away,* Miller thought. Though the killing ritual seemed to have failed, Nathan still spoke in his casual, almost amused manner. Miller really didn't like how Nathan was unfazed by Arun's escape.

"But don't worry, I always plan for contingencies," Nathan went on.

Ice filled Miller's entire body.

Nathan lifted his phone to his ear. "Charges armed?"

Beside him, Miller heard Dipika give a soft gasp.

He's going to blow them up, Miller realized. He then felt something hard press into his lower back, startling him.

"Here," Dipika whispered—she was secretly handing him something.

He took it—it was cool and metallic.

"Ready to watch your friends get blown to hell?" Nathan asked.

Before Nathan could say anything else, Dipika rushed toward him, holding something in her hand. Miller didn't know what it was until the very next moment—when she jammed the Taser into the Nathan's ribcage.

His entire body seized, eyes round as the electrical charge coursed through him. He collapsed, incapacitated and twitching on the grass. He dropped his phone nearby, no longer able to keep a grip on it.

The guard reacted quickly. He caught Dipika's wrist and twisted it sharply. She cried out as the Taser fell from her grip. He expertly kicked her knees from under her, buckling them and bringing her down in a practiced hold Miller knew she'd never be able to break out of.

Miller looked down at what Dipika had given him—the can of pepper spray, the same one that had been meant for Rand.

There was little he could do to fight off this guy who was built like a tank. His nerves froze him in place.

Memories of schoolyard bullies—who'd always been bigger than him—came rushing back.

But with this simple weapon, maybe he stood a chance. He knew what Rand Casey would do.

Miller rushed toward the guard. The big man saw him coming, but hardly reacted—he'd sized Miller up in a split second and determined him to not be a threat.

But then Miller whipped the can of pepper spray around and depressed the nozzle, shooting a fine mist into the man's face. He immediately released Dipika so that his hands could fly to his eyes. He cried out and staggered backwards.

"Are you okay?" Miller asked as he helped Dipika stand.

"Yeah."

Nathan laid on the ground, still stunned. Finally, the man's face was twisted in anger, which Miller was very pleased to see. Nathan's bulging gaze was locked onto his phone.

Miller picked up the Taser, stepped over Nathan, and retrieved his phone. Someone was speaking when he brought it to his ear.

"—you there, boss?"

"Change of plans," Miller said into the phone. "Nothing's blowing up today."

The only response was a confused silence.

Miller dropped it back into the grass. He then crouched and pressed the Taser into the phone. One second of crackling, blue electricity was all it took to destroy it.

Around them, most of the crowds had dispersed. The

helicopter had grown small in the distance, flying away and out of sight.

"Nice work," Dipika said while she rubbed at the wrist that Nathan's guard had yanked.

"You too." He was earnestly impressed with how quickly—and fearlessly—she'd rushed Nathan. "Come on. Let's get out of here and see if we can get in touch with Rando."

Before they left, Miller used the Taser to give Nathan Bale another shock. Just to be sure.

Clear blue sky was all Rand could see as he tumbled out of the helicopter's cabin.

Rand's stomach flopped the same way it did whenever he dreamt he was falling. Except this was not a dream.

His hands frantically shot out. He gripped the first thing he felt as hard as he could.

He halted in place. His body dangled outside of the helicopter as he clasped the lip of the cabin floor. Both of his hands and forearms immediately started cramping, but he held on. His legs kicked instinctively, searching for something to stand on, but they found nothing but open air. Wind whipped all around Rand, threatening to pry his grip loose.

Below, the cars looked like ants. He could barely make out the white tents of the ceremony they'd fled from. A few blocks away was a field of green grass dotted with small gravestones.

Rand pulled himself up, muscles burning, and

managed to get his head to clear the lip of the cabin floor. He quickly spotted a metal frame beneath the nearest seat, lashed out, and caught hold of it. With a much better grip on something sturdy, he was able to drag his entire body back into the helicopter's cabin.

He looked up. Arun was on his knees, Arthur standing behind him. The black dagger was at his throat.

A hostage situation.

'You're stronger than you look.'

Arun's neutral expression made him seem like he was resigned to his fate.

Rand returned slowly to his feet. His chest heaved, out of breath from exerting every ounce of strength he had to pull himself to relative safety. His arms, hands, and wrists were numb from the effort. Wind whipped at his back, the fall still just a few inches behind him.

As Rand desperately tried to come up with a way out of this, his mind went somewhere unexpected.

The cemetery.

During Rand's fight for his life, his brain hadn't fully registered what he'd seen while he was dangling over the edge.

He reached for another wall-mounted headset and put it on. The pilots were talking to each other.

"—the hell is going on back there?"

"I've cleared us for an emergency—"

"Land us in the cemetery," Rand said into the mic. The pilots went silent. Arthur's black eyes narrowed—the demon apparently didn't need a headset to know what Rand had said.

"Cemetery?" one of the pilots asked.

"Just do it," Rand said. "Now."

A moment later, the helicopter took an abrupt turn, momentarily throwing Rand off balance.

'Already planning your funeral, Randolph?' the demon's voice slithered once again into Rand's mind.

Rand removed his headset—he didn't want the pilots to hear the things he was about to say. He only wanted them focused on getting them to the cemetery.

"There's no point in killing him now," Rand said. "No one's here to witness it."

'But you are.'

"You need a lot more people than just me."

'This man is not the only person worthy of a ritual. There will always be someone suitable.'

Rand figured Arthur would say something like that. But Rand wasn't simply trying to win a debate with the demon—he just needed to buy time. Since they'd soon be near hallowed ground, the demon might rush to finish off Arun.

Arthur pressed the tip of the knife into the soft flesh of Arun's throat. The man's eyes widened as blood spilled from the wound.

Rand was about to leap into motion, desperate to save Arun, but the helicopter veered sharply, causing him to wobble again. His stomach lurched like he was on a drop-tower ride at a theme park. Arthur was thrown off balance as well, preventing him from drawing the knife the rest of the way across Arun's throat.

They were descending—fast.

Arthur's inhuman eyes blinked several times. The tension in his limbs seemed to slacken.

He feels it, Rand realized. He glanced behind him to where the sliding door was still open from Arthur forcing himself in. They were rapidly approaching the cemetery. *It's affecting him.*

Arun must've noticed Arthur's grip loosen, because he took the opportunity—he seized Arthur's wrist and yanked, pulling the man over his shoulder and dropping him onto his back, a well-executed takedown that he'd likely spent hours practicing in a dojo.

The black dagger spun from Arthur's hand, so Rand used the chance to kick the knife across the cabin floor and through the door, leaving behind smudges of Arun's blood. It fell out of view.

Arun went to pin Arthur, but hesitated when he saw that Arthur wasn't fighting back. Instead, Arthur only opened his mouth wide and let out an ear-splitting, otherworldly scream of pain.

Rand didn't hesitate before grabbing Arthur's jacket. He dragged the man by the collar across the cabin to the open door. The pilots had lowered the chopper to about five feet above the cemetery grounds. The limbs of the nearby trees were buffeted, windblown by the rotors.

Close enough, Rand thought, hoisting Arthur over the edge.

He turned to Arun, and they held each other's gazes for several long moments. Arun pressed a reddened hand over the wound on his neck, staunching the blood flow. It seemed Arthur hadn't cut anything critical.

Rand gestured upward, signaling for Arun to instruct the pilots to fly away and leave him. Arun nodded, understanding.

Rand then crouched down and dropped from the helicopter.

RAND LANDED hard on his feet, knees bending into a deep squat.

The gusts from the spinning blades blew down on him as Arun's helicopter lifted off. Over the next few seconds it grew smaller in the sky as it departed.

Arthur lay in a heap about fifteen paces from him. He stirred, sat up, then fixed his dark eyes on Rand, glaring at him. The possessed man grasped a headstone to use as support to get back on his feet, but his strength failed him. He dropped into a sitting position against the flat gravestone.

Black smoke began to rise from the crown of Arthur's head—the same place Vyraxus had entered during Nathan Bale's ritual. The demonic entity rose as an amorphous shadow into the air just above Arthur, teeming there, clearly unable to bear being in direct contact with the sacred and hallowed cemetery grounds. To Rand's relief, the shadow then faded.

Arthur's eyes returned to normal. He blinked several times, looking at Rand but not recognizing him. His face and glistened with sweat, and his shirt was soaked through as well. His eyes rolled back as his head lolled weakly.

Rand lowered himself down beside Arthur. "You're okay. Just relax."

63

Rand threw one of the Arthur's arms over his own shoulders and helped the other man stand and walk.

As he did, he fished his phone from his pocket and called Miller.

"Rando, you okay?" Miller asked immediately.

"Yeah, are you? And Dipika?"

"We're both fine. Where are you?"

"Some graveyard. I have Arthur with me."

Miller paused, likely confused by that response. "Is he... back to normal?"

"More or less." Arthur's knees wobbled as Rand guided him between the headstones.

"Text me your location. I'll come pick you up."

"Sure." Rand hung up.

"May as well leave me here," Arthur muttered as Rand sent their location to Miller. "I already feel like death. Just let me rot in one of these holes."

Definitely returning to normal, Rand thought.

TEN MINUTES LATER, Miller arrived at the cemetery entrance in Rand's Jeep, Dipika with him.

Miller got out and folded down the backseats, so Rand hoisted Arthur inside, laying him flat. Rand rode in the back with him as Miller drove.

"Is Arun okay?" Dipika asked, twisting around to face him.

"He's fine," Rand said, then recounted the story.

"Good thinking," Miller said after he was done. "I'd forgotten Arthur told us about graveyards."

Arthur muttered something, but his voice was too low and weak for Rand to discern what he'd said.

Rand had seen this condition before. This catatonic state often followed a particularly strong demonic possession. It looked scary, but he knew Arthur would recover in time.

"What about you?" Rand asked. "What happened after Arun and I took off?"

Miller and Dipika exchanged a glance, and Rand's heart rate accelerated.

"You... might not want to hear this, Rando, but you and Arun almost got blown to hell," his friend replied.

"What do you mean?"

"Nathan had a backup plan. That chopper was rigged to blow, and everyone on the ground would've seen it."

In the heat of their escape from Arthur, Rand hadn't even stopped to consider that maybe he and Arun *shouldn't* have gotten on the helicopter. At the time, it was their only obvious means of getting away.

Dipika mentioned it might also be compromised, Rand remembered.

"So what happened? Why *didn't* Nathan blow us up?" Rand asked.

Miller peered at Rand in the rearview mirror. "Dipika saved your ass."

THEY WENT to Dipika's hotel, where she quickly packed her things and returned to the Jeep without officially checking out—all of them wanted to get as far away from D.C. as fast as possible.

"When's your return flight?" Rand asked.

"As weird as it sounds, I'd rather ride back with you," Dipika said.

Rand didn't protest. He wanted Dipika to do whatever made her feel safest.

They drove for about three hours before they stopped in a small town outside of Charlottesville, Virginia, and checked into the first motel they found. Although Rand would've preferred to head straight home, he knew it'd be impossible—they were all simply too exhausted. Arthur especially needed to rest.

Rand booked Arthur his own room, laid the man down on the bed, and drew the curtains. He was asleep within seconds. Rand checked on Arthur sporadically throughout the afternoon. He poked his head in just long enough to hear the loud snoring, then went back to Miller and Dipika.

After one check, Rand spotted Dipika sitting on a bench near the entrance to the motel lobby. She held her phone in front of her like she was on a video call. Rand was too far away to make out what she was saying, but figured he knew who she was speaking to.

Dipika noticed him and gestured for him to come over, then handed the phone to him. Arun's face filled the screen. A thick square of gauze was affixed to the side of his throat.

"I'm glad to see you in one piece," Arun said.

"Same to you."

"I owe you an apology, Rand. I *did* believe you when you said I was in danger, but I... I never expected anything like that."

"I probably wouldn't expect it, either."

"You're a good man, Rand. The world could use more people like you."

Rand didn't know how to respond—he rarely heard people say things like that. Usually, he was chastised for his work with the supernatural.

"I want to see you again soon," Arun said. "Under normal circumstances, next time."

"I'd like that." There was a lot that Rand wanted to discuss with Arun, mostly having to do with Tara.

"Take care," the other man replied.

Arun hung up, and Rand handed the phone back to Dipika.

She took it, and then surprised him by pulling him into a firm hug, her arms securely around his neck.

"Thank you," she whispered.

Rand woke at seven the next morning, which was the most he'd slept in several days. He threw off the covers and pulled on his jacket before going to check on Arthur.

When he opened the door, though, he found the room empty.

"Oh no..."

He looked around. The motel was in an isolated area off a state highway, so he knew there was no way Arthur could have gotten far on foot.

Then Rand saw it—across the road was a bar with a parking lot about three times the size of the building. A handful of eighteen-wheeler trucks were parked nearby, and the exterior was lined with neon signs advertising many different brands of beer.

The trucker bar seemed almost suspended in time, like it had been built in the 60s or 70s and not updated since. Arthur was alone at the bar, hunched over a glass of whiskey.

Rand sat on the stool next to Arthur. "Seems you're feeling better."

The bartender stood in the narrow space behind the bar. She wore a black t-shirt and ripped jeans, and seemed to expertly toe the line between friendly and no-nonsense. "What you drinkin'?" she asked Rand.

"Nothing for me, thanks."

She immediately returned her attention to the stack of papers she was reviewing, checking off items with a blue pen—likely something to do with inventory.

"So what happens now?" Arthur said.

"Well..." That was a good question, and one Rand hadn't thought about yet.

"After all that shit, you want to just dump me off at my

house where I can wait for the Bales to come for me again?"

Rand knew Arthur had a point. "Come back to Louisiana with us."

Arthur scoffed and took a sip of his drink.

"You're safer if you're closer to me." Much like Rand had wanted Dipika to be close by after the Bagged Woman had threatened her.

Arthur looked at Rand for the first time since he'd walked into the bar. After the pools of black his eyes had become after being possessed, Rand was happy to once again see the old man's derisive glare. It was harsh, but it was *human.* "I was safer *before* I met you."

"That's true, and I'm sorry," Rand said. "I didn't know I was being followed, or that the Bales had any interest in you. You were right, and I apologize." Arthur seemed unmoved. "But now... things have changed. Both you and I are better off if we team up."

Arthur was silent for a few long moments, and Rand wondered if the man was about to curse him out and walk away again.

"Two demonologists under a single roof. One old, the other getting old." Arthur took a sip of his drink. "Sounds like a terrible sitcom."

Rand couldn't picture what it would be like to introduce Arthur to Tessa and Bill, much less ask Bill if Arthur could stay there too.

I'll cross that bridge when it's time, Rand thought.

"Fuck it," Arthur said, downing the rest of his whiskey. "Seems to be my only sensible play. So let's do it."

THEY CHECKED out of the motel later that afternoon.

"Should we stop by your house on the way?" Rand asked Arthur as Miller loaded their bags.

"What for?"

"You know, so you can pick up some of your things..."

"There's nothing there that can't be left behind."

Rand doubted that as he remembered Arthur's cluttered living room. "But you have all those books and notebooks from your research and travels," he said. "There has to be *something* in those that's valuable and that I could learn from..."

Miller nodded in agreement.

Arthur ground his teeth as he thought it over. "Fine. Maybe there are one or two things you might find interesting."

"Great," Rand said. "We'll make a quick stop on the way."

Rand unfolded the Jeep's backseat now that Arthur could sit upright again. As they set out for home, Arthur leaned against the window, eyes peering through the glass, seemingly lost in thought. Rand sat in the back with him while Miller drove, occasionally casting glances at the old man. Rand wondered what he was thinking.

A few hours into the trip, Rand took out his phone and called his daughter. They'd spoken only briefly the day before when Rand had told her that he and Miller were okay.

Libby's face appeared on the screen. "Hey, Dad."

"Hey. I just wanted to let you know that I'm coming home."

"Finally!"

"How are you doing?"

Her initial excitement visibly waned as she said, "The same."

Rand frowned. Libby would likely be affected by what she'd experienced for a very long time.

"Is he still around?" Rand asked.

Libby's eyes locked onto something just out of frame. "Yes."

Rand frowned. "We'll figure it out when I get back."

She refocused on him. "Can you tell me now what all happened?" she asked, clearly eager to change the subject.

"Yeah, but before I do that... is your mom there? And Bill?"

"She's right here."

Tessa appeared over Libby's shoulder. She seemed significantly less pleased to see him. "Did you find that weird guy from the internet or whatever?"

From his periphery, Rand saw Arthur slowly turn to glower at him. "We did."

"And?"

"Is Bill with you? I... want to ask him if he's okay with another house guest for a little while."

Tessa's eyes widened. "Jesus Christ, Rand," she said before storming off.

"Well, *I'm* glad you're coming back," Libby said.

"That's good enough for me," Rand said. And it was.

After Rand hung up with Libby, his thoughts wandered to what might come next. The Bale family was still out there and were likely pissed that Rand had one-upped them again. Nathan had told Rand that he wasn't a priority, but at what point would he cause enough problems to *become* a priority?

Probably now, he thought.

He looked at Arthur, who'd resumed peering out the window at the passing trees.

We're coming back with a new ally, but can he actually help us?

Rand knew it wouldn't be long before the looming shadow of the Bales caught up with them. When it did, only then would the real fight begin.

Randolph Casey will return!

To be notified as soon as he does, visit my website to sign up to my email list.

https://rockwellscott.com/free-book/

As soon as you sign up, you'll also receive a FREE gift from me—my supernatural horror novella that is not available anywhere else. You'll be able to download the book directly to your e-reading device in seconds.

HEY THERE.

Thank you for spending your valuable time reading my book, and I hope you enjoyed it.

As you may know, reviews are one of the best ways readers can support their favorite authors. They help get the word out and convince potential readers to take a chance on me.

I would like to ask that you consider leaving a review wherever you purchased this book. I would be very grateful, and of course, it is always valuable to me to hear what my readers think of my work.

Thank you in advance to everyone who chooses to do so, and I hope to see you back in my pages soon.

Sincerely,

- Rockwell

ALSO BY ROCKWELL SCOTT

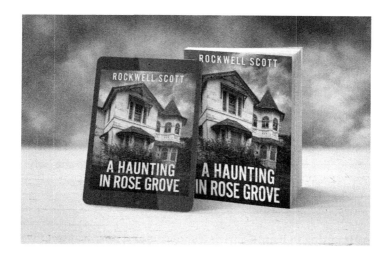

A Haunting in Rose Grove

A malevolent entity. A violent haunting. A house with a bloody history. Jake Nolan left it all behind, but now he must return.

Jake has it all — a new home, an amazing girlfriend, and nearing a promotion at work. Best of all, he feels he's finally moved on from the horrors of his traumatic past. But when he learns that his estranged brother, Trevor, has moved back into their haunted childhood home, Jake knows his past is not quite finished with him yet.

Jake rushes to the old house in Rose Grove — a small town

with a tragic history — to pull his brother from that dangerous place. But it's too late. There, he finds Trevor trying to make contact with the spirit that tormented them years ago.

And Trevor refuses to leave. He is determined to cleanse the house and remove the entity. But the supernatural activity becomes too much to handle, and Jake knows they are both unprepared for the fight. Worse, the entity targets Daniel, Jake's young nephew, and wants to bring him harm. And when the intelligent haunting shows signs of demonic infestation, Jake realizes they aren't dealing with a mere ghost.

Jake attributes the evil spirit for driving his parents to an early grave. Now it wants to claim the rest of the family, and the only way Jake and Trevor will survive is to send the entity back to hell.

A Haunting in Rose Grove is a supernatural horror novel for readers who love stories about haunted houses and battles with the demonic — the truest form of evil that exists in our world.

ALSO BY ROCKWELL SCOTT

The Gravewatcher

Every night at 3 AM, he visits the graveyard and speaks to someone who isn't there.

Eleanor has created an ideal life for herself in New York City with a career that keeps her too busy, just as she likes it. But when she receives an anonymous message that her estranged brother Dennis is dead, her fast-paced routine grinds to a halt. She rushes to Finnick, Louisiana — the small, backward town where her brother lived and temporarily settles into his creepy, turn-of-the-century house until she can figure out how he died.

But that night, Eleanor spots a young boy in the cemetery

behind Dennis's house, speaking to the gravestones. When she approaches him, Eleanor's interruption of the boy's ritual sets off a chain reaction of horror she could have never prepared for. The footsteps, the voices, and the shadowy apparitions are only the beginning.

Eleanor learns that the boy, Walter, is being oppressed by a demonic entity that compels him to visit the graveyard every night. She suspects Dennis also discovered this nightly ritual and tried to stop it, and that is why he died. Because there are others in Finnick who know about Walter's involvement with the evil spirit and want it to continue, and they will do whatever it takes to stop Eleanor from ruining their carefully laid plans. Now Eleanor must finish what her brother started — to rescue the boy from the clutches of hell before he loses his soul forever.

The Gravewatcher is a supernatural horror novel for readers who love stories about haunted houses, creepy graveyards, and battles with the demonic - the truest form of evil that exists in our world.

ABOUT THE AUTHOR

Rockwell Scott is an author of supernatural horror
fiction.

When not writing, he can be found working out, enjoying
beer and whiskey with friends, and traveling
internationally.

Feel free to get in touch!

Instagram

https://www.instagram.com/rockwellscottauthor/

Facebook
www.facebook.com/rockwellscottauthor

Twitter
@rockwell_scott

www.rockwellscott.com

rs@rockwellscott.com

Printed in Great Britain
by Amazon